Busy Bodies

Other works by Zane

Addicted
Zane's Sex Chronicles
Dear G-Spot: Straight Talk about Sex and Love
Love Is Never Painless
Afterburn
The Sisters of APF: The Indoctrination of Soror Ride Dick
Nervous
Skyscraper
The Heat Seekers
Gettin' Buck Wild: Sex Chronicles II
Shame on It All
Addicted with a Twist
Total Eclipse of the Heart
The Hot Box
Everything Fades Away
I'll Be Home for Christmas
The Other Side of the Pillow

Edited by Zane

Honey Flava: The Eroticanoir.com Anthology
Succulent: Chocolate Flava II: The Eroticanoir.com Anthology
Caramel Flava: The Eroticanoir.com Anthology
Chocolate Flava: The Eroticanoir.com Anthology
Sensuality: Caramel Flava II: The Erotica Noir Anthology
Z-Rated: Chocolate Flava III: The Eroticanoir.com Anthology
Breaking the Cycle
Blackgentlemen.com
Sistergirls.com
Purple Panties
Missionary No More: Purple Panties 2
Another Time, Another Place

Zane Presents

Busy Bodies

Chocolate Flava 4

The Eroticanoir.com
Anthology

ATRIA PAPERBACK

New York   London   Toronto   Sydney   New Delhi

ATRIA PARERBACK

A Division of Simon & Schuster, Inc.

1230 Avenue of the Americas

New York, NY 10020

First Atria Paperback edition July 2013

ATRIA PARERBACK and colophon are trademarks of Simon & Schuster, Inc.

For information about special discounts for bulk purchases, please contact Simon & Schuster Special Sales at 1-866-506-1949 or business@simonandschuster.com.

The Simon & Schuster Speakers Bureau can bring authors to your live event. For more information or to book an event contact the Simon & Schuster Speakers Bureau at 1-866-248-3049 or visit our website at www.simonspeakers.com.

Manufactured in the United States of America

10   9   8   7   6   5

Library of Congress Cataloging-in-Publication Data

Zane presents busy bodies : chocolate flava 4 : the eroticanoir.com anthology. —First Atria paperback edition.
        pages cm
    1. Erotic stories, American. 2. African Americans—Fiction. 3. American fiction—21st century. I. Zane editor of compilation. II. Title: Busy bodies. III. Title: Chocolate flava 4.
PS648. E7Z38 2013
813'.01083538—dc23   2012046252

ISBN 978-1-4516-8964-8
ISBN 978-1-4516-8965-5 (ebook)

Copyright Notices

Contents

Busy Bodies

Doing Bris

R. W. Shannon

It was a typical Tuesday afternoon. I had the place to myself, so, I thought, why the hell not? The cool air flowed in through my open windows, but I was careful to close the blinds. I wiggled my hips to the smooth sounds of the radio as I stepped out of my teal shorts. My gray tank top was already on the floor. I walked around the living room of my Georgetown condo, squeezing the full globes of my tits as my pussy moistened. My boyfriend, Jason, had moved in over the weekend and his boxes were everywhere. I maneuvered around them to gaze at my nude body in the hallway mirror.

My dark chocolate skin was covered with a fine layer of sweat from my hour-long jog around the park. I fingered my dark brown nipples until they hardened. My breath hitched as I watched myself run my hands down my torso to curve around the shaved mound between my legs. My brown eyes sparkled with mischief. Turning, I looked at my full ass in the mirror. I smacked the taut muscle before bending over. I realized, too late, that I couldn't see my dark berry pussy from this angle and straightened up. Turning, I pointed at myself in the mirror.

"You're so beautiful, Bris."

I kissed my reflection in the mirror, winked, and then danced my way back into the living room and sat on the couch. Spreading my legs, I teased the soft nub of my clit. The muscle stiffened beneath my index finger. Moaning, I leaned back against the cushions and dipped my fingers down to explore my wet cave. I thrust my finger inside, then stroked my supple wall before pulling it out and doing it again. A tingling sensation engulfed my pussy but I wasn't ready to cum yet.

Normally, just doing this much would've sent me into a fit of giggles before I passed out from embarrassment. When I touched myself, I normally did it in bed, under the cover of darkness. This was all new to me. On my right was the thing that started this whole "me time"; my black cosmetic bag. I had stumbled upon it while I was making room for Jason's things. It was my *emergency kit*. I hadn't used it in the six months that Jason and I had been together. I hadn't needed to. I decided to take them for one final spin before I got rid of them.

I pulled Pink Panther from the case. Panther was a slender, pink vibrator. The shaft was only five inches long. The tip curved up to perfectly caress my G-spot. I licked my lips as I twisted the base to activate the vibrate function. I held the smooth tip against my clit and squirmed as it massaged my bud, once again making me want to cum.

"Mercy . . ." I sighed.

Spreading my thighs farther apart, I thrust Panther into my pussy. My scent filled the room as the tip caressed my G-spot. My body quivered, begging me to allow it to release. *Not yet, Bris,* I told myself. The shaft was slick with my essence but I wanted to wait and see how many orgasms I could coax out of my pussy before I let Panther, and his cousin Black Stallion, go. I took Panther out and held the wet tip to my clit. The need to cum simmered. I cupped my breast and flicked my tongue over my nipple. Closing my eyes, I allowed my head to fall back against the cushions. I shifted to hang my leg over the arm of the sofa, widening my legs.

"Oh . . . God . . . Jason," I panted to my lover, who was still at work. "I want to cum so bad."

"So, do it."

I froze. Opening one eye at a time, I turned in the direction of the voice. Jason stood in the doorway, balancing my favorite flower, lilies, in one hand, Chinese takeout and his briefcase in the other. See, this was why I loved him. He was always thoughtful. Not to mention gorgeous. I got so caught up in gazing at his blue eyes, his thick black hair, and porcelain skin that I almost forgot that I was butt naked on the sofa, legs spread, with a vibrator pressed to my clit.

"Hey . . . you. You're home early."

Removing Panther, I let my leg drop to the floor. I blushed as he stepped closer to me to plant a kiss on my forehead. Silently, he doubled back to close the door. He moved around the boxes to set the food and flowers on the kitchen counter. I watched him. The fabric of his black suit molded around his muscular physique. I licked my lips as I again became aroused.

We met on the Metro, the blue line, as he was going home from his job as a tax accountant and I was leaving my job as a curator at the Smithsonian. We'd been eyeing each other, trading pleasantries for a year before he finally asked me out. We'd been together ever since.

"Yeah, I thought I'd surprise you."

"Surprise," I mumbled.

I picked up the leopard print pillow and held it in front of me. When he returned, he took the pillow from me and threw it across the room. After removing his jacket, he sat in the armchair, positioning it so that he could see me. All of me. I gulped. I'd never done anything like this in front of him. Our sex life was, how could I say this, ka-*bam*! He was everything that I'd ever wanted in a partner, and more. He'd asked, but I'd been shy about telling him about my fantasies—what I needed, more or less. Maybe I could finally let go of this last hurdle and let him in.

"You don't have to stop."

"I know, but . . ."

"Bris. I'm serious. Keep going."

"Okay."

I didn't know how I expected him to react when he walked in on me masturbating, but this wasn't it. He leaned forward in his chair, resting his elbows on his knees. My pussy clenched. She was ready to go again. Reaching between my legs, I stroked her. She was still stiff. Each caress sent a tremor down my spine. I squirmed, trying so hard not to cum. Yet.

"Babe, I can't see."

I opened my legs for him. He grinned. I expected to feel weird doing this, but I didn't. I discovered that I liked him watching me. As I stroked my clit, I caressed my left breast. My nipple tingled when the palm of my hand brushed against it. I traced a circle around the dark orb with my fingernail. I looked at him. He was unbuttoning his shirt. As his muscular chest came into view, an inch at a time, my breath caught in my throat. Oh. Damn.

"Are you wet?"

Nodding, I plunged my fingers deep into my pussy. Boy, was I wet. My essence sloshed out of my opening, dripped down the path of my skin to soak the cushions beneath me. Moaning, I bit my lip as the muscles clenched around my index and middle fingers. I pinched my rigid nipple between my fingers. My eyes slid closed. Man. This felt so good. I almost forgot he was sitting there, watching me. I could probably cum right now and . . .

"Taste it."

I opened my eyes. "Huh?"

His shirt was all the way off and draped over the arm of the chair. "I think you should taste yourself."

I gasped. I'd never . . . Oh . . . fuck it . . . I removed my fingers and put them into my mouth. I was sweet with a little bit of tang. I licked my fingers clean before spreading my legs wide and pushing them as far inside me as I could. My core was moist and warm. The right temperature to cum. My thighs trembled as I traced the ridges deep in my core. My body relaxed as my pussy tensed, ready to release the orgasm that had been building.

"Jason . . ."

"Yeah?"

"I . . ."

Before I could get the rest of the sentence out, my orgasm rushed out of me. I called his name as I came. I left my fingers in place until the tremors stopped, only because I couldn't move. Sated, I closed my eyes. My stomach growled. There was a container of sweet and sour shrimp with my name on it. I also wanted to take a quick shower before I ate. At least, I thought that was the plan.

When I looked up, he had removed his pants and was walking toward me. Clad in only a pair of boxer briefs, he removed my fingers and sucked my essence off them. My clit began to throb again. With my fingers still in his mouth, he sat beside me. My fingers slipped out of his mouth as he bent toward me and kissed me passionately.

"You taste so good."

"Thanks."

He kissed me on my neck. That should've been my first clue that he had something up his sleeve. His fingertips danced on my bare thigh. My flesh tingled where he touched. Damn. Before I could blink, my nipple was in his mouth. He suckled slowly, causing the arousal to build again in my pussy. I opened my legs to ease my pulsating clit. I moaned as his fingers inched up my thigh to find and explore my clit.

"I know you're not done," he whispered. "You're still wet."

I shivered as he stroked my opening. No, normally I wouldn't be done, but I didn't want to bring out Stallion. I wasn't ready to answer the barrage of questions Stallion might cause. His feather-light caress was making my pussy clench. Panther rested on my thigh. As I moved him toward the case, the large bulge in the black snakeskin leather drew Jason's attention.

"How many more do you have?"

"Just one." I zipped up the case, but he took it from my hands and unzipped it. Damn it!

"You gonna use the other one?"

"I wasn't."

"Why not?"

He halted his words as he peered in the bag, then looked up at me with one eyebrow raised. He pulled out Stallion. This dildo was twelve inches of thick, deeply veined cock. I saw the question in Jason's blue eyes. I knew what he was thinking: that his dick doesn't measure up, but it did. Jason's cock filled every inch of my pussy and satisfied me thoroughly. Suddenly uncomfortable, I sank down in the cushions of the sofa and closed my legs. I flashed him a sheepish grin while he turned it over in his hands.

"Is this what you like?"

"Well . . . no . . . I mean, Kel had dared me to get it so . . . I hardly ever used it."

I had gotten Stallion on a dare from my best friend a few years ago. Jason pulled out the small tube of lubricant that was also in the cosmetic bag. The lube was strawberry scented. The same aroma drifted from Stallion's shaft, though I'd washed it thoroughly after the last time I used it. I gulped as I watched him twist the base to activate the vibrating function, but I had broken that feature long ago. I curved a strand of hair behind my ear and attempted to sit up. I reached into his lap and patted his erection.

"I like your cock better."

"Sure," he teased as he kissed me. "I'd still like to see you take it."

With a look of pure desire in his eyes, Jason pried my thighs farther apart. He paused to coat Stallion with lube before inserting just the tip into my pussy. I grasped his wrist before he could push it in deeper. This wasn't how I liked to use Stallion. See, I liked to prop Stallion up and ride him like a cowgirl, but I didn't think Jason was ready for all that. Or maybe I was the one who wasn't ready.

On wobbly legs, I stood and turned around to face the back of the sofa. He held Stallion in place while I straddled the massive shaft. Stallion was too thick and deeply veined to take all at once. I pushed the tip inside me, then stopped to allow my muscles to stretch around its girth. My essence dripped around the shaft, coating the latex to make it easier to slide in another inch. Leaning over, I kissed his lips as my pussy slid down another inch of Stallion's shaft.

Slowly, I moved up and down the shaft as I gripped the back of the sofa. Closing my eyes, I moaned as the hard veins caressed the walls of my pussy. Okay, so I'd used Stallion. A lot. It was because of the way it massaged my pussy like a pair of fingers.

Its tip hit my G-spot like a dart piercing a bull's-eye. And when I would cum, it was so hard that I almost passed out. Jason's lips on my thigh only heightened my arousal. He continued to hold Stallion steady as I bobbed up and down on the shaft.

"You like that, huh?"

I moaned in reply. He spanked me. The flesh on my ass stung but it didn't make me stop. Instead, I bobbed faster. The sofa shook beneath my thrusts. My head rolled back. He smacked my ass again. My walls contracted and I came again. When he removed his hot hand from my ass, my skin immediately felt cool. I slowed down. Opening my eyes, I snuck a peek at him. He was coating Panther with the lube. My breath caught in my throat. I thought I was done but, suddenly, his fingers were on my anal opening. Caressing and teasing the tight flesh.

"What are you doing?"

"You'll see."

I never told him that was a secret fantasy of mine: double penetration. My body trembled in anticipation as he kissed my shoulder. He released Stallion's base to concentrate on what he was going to do behind me. My eagerness caused me to flinch when he touched my shoulder blade. My pussy tightened around Stallion. I reached between my legs and stroked my clit. The nub had softened but my fingers worked my clit into a hard peak.

"Lean forward."

I did. The tip of Panther's shaft pushed into my opening. I gasped, gripped the back of the sofa so tightly with my free hand that I was afraid it was going to tear off in my hands. The swipe of his tongue against the sensitive skin of my anus caused my nipples to harden. I released my clit to hold Stallion in place. I'd used Panther in my backdoor area once before. My muscles relaxed to allow the pink vibrator access.

Jason worked my back door with Panther as I fucked Stallion. Both shafts tapped all of my pleasure centers at once. Panting, I fucked them as if my life depended on it. He didn't know it, but Jason had just opened a can of worms. With his free hand, he spanked my ass.

"Ride it," he breathed. "Ride that shit!"

My tits shook. My ass shook. When I reached for his cock, which was now sticking out of the fly of his boxer briefs, he knocked my hand away. Before I knew it, I had cum again, and again. When I was certain that I was going to pass out from the pleasure, the orgasms stopped. He removed Panther so that I could climb off Stallion. I collapsed on the sofa, trying to catch my breath as he went to the bathroom to wash them off.

"Mercy . . ." I sighed.

Every inch of my body ached. My throat was raw from screaming. My pussy was sore but when Jason returned, I knew that I'd be ready to go again. He set the bag on the coffee table before climbing behind me and wrapping his arms around me. I exhaled when he kissed my temple. His erection pressed into my hip. He had to be going crazy but he never let on.

"I was going to throw them away," I tell him. "I mean, after I used them one last time."

"And now?"

I twisted around in his arms and kissed him. The whiskers of his five o'clock shadow tickled my chin. I worked the waistband of his briefs down his hips to free his cock. He groaned as I stroked his length. I loved the warmth of his cock. The pulsating vein that ran down the side. While I preferred him to plastic, I thought I'd keep Stallion and Panther around for a little while longer. Releasing his lips, I dipped my head to wrap my mouth around his cock.

A LUSTFUL GIFT TO THEE

She lies upon a tangled rug of red cloth
late stoned nights
lost in dark moments of sensual sound
his words seem unreal
"Touch yourself"
he whispers, watching
"Feel your hand, your fingers"
he senses the smoothness of her skin
as her fingers slide upon her body
caress the curve of her breast
"Look at me, this man who hungers for you."
She opens dark eyes
heavy with lust
her fingers
feeling him
"Your cock is hard in my hand"
she breathes
"I want to feel you, feel your hunger for me"

"Fuck"
she moans to the darkness
shivering
shaking
urgent
her breath heavy
he watches
the rocking of her breasts
"Fuck me—Fuck me"
her voice urgent

demanding
primitive lust
seizes her body
sends her shuddering

Author Unknown

Birthday Special: The Gift of Trois

Cee Wonder

It is amazing what people will do when they are caught up in the moment. My girl, Sam, and I have been in a relationship for some time now. We have a pretty fulfilling sex life, and we are comfortable discussing sex. Recently, when Sam spent the night at my place, we watched the movie *Trois*. The story line involved a husband and wife attempting to add excitement in their bedroom by having a sexual liaison or threesome with another woman.

After the movie, as we shared pillow talk, I brought up the topic of ménage-à-trois and asked for her thoughts on it. We lay facing each other with Sam's head nestled in the crook of my arm and chest.

"Hey, baby. What do you think about us getting down like that?" I asked as I lightly traced my fingers around her navel and grazed below the waist of her panty, just above the entrance to her manicured love garden. I looked down at her when I felt her body rhythmically react to the effects of my touch. Sam looked at me with a smirk and a look of disapproval on her face, as she studied mine.

"No, sir. I don't think so. I ain't the one. Uhm, nah, that's not my thing" was her response as she appeared to entertain the possibility of her participating in some three-way action.

Our conversation continued with us talking about different scenes from the movie that we thought were very sexy and arousing. Sam teased my nipple with her fingernail and made a trail down my stomach until her fingers found the tip of my dick. Her hand explored my girth and length.

"Somebody's not sleepy," she moaned, and chuckled slightly as she felt the hardness and the moisture of my excited alter ego.

"Would you have a threesome?" Sam asked as she made her way down my body and her warm, wet mouth slowly but firmly took me in.

"I have entertained the thought," I said, panting from the oral pleasure I was receiving.

She eased her way up toward me and positioned my erection at the entrance to her sweet spot. Inch by inch I was being sucked into her pleasure treasure. Sam rode me intensely until she buried her nails into my chest and tensed up.

"I'm cumming," she screamed, and shook uncontrollably.

It wasn't long before I joined her.

"Oh, shit! I'm cumming, too."

Heavy breathing filled the room as she collapsed on top of me. At some point, we both drifted into a deep coma-like sleep.

Sam's birthday was coming around the corner. She had planned her own birthday party. As I made plans to attend, I invited my homie, Sarge, to roll with me. That's the nickname we gave him because he was a military veteran. He was a big guy like Terry Crews, who played Damon in *Friday After Next*. Also, Sarge was a workout freak. I had introduced the two of them in the past. After he agreed to tag along, Sarge felt compelled to buy a gift.

We drove to the mall together the day of the party, which was Sam's actual birthday. I told Sarge that she liked lingerie from Victoria's Secret. My plan was to buy her a bottle of Lemon and Sugar perfume by Fresh. As we walked and browsed the latest line of lingerie in Vickie's Secret, as I call it, Sarge and I took in all the eye candy, elbowing each other, grunting and nodding for each other to look in one direction or the other, appreciating the beauty and booty that God created. He decided to buy a canary-colored underwear set that included a wife beater and boy shorts. I thought about how good it would look on Sam's body. She is petite, standing about five foot four and 110 pounds, slim, with nice breasts and bubble butt. Mmmm, I'm having a nature rising moment just describing her. After I made my purchase, we left the mall to go get ready for the party.

When we made it to the party, it was already in full swing. There was food galore, a live band, and a deejay. People were standing near the speakers bobbing their heads and moving their bodies to the beat in subtle fashion. There was a group of Sam's friends and family sitting around a table playing card games, and others were feeding their faces and engaging in conversations.

Sam's mother approached me, and we embraced. I introduced her to Sarge and the two of them shook hands. Sam made her way out of the kitchen and came up to me and gave me a kiss.

"Happy birthday, baby," I whispered to her after the kiss and presented her with the gift I'd bought for her.

"Thank you," she said, smiling like a schoolgirl.

"Damn, you look good enough to eat."

"Behave, please" was her reply while playfully hitting me on the shoulder.

"You remember Sarge?"

"Yes, I do. How are you?" Sam responded, looking at Sarge.

"I'm fine. Long time no see. Happy birthday." He smiled, extending the gift bag to her.

"Thank you. Go mix and mingle and have fun," she told the both of us. "I'm the host as well."

At the sight of seeing Sam looking so damn good, I don't know what came over me. Lust was on the brain. She wore a black lace and nude corset with some cheek-a-boo cuffed shorts and a pair of black peep-toe stilettos. It took every ounce of mind control to talk myself out of dragging her to an isolated part of the house for some quick action. At that moment I decided that I would make this birthday a memorable one that would push Sam's sexual limits. Sarge had no idea what I was up to.

In the past, when we would have real talk, I would share with Sarge some intimate moments that Sam and I had experienced.

"Man, my girl, Sam, got some bomb-ass pussy. Bro, I'm talking 'bout like your boy Plies says, it gets wet, wet. She got a major head game, too. Her jaws are so strong. She can suck a golf ball through a water hose."

"Damn, dawg. She got it like that? Just the thought of it is making my dick hard," Sarge said, laughing.

The party was beginning to thin out. I made myself comfortable on Sam's bed, turned on the TV, and relaxed while she continued to play the host role. Eventually, she came and joined me, making sure I was taken care of and satisfied while she sipped on a glass of wine. I gave her a reassuring kiss and squeezed her ass to let her know I would definitely be okay later, if you know what I mean. We could still hear the sounds of the music and faint voices of the remaining guests outside the bedroom. Sarge joined us later and sat in a chair at the foot of the bed and watched TV.

Still in host mode, Sam offered to get Sarge something to

drink as she left to go check on her remaining guests. When Sam left the room, Sarge was going on and on about how he was enjoying himself.

"Man, your girl did this thang up right. I'm glad I came."

"Wait till I tell you what I got in store for her." I transitioned to tell Sarge what I had in mind. "Say, bro, would you like to hit Sam?" I asked.

He looked at me with disbelief and asked with a nervous laugh, "Are you for real? Man, you are crazy."

My look must have said it all.

"You are for real, huh? Okay," he said, letting me know he was game.

After she had returned to her bedroom and had given Sarge his drink, Sam exhaled and sat on her bed with her back against the headboard and her legs stretched. I sat next to her on the edge of the bed.

"Are you having a good time, baby?" I asked as I took off her shoes and began to rub her feet.

"Yes, this is really nice," she stated, satisfied with the outcome of the party.

I could tell she was buzzing from the wine she'd had earlier. With her disposition being very mellow and in chill mode, I decided to test the waters and put my plan into motion. I asked Sam to take a look at the gifts we'd bought her. She unwrapped the fragrance I bought and opened it.

"This smells nice," she said after one whiff. "Thank you again, baby."

When she saw what was in Sarge's bag, she smiled, stated how much she liked it, and thanked him, too.

"Go try on Sarge's gift," I urged with a smile.

"I don't think so," she replied with her head tilted downward and looking up at me, giving me that look that asked what are you up to.

I whispered, "Happy birthday," as I leaned in to give her a kiss, only this kiss was more sensuous. I gently tugged at her bottom lip, causing her mouth to give slightly, letting her lips part. I then licked across her upper lip before exploring the inside of her mouth with my tongue.

"Mmmm," escaped her mouth.

While the kissing continued, I started to massage her 36 C-cup breasts. For a brief moment, her breathing began to become unsteady and choppy when I began to unbutton her blouse. With little resistance, Sam grabbed the top of my hand to stop me, while looking in the direction where Sarge was seated.

"We have company."

"There's nobody here but us," I whispered as I continued with my quest and was very successful in freeing her twins. I took one of her breasts in my mouth and gave Sam's nipple a soft bite. I used my tongue to spiral around her nipple and began to suck moans out of her.

"Mmmm," she moaned while stroking the back of my head.

My tongue slithered like a black mamba snake up her chest, licking the nape of her neck up to her earlobe. Ever so gently, I caressed her face and brought her lips to me once more, and we kissed.

"I told my boy you have some good pussy," I whispered, informing her that Sarge knew of some of our sexcursions.

"Oh, really? And why would you do that?"

That seductive look in her eyes said it all. Without any resistance, Sam allowed me to remove her shorts, and I started working my way down to eat her pussy. In the midst of making my way downtown, I managed to unbutton and unzip my jeans to free Willy, my seven inches of dangling fury. Sam's pussy was extremely wet and warm. The moisture probably made itself visible through her panties. I was too consumed with trying to get my eat on to find out. I used my thumb and index finger to part the lips of her pussy, allowing her swollen sex antenna to receive an oral transmission. After giving that clit my version of birthday licks, I climbed onto the bed and positioned myself so that Sam could suck my dick. I stood up and grabbed the headboard with one hand for balance and squatted in front of her. When Sam opened her mouth, I teased her by just allowing her to taste the underside of the head of my dick with her tongue, sampling the pre-cum that had eased out from the excitement. She began to suck me in as if her mouth were a vacuum, inch by inch until she reached the base and her nose teased my man forest.

While I was enjoying some major oral surgery, Sarge sat with his eyes glued to the TV as if he was in a trance. I knew that there were still people partying on the other side of the bedroom door, and my adrenaline was at an all-time high because of what was ultimately about to go down.

"I told Sarge how good your pussy tastes," I whispered. "He wants to eat it for you."

She couldn't respond because her mouth was full of my dick.

"Hey, bro," getting Sarge's attention. "You wanna taste this pussy? I told you it was good. Come and get this pussy," inviting him to join in.

Without saying a word, he leaped from the chair in a single bound and attacked her pussy like a flesh-eating piranha. While still with her back somewhat against the headboard, Sam was semi-naked. Her shorts had been tossed on the floor and her blouse and bra were hanging off her shoulder. I continued feeding her mouth my dick, and Sarge sopped her pussy like it was biscuits and gravy. By now, I knew Sam was down for whatever.

"Sarge wants some of that pussy."

As Sarge took off his clothes, I face fucked Sam before climbing out of the bed and making my way over to the chair to sit down. Sarge returned to the bed, and I witnessed his face disappear between Sam's legs. Once he came up for air, I sat and watched the two of them transform into one as Sarge drove deep into Sam's love canal for about fifteen minutes. Sarge handled Sam's petite frame like a rag doll. He held her legs up in the air and was hitting that pussy like a man just released from prison after doing time for ten years. As I watched the two of them have some one-on-one action, I gave my right hand a workout by stroking my dick. I was always curious what Sam would look like getting her sex on. It turned me on big time to witness it. As he dug deep into her tunnel, Sarge said over and over, breathing and sounding like he'd just finished a set of weights at the gym, "Happy birthday! You know you special."

He rolled over on his back and pulled Sam on top of him while still keeping his dick inside her pussy. Riding dick is what gets her off, too. Sarge held Sam by the ass and was helping her ride him. After a few good bucks, I knew Sam was cumming because I saw her trademark orgasmic tremble. Witnessing her enjoyment from a distance was like a thing of beauty and seeing that shit sent me over the edge, too. For a brief moment as I was cumming, Sam and I made eye contact.

During her recovery from that big "O," Sam stroked Sarge's dick with both hands till he unloaded what looked to be a year's worth of cum. He lay motionless for a short period of time. Sam climbed down out of the bed and came over to me. She sat in my lap and laid her head on my shoulder while I held her close and stroked her shoulder.

"You have fun? Did you like your gift?" I said as I was caressing her cheek and stroking her shoulder.

"Whew. You are so bad. I'm going to sleep good tonight" was all she said. I tilted her face up toward mine, looked her in the eyes, and kissed her long and passionately.

Sarge got dressed. I got dressed and drove him home. Afterward, I drove back over to Sam's place. I stripped down naked and climbed in bed with her. I noticed Sam had showered, changed into the new lingerie, was wearing the new fragrance, and was snuggled in a fetal position. As we spooned, I slid her panty aside and put my newfound hardness in her still wet and warm pussy.

"Mmm," I heard her say as I pulled her close to me and kissed the back of her neck.

"Good night, baby."

"Good night."

Man at Work

Harold Armstrong

As darkness covers a quiet city, an overhead light brightens the kitchen of a small apartment. Derek Parker is sitting at a round, wooden table, wearing a white, V-neck T-shirt. Derek is twenty-four, six foot one, 170 pounds. He has an athletic build, a dark complexion, and a short, neatly trimmed haircut. He is a full-time student, working toward a degree in business. The table is cluttered with books and papers since Derek is cramming for a midterm exam. He is busy, taking notes, when his wife calls his name.

"Derek!"

Derek is married to his high school sweetheart, Tracy. She is twenty-four, five foot seven, with a petite frame and short, dark hair. Tracy has dimples and a deep brown complexion. She walks into the kitchen and stands over his right shoulder. She is wearing a pink chiffon baby-doll nightgown.

"Derek?"

He is still focused on his books when she taps him on the shoulder. He turns his head momentarily.

"Hey, baby."

"Derek, I've been calling you."

"Oh, sorry, I didn't hear you."

Derek continues to scribble notations on his yellow legal pad.

"Derek, it's after midnight. When are you coming to bed?"

"In a minute, sweetheart."

"You've been saying that for the last three hours."

Derek flips a few pages in a textbook and continues taking notes. Tracy has a playful smile as she begins to massage his neck and shoulders.

"Can't you at least take a break, even for a few minutes?"

"In a minute, sweetheart."

Tracy's smile disappears. She stands behind him with her hands on her hips, staring daggers at the back of his head. She storms out of the kitchen and seconds later, a door slam echoes through the apartment. A short time afterward, a low buzzing sound emanates from behind the bedroom door.

Meanwhile, a couple in another part of the city are having a romantic, candlelit dinner. Shayla is twenty-five, five foot six, 145 pounds. She has a medium brown complexion. She is a thick, busty girl, with long dark hair and red strands blended in with her regular hair color. She has a cute baby face and chubby cheeks. She is married to Kevin Clark. Kevin is twenty-five, six foot two, 220 pounds, with a muscular build. Kevin has a dark complexion and his entire face and head are clean shaven. Kevin is a pastry chef at a popular restaurant. He and his wife are having a special dinner to celebrate their one-year anniversary. They are very much in love and can't help grinning at each other across the dining room table, while soft music plays on the stereo. Shayla is wearing a red strapless gown, and Kevin is wearing black on black, with a red tie.

"How's the roast beef, Shayla?"

"Tender and juicy, just the way I like it." She giggles and takes a huge piece in her mouth. "I can hardly wait for dessert," she adds.

"You won't have to wait much longer," he replies. "But first, may I have this dance?"

He rises from the table and extends his hand. She places her hand in his, and he helps her out of the chair. He escorts her into the living room, and they embrace, swaying back and forth to the rhythm of the music. He spends a few seconds nibbling on her earlobes, then his lips explore the slope of her neck. His hands slide up her curves, and with his fingers, he tickles the underside of her arms. She laughs and pulls away from him. He uses the moment to walk over to a nearby mobile cart and lifts the lid off a cake dish. He reveals a yellow cake frosted with white icing and topped with plump, bright red strawberries. He carefully plucks one of the strawberries off the top and carries it over to Shayla.

"Happy anniversary," he says.

He holds it up to her lips. She takes a small bite, then invites him to take a bite. She holds the final piece between her teeth. Their lips meet and his tongue pushes the rest of the fruit down her throat. They share a long, passionate kiss. Then Shayla pulls down the top of her dress, revealing her full, ample breasts.

"Happy anniversary," she says in her high-pitched voice.

She helps him remove his tie and unbuttons his shirt. Her hands caress his muscular chest. He cups her breasts and his fingers gently massage her puffy nipples. Her hands move down to his waist. She unlocks his belt and unzips his pants. She reaches inside his boxers and takes a firm grip on his dick. As she begins to massage it, she feels it bulging within her grasp. They kiss and caress each other, then Kevin helps her out of her dress and pulls her down to the carpet. She helps him out of his boxers while he removes his shirt. With one hand she strokes his dick and with the other, begins to feel his balls.

She smiles playfully, then leans closer and allows her tongue to tease his balls. Her tongue moves upward, following the contour of his throbbing dick. Her tongue reaches the tip and she teases his swollen dick head. Slowly, she glides her tongue back down one side of his shaft, then right back up the other side, down the front and up along the other side again. She repeats the process several more times before allowing his hard, brown dick to fill up her jaws. Her head moves up and down on his shaft. She gently sucks it on the way up, and on the way down, the edges of her teeth graze the skin. Then she begins stroking the base of his dick while sucking on the end. She lets go of him momentarily to position herself on top of his face, allowing him to taste her bushy pussy. Then she stretches forward and resumes sucking on his massive dick.

After several minutes, she moves her body closer to his waist and while holding his dick in place, she eases down on top of it. Kevin enjoys watching her apple bottom bounce up and down on top of his dick. Shayla moans each time her wet pussy slides down and fills up with his big, hard dick. Then she begins to swivel her hips from side to side, grinding his cock deeper inside her warm pussy. She turns her head and smiles at him, seeing the pleasure on his face. She swivels her entire body around and resumes the up and down motion.

He watches her big breasts bounce up and down and reaches up to hold them. Shayla places her hands on top of his. She rides him intensely as his hands move down to her waist, helping her up and down, faster and harder, and minutes later, with the vigorous sensation increasing, they both reach an exhausting climax and cum at the same time. With a satisfied grin on her face, Shayla climbs off and crawls over to the pastry cart. She slices a big piece of cake, lies on his chest, and offers him a bite. He takes a huge bite, then she takes a huge bite as well. Each of them has white icing on their upper lip. They share a laugh while continuing to eat their anniversary cake.

The next morning, Shayla is driving to work with her coworker and best friend Tracy in the passenger seat. She is telling Tracy about the intimate, candlelit dinner that she and her husband had last night.

"Then, after dinner, we danced for a little bit, then we got naked and . . ."

Shayla glances across the front seat and notices that Tracy seems to be fighting back tears while gazing out the window. As she pulls into the employee parking lot, she finds the nearest empty spot and parks the car.

"Tracy, what's wrong?" Tracy doesn't respond. "Whatever it is, you can tell me. I won't tell anybody."

Tracy turns and glares at Shayla. "You mean like the time in high school, when you told everyone that I was in the broom closet giving Derek a blow job?"

"I told you, it just slipped out."

"There was a crowd of people waiting with cell phone cameras when we opened the door."

"I thought you were gonna swallow, or at least wipe your face off before you came out."

Tracy folds her arms and turns her head away from Shayla.

"Come on, Tracy, you're obviously upset about something. It'll help if you talk about it."

Tracy sighs and turns back to her friend, looking for some reassurance. "You promise not to tell anybody?"

Shayla tries to look and sound sincere.

"I promise."

Tracy pauses, then explains to Shayla how, for the past four months, she and Derek have not had sex.

"Wow! You haven't had any dick for four months?"

Tracy nods and as her eyes begin to swell with tears, Shayla reaches into her purse and pulls out some tissue, then hands it to Tracy.

"Have you tried wearing something sexy?"

Tracy explains that she tried wearing sexy sleepwear but Derek wouldn't take his eyes off his books long enough to notice. Shayla consoles her friend by allowing Tracy to cry on her shoulder.

"Don't worry, we'll think of something."

Later that evening, Derek is in the front room of the apartment, pacing back and forth, waiting for Tracy to arrive home. After wearing a groove in the rug, he stops upon hearing a key in the lock. The door swings open, and Tracy is surprised to see him.

"Derek? I thought you were going to be at the library."

"I changed my mind. Where've you been?"

"Shayla took me to the store after work."

Tracy walks over to the kitchen table and pours out a plastic bag full of size AA batteries. Derek looks at the batteries, puzzled, then follows her into the living room.

"I had an interesting chat with your friend Shayla today."

"What about?"

"About you and me!" he says, his voice rising.

"Derek, what are you so upset about?"

"I don't like the idea of you telling other people about our personal business. If there's a problem, then you need to talk to me about it!"

Tracy raises the level of her voice to match his. "Well, maybe if you were taking care of your personal business, I wouldn't have to talk to someone else about it!"

Derek suddenly gets defensive. "What do you mean by that?"

Tracy explains that she resents the fact that he pays more attention to his schoolbooks than to her, and that she would even be happy if once in a while, he told her to have a nice day at work.

Tracy bolts into the bedroom and slams the door behind her. Seconds later, she comes out of the bedroom, marches defiantly into the kitchen, grabs a pack of batteries off the table, and marches back into the bedroom, slamming the door again. Derek responds by heading out the front door and slamming it behind him.

Later that same evening, Derek goes to visit his best friend, Kevin. He and Derek are in the basement, drinking at his custom-made bar set. Derek is sitting somberly at a barstool and drinks down the last of his second beer. Kevin watches him patiently from behind the bar.

"You want another one?"

Derek nods and Kevin retrieves a bottle of beer from a nearby fridge, opens it, and hands it to his friend.

"I hope before you finish this one, you get around to telling me what you're so upset about."

Derek sighs.

"Tracy and I had a fight."

"Yeah, I figured that much. What was the fight about?"

Derek takes a drink from the bottle, then explains that he has not been intimate with his wife for several months.

"Why not?" Derek gives Kevin an awkward glance. "Oh, that. Look, it's nothing to be ashamed of; it happens, and I think I know why."

"I'm listening."

"A little something called male ego."

Derek looks puzzled. "What do you mean?"

Derek listens carefully as Kevin explains to him that he most likely feels inadequate due to the fact that his wife is supporting the two of them while he goes to school.

"You really think that's it?"

"Sure. Once you graduate and start working, you'll be good as new."

"I've got a few years to go before I graduate. What do I do in the meantime?"

Shayla's high-pitched voice echoes from upstairs. "Kevin, are you two going to be down there all night?"

"We'll be up in a minute, sweetheart!"

Derek shakes his head. "I have to ask, man, doesn't her voice get on your nerves?"

Kevin chuckles. "Sometimes, but I love her, squeaky voice and all. Plus she gives great head. Now listen. What you have to do is get freaky."

"Freaky? You mean, like sex in a closet?"

"Yeah, but it's not just where you do it, it's how you do it. Let me give you a few suggestions."

Kevin spends the next few minutes giving his friend some ideas on how to solve his intimacy problem. Then Derek goes home to his wife, and Kevin stops in the kitchen to get a jar of honey before heading upstairs to his own wife.

The next morning, Shayla is in the lobby of the office building, waiting nervously for Tracy to arrive. A short while later, Tracy arrives and gives her friend a curious look.

"Okay, Shayla, why did I have to take the bus to work?"

"Sorry, I had an errand to run. Your eyes are red; have you been crying?"

Tracy answers reluctantly. "Yeah."

Shayla is looking around, not listening to her friend. "That's great."

"Shayla, are you listening?"

"I'm sorry, I mean, why were you crying?"

"Derek and I had a terrible fight last night. When I woke up this morning, he was gone." Shayla is still looking around nervously. "Shayla, what is going on?"

"Hmm? Oh, Tracy, you need to fix your makeup."

"Really?"

"Oh, yeah, girl; you look a hot mess."

Tracy starts to look through her purse for a small mirror, but Shayla has a better idea.

"No, no, not here. Go in the restroom!"

"Why?"

"The lighting is better in there."

"Shayla, are you okay? You're acting really strange."

Shayla escorts Tracy to the nearest ladies' room, just to the right of the foyer.

"Yeah, yeah, yeah, I'm fine. Now, go on in there and make up."

"What?"

"I mean . . . go fix your makeup."

Tracy looks curiously at Shayla before entering the ladies' room. Once inside, Tracy is fumbling through her purse, and is surprised when she looks up and sees her husband. "Derek?"

He walks toward her slowly, with his finger to his lips. "Shhhh, don't say anything," he whispers.

Their lips meet, and his tongue explores the back of her

throat. He quickly removes her skirt and blouse. She is totally submissive as he unhooks her bra and removes her panties. He leads her over to the sinks where he's placed a container of chocolate-flavored massage lotion. He begins at her shoulders, slowly pouring it on and watching it glide down her naked body. He starts licking the lotion off her plump, cupcake-shaped breasts while it drips down her smooth, brown body. His tongue teases her nipples and they become puffy and hard, while he sucks the sweet syrup off them. He drops to his knees and uses his tongue to catch some of the lotion dripping down her chest. He holds it there, then slides the tip of his tongue inside her pussy. The lotion begins to heat up and the warm sensation causes her to tingle all over. While swirling his tongue around inside her pussy, his finger roams between her cheeks and finds her asshole. She clenches at first, then relaxes as his finger ventures inside.

"Oh, Derek," she whispers. Then he rises and pours some of the lotion all over his bulging hard dick and invites her to taste it. She drops to her knees and wraps her lips around his pulsating dick head and slowly takes more of his dick inside her mouth, tasting that warm, sweet chocolate, hungrily sucking it off his thick, brown dick. She starts rubbing his balls, and his dick begins throbbing inside her mouth. She grabs it and her hand glides up and down his shaft, stroking it firmly. She eyes his thick, hard, wet dick and rubs her pussy, aching to have it inside her. She turns and bends over the counter, inviting him to take her from behind. She is overjoyed to feel his warm, hard dick slide between her soft pussy lips and his body pressed tightly against her pulsing wet clit.

Meanwhile, Shayla is standing guard outside the restroom door, when an older white lady tries to enter.

"I'm sorry, this one is out of order at the moment."

The lady looks confused.

"Out of order?"

"Yeah, there's a man at work in there."

"What's he doing?"

Shayla thinks quickly. "Right now, he's laying some pipe."

"Oh, I see."

Satisfied with her answer, the lady walks away and Shayla exhales. Then she takes out her cell phone, turns on the video recorder, and peeks inside the restroom. Derek pours the rest of the lotion down Tracy's back. He leans over and his tongue hugs the contour of her back. He feels her round, soft booty and rubs the lotion all over her ass, then he begins to slap her ass firmly, listening to the sound echo throughout the restroom. He starts pumping his dick in harder and faster, his balls smacking up against her.

He tells her that he wants to cum on her ass, and she says, "Go ahead!"

His dick is glistening with her pussy juice as he slides it out and, seconds later, he shoots his baby gravy all over her booty, making a hot, sticky mess. Tracy reaches back and rubs his warm cum, mixing it in with the lotion. She brings her fingers up to her lips, sliding two fingers in her mouth, to taste the creamy mixture. They both try to catch their breath and slow their racing heartbeats.

Derek slaps her booty one last time and leans forward to whisper in her ear, "Have a nice day, baby."

The Siren

Eva Hore

We were taping auditions for the lead role in a new pornographic movie. I was tired of analyzing all the different body types, positions, and attributes. The director was searching for a new face, body, and that element that shines through when you're filming.

We'd been at it since early morning and now it was nearing eight at night. It was time to call it a day. I was exhausted and so were the rest of the crew; that was, until this sultry black siren, nearly six feet tall, glided into the room. The air was charged with testosterone as every man became aware of her presence.

"Hope I'm not too late," she purred.

Oh, God, her voice. It was like liquid, falling off her tongue to spill its way around the room. Every eye was on her. John, the director, seemed to have lost his ability to speak. He was always in control, and this was the only time I'd ever seen him react this way. He was speechless.

Finally, he found his voice. "Ah, yes, name, please."

"My real name or my stage name, darling?" she asked, advancing on him like a predator about to devour its prey.

He actually stepped back a fraction as she approached. She towered over him. He stood there, potbellied, balding, his mouth open.

"Delight. It's both my stage and real name. I have nothing to hide and I'm proud of who I am," she said.

"I'm sure you are," John said, and then with more assertiveness, "perhaps you'd like to show us your stuff."

Show us your stuff. Couldn't he have thought of something more professional to say? He sat on his director's chair and I began to roll the film. To say she knew how to work the cameras was an understatement. She was born for it.

She began by shaking out her thick black hair. It fluffed up around her face, softening her already beautiful features. It was as though I had a dimmer on my lens—everything else around her just faded out.

Then she was kicking off her shoes and peeling out of her skin-tight leather trousers. They were bright yellow and as she inched them over her gorgeous ebony backside I saw she was wearing a matching G-string. She kicked the trousers off her feet, licked her lips, and smiled at me.

Giggling, she turned around, flipped her hair over her shoulder, and peered coquettishly through her dark black lashes at the camera. Her smoky eyes bored into mine as she pointed that sexy butt straight at me, bending over to run her hands slowly up from her ankles to her hips. She turned; her hands skimming over her flat, taut stomach before she played with the front of the G-string, pulling it down a fraction as though beckoning us to take a peek.

Man, was she hot!

Her shirt was also skin-tight and yellow, her huge breasts practically spilling out, her cleavage straining against the buttons as they threatened to burst forth. Her white painted fingernails toyed with each button before unfastening them. The whole time she didn't take her eyes off the camera, licking her top lip with the tip of her pointy wet tongue. Man, did she have sex appeal. No one in the room spoke; we were frightened we'd break the spell.

Finally, opening the shirt, she flashed her breasts at us, wiggling them before closing the shirt again. She teased us for a while before she slipped it off her shoulders and allowed it to rest at her elbows. With her arms pulled slightly back, her melon-like breasts jutted forward, her dark nipples only just visible under the lace bra as she paraded around the room.

Dropping the shirt to the floor, she sashayed away from me. This beautiful goddess sauntered to the doorway. She turned, flicked her hair back, and then grabbed hold of the door jamb. With her honey-toned legs spread, she lowered her body until her pussy was nearly on the floor. What flexibility. Up and down she rode the frame, letting go with one hand to suck on her middle finger.

With her red lips pouting, she trailed that finger down her neck, over her voluptuous breasts, and into her bra. She let out a soft moan as she pinched her own nipple before continuing on to her G-string, where she taunted us further by slipping her hand in to cup her own pussy.

"Hmm, very nice," she breathed, nostrils flaring as though aware of the fragrance of her scent. "Very nice."

I caught myself holding my breath as my own pussy began to throb. She was walking toward me now, coming closer and closer. I zoomed in on her amazing breasts.

"You want to see some pussy, hmm? Or what about these gorgeous titties?"

I was speechless; we all were.

"Well, pussy or titties? Can't make up your mind? I'll decide for you," she purred.

Staring hard at the camera as though staring straight into my soul, she unclipped her bra and discarded it. I held my breath, my face flushing. Her huge breasts swayed, enjoying their freedom. Dark brown nipples beckoned me. My mouth opened and my tongue searched like a snake seeking warmth, longing to latch on to one and suck it into my mouth.

She pushed her biceps together, her cleavage nearly reaching her chin. Enjoying her own massaging, she lifted her breasts into her palms, weighing them as if each pound of flesh made them more appealing. She lifted one up toward her mouth, the nipple rigid as her tongue flickered over it.

"You want to taste it, too? Want to bury your head in here?" She indicated the space between her breasts. "Or are you more interested in what I've got down there?" she asked.

I had to lower the camera, follow her as she bent her head forward seductively, slipping her fingers into the sides of her G-string. Everyone gasped as she tore the flimsy material off and licked at the crotch, staring at me mischievously with a slight smile on her lips.

All the guys on set were jealous, I'm sure; me, I was in awe of her.

"Oh yeah, that tastes good," she whispered. Then she held the G-string in her hand, her beautiful upturned nose delicately sniffing. "Ah, yes, what an aroma."

Totally nude, she walked gracefully to the white couch. She lay back against the armrest, her hair framing her face. The darkness of her skin against the starkness of the white background made her beauty even more apparent.

The camera and I moved toward her as though one. I panned down from her face, over her luscious breasts with those dark nipples just begging for me to touch, and onward over her mound to her pussy. She had a wiry black bush. Pubic hair was growing wild over her mound. This was new; most girls loved to display themselves with a Brazilian, totally waxed and free of hair.

I wanted to kiss her sexy mouth, to throw myself down on her gorgeous body, but that, unfortunately, was not my job. I longed to be the star in my own porno movie, but I was not one of the attractive ones.

I focused in on her pussy, which she so kindly opened up for me. Her white fingernails roamed through her black pubic hair and into the folds and I realized why she'd painted them that way. It was as though her pussy was an entity on its own and the nails actually made it come to life, like a living breathing pulsating object, to be admired, lusted after, and of course used.

"You like what you see?" she asked me.

I didn't answer, too busy making sure I'd gotten all the important bits in the shot.

"Hey, I asked you a question. You like looking at my snatch? Look at it, take a good look, because you'll never see another one this good again."

I had to agree with her on that one. She'd had her fingers inside and now brought one up to her lips, to lick, to roll her tongue around.

"Hmm, tastes good, too."

In walked the star of the film we were shooting. She sauntered over to Delight, confident of her ability to perform for the camera as well and already nude. Her eyebrows rose just a fraction when she caught sight of this amazingly sexy woman who had the potential to steal her limelight.

Delight was a smart girl. She was giving nothing away. She was there to impress and she was certainly getting our votes.

Paula, the star, slapped Delight on the thigh before lowering herself to kneel in between those amazing legs. I moved in for a closer shot. Her tongue shot out tentatively to flicker at Delight's clit. She showed her appreciation by moving her pelvis upward, wanting Paula's tongue to do some more work as she stared sexily at the camera.

"Lick that pussy, baby; lick it like you've never licked one before. Taste it. There's no other pussy that tastes as good as mine," she said as she grabbed Paula by the head and held her an inch away from it. "Can you smell it, baby? Are you enjoying my scent, hmm? Breathe it in."

Paula was taken aback. She was used to being the star, calling the shots. Now here was this red-hot woman, with the most amazing body anyone's ever seen, and even though I'm sure Paula wants to pull back, make Delight beg for her, she doesn't. Her tongue flickers out and hits her clit.

I notice she's making sure she's got her body more in the shot, her face and hair hiding Delight's delicious pussy.

"Ah, yeah, baby, lick it. Come on," Delight says with that silky voice.

Paula's head disappears between Delight's thighs and I have trouble getting the shot, she's nuzzling into her like I've never seen her do. She seems to be working hard at it, trying to take control, sucking and licking like she's never tasted one before, like this is her first lesbian movie.

I'm picturing myself there, naked, my body sandwiched between the two of them. How awesome would that be? My hands are all over Delight's gorgeous breasts and I suck a nipple into my mouth, draw back on it, before gobbling as much as I can into my mouth. I'm fingering her cunt hard, her beautiful breasts jiggling, her warm brown arms reaching out to me, to pull me into her.

Then her dark fingers are tearing at the flesh on my back, my body can only take so much, and I'm just about ready to . . .

"Hey, whoa, back on that, baby, there's only so much a girl can take," Delight says as she pulls Paula's head away, dragging her up to her breast. Paula nuzzles in, suckling like a baby hours late for a feed. She's eyeing the camera as she does it, her body again more into the camera than the action.

She's putting on a good show, but inside I imagine she's seething. Everyone in the room knows Delight's body is the showstopper. Paula is gorgeous and has been around for years but Delight would bring something exciting into our production if she gets the job, and I'm thinking she's a sure thing.

"Oh, yeah, that feels sooooo good," Delight purrs.

The guys are all looking on as though they are wishing they were between her legs, their faces buried at her breasts. I almost laughed at their hard-ons, visible through their trousers.

"Come on, baby," she says, as she pulls Paula up farther, her mouth pouting, tongue flicking over her teeth, wanting Paula to kiss her mouth. Their tongues lock and she lifts her legs, wrapping them around Paula's back.

I'm trying hard to hang on to what I've been taught. Look for the best shot. The best angle. Watch the lights, shadows, etc. It's too much for me. My pussy and emotions have a mind of their own and they want to be smothered by this amazing woman.

The contrast of their flesh as they wrestle with each other is something to behold. Delight's legs, wrapped around Paula's white back, are kicking into her flesh, while pulling her in even closer.

Sweat is pouring off Paula. I've never seen her work so hard. Usually it's the others who are desperate to put on a performance better than hers but here she is desperate to be the continuing star.

She kisses Delight deep and long, and for a second I think

she's come. She licks Delight's chin, her eyes, cheeks, and then smashes her mouth into hers. I can just see her tongue, slipping all over Delight's mouth. Licking her cheeks, her eyes, ears, throat, and then back down to those amazing jugs.

It's one of the most passionate kisses I've ever seen on film.

"That's enough now," Delight says, pushing Paula away from her.

"What . . . hey . . . I make the decisions," Paula said, trying to regain some composure.

"I'm sure you usually do," she purred, "but this is my audition and I think I have every right to make sure *they're* appreciating the exhibition I hoped to show."

"Huh," Paula says, staring over at John.

I've never seen John like this. He's floundering like a fish out of water. He's got his cock out, stroking it, and it looks like it's about to explode. I should know. Hell, I'm his cameraman; I've seen him interview many women, but not like this. He stumbles over to Paula, his cock jutting forward, leading the way.

"I think I'd better have a look at what you've got there," he says, coming between her legs.

"Yeah, sure, baby," she says. She's not stupid; she knows who signs the checks.

Paula smacks her pussy hard, enjoying the sensation as John looks on. "Bring it here, baby, and you'll never want another pussy again."

He laps at her, licking long and hard from her hole all the way up to her clit. He lingers over it, sucking and licking, his cock growing bigger by the second.

I didn't want to do anything to break the mood. They seemed to be in a world of their own. I zoomed in instead of actually coming closer, not wanting to distract them from their lovemaking. This wasn't just fucking, it was something more, something I've never witnessed between two people.

He looks up at her, his face covered in her juices. Scrambling up her body, he thrusts himself into her as his tongue seeks out her mouth. They fuck on and on, sweat pouring off both of them. The guys and I watch, every one of them has a hard-on; we're all dumbfounded by this spectacle.

In the meantime, Delight is appalled at what is going on during her audition. She finds her clothes and dresses quickly. "Excuse me," she says, making to leave.

"What?" John was so caught up in Paula, he'd lost direction of what he was supposed to be doing, which was of course making sure he signed Delight to a contract.

Paula's plump butt grinds into John and her tits are practically resting on the couch. John tries to lower his hand down to grope one, but they're swaying back and forth under his pounding.

"I'm leaving," Delight says angrily.

I've stopped taping John and Paula and am now focused on Delight, who is angry, standing at the edge of the couch, staring down at the two of them.

"Wait," John says, reluctant to leave Paula.

Paula pushes back into John. She peers back over her shoulder and I catch the look, the look of entrapment. She's snared him and she knows it. John is of two minds on what to do and takes no time in coming.

"You're disgusting," Delight says to John. "I wouldn't work for you if you paid me a fortune."

"Wait," John says. "I want you to be the new star in our movie."

"What?" Paula jumps up angrily.

Prime Piece of Property

Nadia

I am sitting here with my husband and this real estate agent trying to negotiate a price for this beautiful house, but I can't stop my pussy from pulsating at just the thought of fucking the shit out of this agent.

My husband and I have what most people would consider an ideal marriage: nice house with the picket fence, expensive cars, excellent careers, a set of beautiful twin girls, and even a great sex life, so why in the hell am I sitting here flooding like the Mississippi River from just being in this stranger's presence? This agent is picture-perfect, though—he has skin the color of milk chocolate, a baritone voice that would put the Allstate insurance guy to shame, a nicely shaped bald head, and a well-groomed goatee. Fuck, if my husband wasn't sitting here with us, Mr. Milk Chocolate and I would probably be screwing on his mahogany desk by now.

Having these types of thoughts running through my head was unlike me because I had never been this type of woman. A year and a half ago my husband decided he wanted to cheat on me with the water girl down at the gym. The fucking water girl! He confessed to me and we talked about it and all that shit. I forgave him since it was his first slipup, but I never forgot it. And ever since then every fine-ass man that crosses my path, all I can do is think about how he could please my walls in bed. I know two wrongs don't make a right but I was like fuck it, I'm still going to get mine, at least once!

"While your offer sounds good, I would like a few days to talk this over with my wife, Mr. Johnson, and we'll get back in touch with you soon as we come to a decision," said my husband, Richard.

"Well, here's my business card, and one for you as well, Mrs. Mitchell. Feel free to contact me anytime regarding your decision."

That's just what I plan to do, Mr. Milk Chocolate, contact your ass anytime. I hope my husband didn't pick up on the vibes Mr. Johnson and I were giving each other. The look of passion that occupied his eyes when he handed me his business card made my insides get an instant fever.

He walked us to the door and thanked us for coming to take a look at his property. I knew he was checking out my *property,* too, because all the men did. I had to give it to myself, I have one of those video model–type bodies: ass for days, succulent titties, and killer legs. And on this particular day I was working the hell out of my low-cut, pencil-straight dress with my stilettos.

Once my husband and I got into our C-class Benz, he started the car and looked at me. "So what do you think, baby?"

What do I think; I think I want that man to fuck my insides until I scream bloody murder, that's what I think. Lawd knows I couldn't say that, so I had to instantly clear all my nasty thoughts.

"Baby, I really don't need any more time to decide if I want this house. I love it! It has everything in it we're looking for in our dream home: a pool, his and hers closets and bathroom space, your man's den, our own offices, and a mini theater. I'm sold!" I said with a little giggle.

"You're right, baby, I love it, too, but I think I can get him to—"

Ding, Ding.

I picked up my phone and it read *Facebook Alert*. Richard knew that sound all too well and hated it because he says I don't pay any attention to him when I'm reading my Facebook messages. Shit, that's business, and I'm sorry that he can't understand that, but it's how I make a living, and right now business is booming. I glanced at a message and it was from Lisa, one of my good friends. *I'll hit her later so I don't hear his mouth.* She probably was just commenting on the picture I posted not long ago.

"As I was saying," Richard said with disgust in his voice, "I love the house and it does have everything in it that we want, but I think we can get him to come down on the price. It's been on the market for close to a year so I'll use that as my bargaining tool. I also need to see what the other houses in the area are going for before I lock myself into a contract."

Bargaining tool? What the hell was he talking about; everybody knows that pussy ranks as the number-one bargaining tool that has been proven to work since before George Washington was playing with peanuts.

"Cool, babe."

So while my husband was trying to figure out how he would talk Mr. Johnson down on the price, I was plotting on how I would go down on his dick like no other woman ever had before. That way we would both get what we wanted: me—a pleased pussy; my husband—a lower price on the house. I still don't know why I even wanted to fuck Mr. Johnson so bad because like I said, sex was good on the home front, but it was just something about the way this man carried himself. He was different. He had a certain arrogance, or what the teeny boppers called "swag," about him, and I just wanted a little piece.

Later on that night, I couldn't even sleep. Mr. Milk Chocolate was on my mind heavy, so at about 2:45 a.m. I climbed out of the bed I shared with my husband, who was dead to the world, took Milk Chocolate's card out of my zebra-print wallet, and headed over to the guest computer in the den and logged on to my Facebook account. I'm sure he had to be on it—everybody has a page, from the hoodest of the hood to the most elite professionals.

"Alexis Johnson, cute name," I whispered to myself as I typed it in the search bar. "Bingo!"

After searching through about eighty-seven motherfuckers with the same name, I finally found him. I sent him a friend request, along with an empty private message with only a subject that read: *So contact you anytime, huh?* I hit the send button, logged off, and crawled back in bed with the hibernating bear, but went to sleep with Milk Chocolate's pleasure piece on my mind.

The next morning came around and I woke up with a soaking wet canal.

Monica, you are too old to be having wet dreams, girl. Get it together. This man really has me going, I thought to myself.

After taking my shower to clean the natural disaster that had happened overnight between my legs, I threw on some loungewear to see my family out the door for the day. I kissed Richard, Ciara, and Chelsea as they all walked out heading for school and work.

I am a well-known event planner in the city and I conduct my business from home so I don't have to commute to work like my husband does daily. It's lovely at times, but takes a lot of self-discipline.

"First things first, let me see what kind of events I have in store for today. Sweet Sixteen . . . bridal shower . . . divorce party . . ." reading my Facebook subjects out loud.

RE: So contact me anytime

"Oh, shit! He responded," I said in a very low voice as if someone were still at home with me. "Well, let's see what you're talking about, Mr. Milk Chocolate."

Open.

"*Hi, Mrs. Mitchell. Yes, I said to contact me anytime you guys were ready to make an offer, or if you have any questions regarding the house. Actually, I will be over at the property today at ten a.m. if you would like to stop by and take another look.*"

Well, that gives me two and a half hours to get myself together. I got to make sure everything is on point for our "meeting."

My thoughts were interrupted by my Brandy "Best Friend" ringtone, which told me that Lisa was calling.

"Hello . . . hey, chick . . . I'm getting ready to go to a meeting . . . with Mr. Milk Chocolate . . . I'll explain later . . . okay . . . bye."

Lisa called me every morning to chitchat and catch up on the events of the day before since we both really don't have much time to talk for the rest of the day after that.

A couple of hours later I arrived at my dream home, which was the *baddest* house on the block, kind of like myself. I rang the doorbell and waited for him to receive me. I had on my white halter sundress that stopped right above my knee and showed off my curves. My feet were freshly manicured and polished with a burnt orange color. My naturally curly hair was pulled back into a ponytail and my skin was glowing as if the sun personally blew me a kiss. I was flawless and I knew it. I guess you could say I had a certain "swag" about me, too.

When he opened the door, my cockiness disappeared. I stood there speechless. What the hell was I going to say? I mean, all this *man* standing in front of me was too much, but now was not the time to freeze up. It was time to go hard or go home. There he was in my presence again, and there was the Mississippi waters stirring up in my lace panties again. I'm not sure what fragrance he was wearing but it sent shockwaves through my body that traveled from my nose to my clit. And I knew before I left this house today he would be nibbling, biting, and sucking on it like it was his last supper.

"Hi, Mrs. Mitchell, come on in. Is your husband accompanying you today?"

"Hi, Mr. Johnson, how are you? No. My husband had to work today, so I came alone."

"I'm fine, thank you. Please have a seat."

Yes, you are.

"So, Mrs. Mitchell, did you want to take a look at the house again, or do you have any questions, or just tell me what's on your mind." He chuckled.

If I told this man that his golden rod was on my mind, he'd probably fall out of his chair, or maybe not.

"Well, we both love the house but my husband thinks that it's overpriced. I would just like to get a second tour, if you don't mind showing me again."

"Certainly, not a problem, Mrs. Mitchell; we could definitely do that."

"Please, feel free to call me Monica."

"Okay, Monica, and you can call me Alexis."

We started off on our journey touring the house again. All of the rooms had hardwood flooring except for the bedrooms; there was plush carpet in each one of those. The windows were thirteen feet tall. There were also some really nice pieces of furniture left behind from the last owners, who'd decided not to take it with them when they left. There were no complaints on our end, though; we could find somewhere to use it.

Our last stop on the house tour was the master bedroom. This room was beautiful. It had a double-sided fireplace, a chandelier, and even a pole! Once you stepped out onto the balcony, there was a beautiful view of the lake that ran behind the upscale subdivision. There was nothing at all that I would change about this house, I loved it, but right now Alexis was the prime piece of property I wanted to acquire.

The sexual tension had been building up throughout the tour. My pussy had been pounding like I'd been locked in a department store bathroom after hours, trying to get the security guard's attention. I could only imagine what was going on in his pants.

"And here is the final room, the master bedroom. Do you have any questions?"

"Yes, I have one."

Oh shit, just say it, girl, before you get too nervous and make a complete fool of yourself.

I continued, "Alexis, are you craving me right now as much as my body is craving you?"

Without saying a word, Alexis took maybe two steps toward me and kissed me on the lips. Our kisses grew harder and harder, filled with passion. His strong hands were rubbing the small of my back and when he pulled me closer to him I could feel the bulge in his pants. That sent my body into ecstasy overload. Not long after, he pulled my dress down and started sucking on my breasts while pushing them together, as if he could fit them both in his mouth at the same time. My moans grew louder the harder he sucked on my breasts. So I started unbuttoning his shirt and unbuckled his pants because I needed him inside me.

He wasted no time, and told me to get on all fours. I did as I was told and I just knew he was about to please me from behind with his golden rod, but that wasn't the case. On his back, he slid under my black panther like he was a mechanic at the body shop, and working on my pussy was his job. He gripped my thighs as his warm, thick tongue began to trace the folds of my pussy, causing my body to become weak.

Shit, this was something new to my body because Richard had never tasted the black panther before. He never performed oral sex on me and would never let me perform on him. He thought it was disgusting, and it fucked me up because I was trying to figure out what day and age he was living in, to where a man didn't practice oral sex! I still married his ass, though; the sex game was still good.

Mr. Milk Chocolate must have loved giving oral pleasure because he stayed beneath me longer than I thought he would for a woman he'd just met. But like I said, I wasn't just any woman, I was a bad bitch. By this time my jowls were starting to clench because I couldn't wait any longer to taste him.

I told him, "Let's trade places."

At this point, his pants and boxer briefs were fully removed, and the golden globe sprang out of his pants as if it was about to yell out, "Surprise!" I gave it a look of desire and then I licked his shiny head before engulfing more of him into my mouth. I got my mouth really wet with my warm saliva and took all of him that I could fit inside until the eye of his head searched the back of my throat. I caressed his balls with my hands while I was pleasing him with my mouth.

"Damn, baby, you feel so damn good," he moaned while grabbing hold of my fluffy ponytail.

I took a quick leave from his magic stick. "Well, if you liked that, then you'll love this."

I took the Pop Rocks from my purse that I had left over from one of the kids' events I'd put on last week, placed them on my tongue, and started back on the job.

"Oh, shit!" he yelled, while his body jerked.

"Some people want it all, but I don't want nothing at all, if it ain't you, baby . . ."

My Alicia Keys ringtone alerted us that my husband was trying to contact me, but I couldn't stop right now, because I was doing us both a favor. I was working on this man's dick like it had been bitten by a poisonous snake and I was trying to save his life by sucking out the venom.

After I finished pleasing him with my warm, inviting mouth, it was time to feel him inside me. He took a condom out of his taupe-colored slacks, laid me on my back, and proceeded to please me. That first thrust was unbelievable and it made my body melt. He slowly slid his piece out, just leaving the head in, and once again, another forceful, yet gentle thrust followed. At this point, I could feel my nectar flowing out of me and drizzling between the crease of my ass, while glazing his dick at the same time. He was passionately sucking on my neck and full breasts while pushing inside me. And I was holding onto his firm ass as he was driving deeper and deeper into my warm, wet insides.

Alexis then took my legs and placed each one over his shoulders so that he could explore deeper. He felt so damn good, I was starting to think, *Could this be a onetime affair? I really don't know.* He still wasn't done with my ass; he took me over to the bathroom counter, sat me in between the his and hers sinks, and once again he glided his dick, glistening with my juices on it, in and out of me. First with slow, long strokes, and then with fast, hard pumps, and before you know it Alexis gave me my first orgasm. But I was nowhere near ready to stop and by the look in his eyes, neither was he.

We then moved to the living area of the master bedroom. He bent me over the arm of the sofa, which was one piece of the furniture that was left behind, and he entered me again. This time there were no slow strokes, only fast and hard just the way I wanted it. I wasn't looking to make love to this man, I just wanted to fuck him. So I accepted all of his forcefulness and worked my ass back on him, moving my hips in circular motions so that I could feel his dick in every inch of my pussy. He licked his thumb and placed it right over my anus and rubbed it vigorously. And not long after, I was cumming again, but he still hadn't gotten his nut from me so now it was time for me to return the favor.

Once I got what I needed from Mr. Milk Chocolate, I guided him to the seat of the lavender-colored sofa, straddled his magic stick backward, and sat down on top of it slowly until every inch of him was inside me. Up and down I went while he kissed my back and squeezed my C-cup breasts. Our moans grew louder and louder. We both were excited from the gyrating moves I was giving out, and we climaxed together.

On my twenty-minute ride home from the dream house, I called my husband back but he didn't pick up. So I returned Lisa's phone call and filled her in on what I'd just done and how I had already "christened" the house with Mr. Milk Chocolate. She didn't judge me but told me to promise that I wouldn't do it again, because she knew I wasn't that type of woman. I promised her I wouldn't because I felt like I had gotten my revenge, so I was good. And we said our good-byes.

"*Some people want it all, but I don't want nothing at all, if it ain't you, baby . . .*"

"Hey, baby, I tried calling you back but I couldn't reach you," I said.

"I know. Monica, you're not going to believe this, but Mr. Johnson called me back and told me that they were willing to come down on the price of the house. So, baby, that house is going to be ours in a couple of days!"

We both screamed and yelled because it *was* our dream home. A few days later, we met with Mr. Johnson to seal the deal. We put our signatures on all the needed paperwork. He shook our hands and said, "Congratulations, enjoy your new home," and handed us the keys and paperwork with a beautiful smile.

Richard and I kissed and he hugged me so tight that he lifted me off the ground a few inches. On the way out of the signing, Mr. Johnson walked us out of the office and congratulated us again. My husband told him, "Thanks again, but we got to get out of here to go christen our new home," while looking at me passionately.

I don't know why he's thanking Mr. Johnson; he should be thanking my pussy!

I turned back to Alexis, smiled, and said, "Yes, thank you, Mr. Johnson."

I gave him a wink and he winked back.

On the Eve of Tomorrow

Ran Walker

Grant Darby could barely hear the light knocking at the front door, and had the apartment still been full of boxes and furniture, he might not have heard it at all. He was surprised by how quickly he could move through an empty apartment. Except for the day he'd moved in, he had never seen the place this bare. The power would be turned off the next day, probably shortly after he left the apartment for the last time, headed to Virginia for grad school. Still, he had chosen to stay there one last night, although his roommate had gone home to Knoxville earlier that week. Only one person knew he was still in Atlanta—and she was at the front door right now.

He opened the door casually, as if he had not been waiting for her the last hour.

"Come on in," he offered, needlessly, as she walked into the dark apartment. Only the streetlights outside glinting through the blinds gave any kind of lighting to the front room.

"No power?" Kamara said, a slight chuckle in her voice.

"It's on until tomorrow."

"I see. So this is for me, then?"

He smiled and took her hand, guiding her down the hall into the master bedroom in the back of the apartment. The blinds were parted, angled downward so that they could look out, but no one could look in.

"They never did fix your front door," Kamara said.

"I guess it doesn't matter now," he responded. He had reported the hole in the outer part of his door when he moved into the apartment complex, and the front office had assured him it would be fixed. They never came to fix it, though. At first Grant had started to go down and raise hell, especially since he was the only one in the building paying full price for his rent, but the hole didn't go all the way through the door and since none of his company seemed to complain about it, he let the issue go. In fact, as time went on, the hole became part of the apartment's character, a reminder that he had slummed it his last year in college before heading on to Virginia.

"Want anything to drink?" he offered.

"Do you *have* anything to drink in here?"

"Some bottled water left over from when I loaded up the truck."

"Sure, then."

As he walked back toward the front of the apartment to the kitchen, he marveled at the fact that Kamara had even come. She was not his girlfriend and would probably never be, now that he was leaving Atlanta. He had run into her the previous day while combing the bookstore for college and Greek paraphernalia to take with him. They had had three classes together over the past two years and had always been cordial, but it wasn't until they pledged and became fraternity brother and sorority sister that they began to talk more regularly. Even then, he had suppressed his attraction to her because there was already so much hooking up going on between the frats and sorors. Still, he considered her a good friend and had even had her over several times throughout the year, just to hang out and play Xbox with his friends.

As he stood at the refrigerator door, he was thankful that she had not left him hanging. At least now he would have someone he could talk to so that he wasn't stuck with only the silence of an empty apartment to keep him company. All of his other friends had already headed out of town, either for the summer break or just to move on to the next thing.

Cracking the refrigerator door, Grant noticed that there was only one bottle of water on the bare shelf. He removed it and carried it back to Kamara.

"You weren't thirsty?" she asked.

"There was just one bottle."

"You want some of this one?"

"I'm good."

"You sure? I don't have cooties, you know," she said, turning the bottle sideways in her hand and swiveling it like a bottle of juice.

"Have you noticed that when guys shake bottles, they do it like this," he said, lifting and lowering his hand in a line just in front of his crotch. "But when women shake a bottle, they twist it like you just did."

"Really?" she responded. "I have my theories about that."

"Hey, don't knock my only hobby."

They both laughed, and he might have been embarrassed being so mannish with her, except for the fact that sex wasn't foreign to their conversations. At various points they had had conversations about nearly everything under the sun, sex included. He had just never made a move. Now that he was spending his last night in Atlanta and she had come over to keep him company, the thought crossed his mind that there might be more to their situation after all.

"I guess I should have kept some chairs or something," he said. "You don't mind sitting on the floor, do you?"

She shrugged and took a seat on the carpet, her legs crossed, positioning herself directly across from him.

"Got any music to listen to?" she asked between swallows of water.

"Just what's on my phone."

Grant pulled his phone from his pocket and began scrolling through his playlists.

"Hey, remember this?" he said, turning up the volume on his phone and tilting the speaker upward for her to hear.

"Oh, shit!" Kamara said, jumping to her feet. She began nodding her head up and down to the beat. "We used to set it out to this track!"

Grant stood up, holding the phone up. "Go 'head, 'Mara. Do it up for all the treys of the world."

As Nicki Minaj's "Moment 4 Life" filled the empty room, Kamara flashed her sorority sign and started performing the party stroll that her chapter had designed for the song. Grant nodded his head to the beat as he admired the way her body moved. Seeing her rocking her hips in sync with the song made him smile. He had always thought she was cute, but seeing her now, in motion, and with such focus, made her much more than cute; she was *sexy*.

As the song ended, she reached for the bottle of water and finished it off.

"I love watching you move," he said, before realizing how loaded his statement must have sounded.

She took her seat on the floor again, screwing the cap back on the empty bottle and setting it in front of her. "Thanks."

Grant sat down across from her and reached for the bottle. Without thought, he began to spin it in a circle. Kamara laughed.

"What?" he asked.

"Reminds me of that game."

"Oh," he said, continuing to spin the clear, hollow bottle. "You must have had your first kiss playing Spin the Bottle."

"No way. I played that game one time, but there were just too many ugly boys there for me. I was so glad it never landed on me. This one time it came close, like between me and this other girl, and we argued for like ten minutes over who the bottle had landed on. Finally, ol' girl just said, 'fuck it,' and kissed that boy. Couldn't have been me," she said, laughing. "You ever play?"

"Nope," he said. "I used to hear about other people playing it. That and 'Sleepers' and all those sixth-grade games."

"You've never been *slept?*" she asked, incredulous.

"I haven't been anything-ed," he said, lifting the bottle from the floor and flipping it in his hand repeatedly.

"I feel like it's my duty to make sure you experience something before you move away and start your life in the 'real world,'" she said, placing air quotes around the last two words.

Looking at the bottle, Grant imagined what it would be like to kiss Kamara. "I have an idea."

Kamara nodded. "I'm all ears."

He could feel his stomach begin to tense. If she was down, this would be a wonderful experience, but if she wasn't, then she'd probably leave or steer the rest of the evening's conversation into such platonic territory that he might as well just unroll the sleeping bag now and get an early start on the next day.

"We can take this bottle and spin it," he said.

"Yeah. That's an original idea," Kamara offered, her voice tinged with sarcasm.

"No. Here's the catch: If the bottle lands closer to me, you can tell me where you'd like me to kiss you, and if the bottle lands closer to you, I'll tell you where I'd like you to kiss me."

The fact that they had never kissed before seemed like an irrelevant point to Grant. He waited nervously, watching her consider his proposition. The fact that she did not flat-out say, "No," made him even more nervous.

"Who spins first?" she finally responded.

Grant smiled and sat back down across from Kamara. He handed her the bottle. "You go first."

She looked at him, a semi-smile resting on her lips, and lowered the bottle to the carpet, spinning it around with a quick flick of her wrist. The bottle spun in a circle very quickly before slowing down and angling just to his right side.

"Okay," she said. "I want you to kiss me here." She pointed at a spot toward the back side of her neck.

Grant rose to his knees and leaned toward her. As she turned her head away from him to better expose her neck, he placed his mouth against her soft skin, his tongue dancing in tender swirls along the length of her neck. He listened for a moan—or anything—but Kamara sat silently, allowing him to finish his kiss, before turning her attention back to the bottle. "Your turn," she said.

Still savoring the taste of her skin, he leaned over and spun the bottle. Again, it landed just to his right.

"This must be my lucky night," Kamara offered. "I can get you to kiss me anywhere?"

"Sure," he responded.

"I want you to kiss me here—on my tattoo," she said, lifting her T-shirt to reveal a small, flower-shaped tattoo on the left side of her right breast, just above the fabric of her bra.

For a moment, Grant stared, taking in her flawless, caramel-complexioned skin. The T-shirt had been loose fitting, but now he could see her full breasts, in all of their glorious splendor, perky and awaiting his attention. He leaned in slowly, enjoying the view as his body proceeded to close the gap.

His tongue immediately danced upon her skin, tracing the outline of her tattoo as she raked her fingertips lightly across the back of his head. In his eagerness, he gently pulled down her shoulder strap, exposing her nipple. He took it into his mouth, his tongue fluttering along her areola. This time she moaned.

For a moment, he moved back and forth between her breasts, his tongue leaving a faint trace from nipple to nipple. When Kamara's hand pressed his chest, pushing him back, he had trouble leaving her topless form. He started to ask why she was pushing him away, until he noticed that she was pointing at the bottle lying on the floor off to the side.

"My turn," she said, as she adjusted herself. Her bra and shirt remained on the floor beside her as she leaned over and spun the bottle again. This time the bottle rotated back toward her as if magnetically drawn to her skin.

A smile spread across Grant's lips.

"So where do you want me to kiss you?" she asked, her beautiful body illuminated by the mild glow of the streetlights trickling through the bedroom blinds.

He knew where he wanted her to kiss him, but he didn't want to be too forward. As he hesitated, Kamara crawled over to him and began to unfasten his jeans. Propping himself up with his hands, he lifted himself so that she could remove them. With his eager erection straining at the fabric of his boxers, he watched as she lowered her face to his waistband, tugging at it with her teeth. When she unleashed his manhood into the darkness of the room, he closed his eyes, leaning back. He could feel her envelop the head in her warm, wet mouth, massaging the length of his shaft with her hand. Patiently, she ran her tongue along the length of his erection. He had not been this hard in a long time, and he wanted only for her to take her time—bottle be damned.

Once he could feel the buzzing glow of an orgasm collecting between his legs, he stopped her. There was only one thing he wanted more than to cum and that was to return the favor.

Pulling himself away from her, he leaned over and kissed her passionately on the lips, rejoicing as her tongue met his. As he placed the palm of his hand along the side of her face, just beneath her flowing hair, he whispered for her to lie down.

Kamara lay down, lifting her hips from the floor so that he could remove her jeans and panties. Even in the darkness, Grant could see that she had trimmed her hair down low. Gently he tugged at her outer lips, allowing the hood to slide gracefully over her pearl. He continued this for a moment, drawing as much excitement to that area as he could, before he lowered his face and allowed himself to taste her. The salty-sweetness of her moist flesh invited him to run his tongue along the length of her vulva and into her vagina, before returning to her clit, careful not to put too much pressure on her sensitivity. As she began to rock herself against his face, he moved with her rhythm, matching her beat for beat.

He could feel her contracting against his chin as her legs tensed. He looked up, hoping to make out her facial expression in the dim light. All he could see was her head lean forward and then tilt back, her face lifted toward the ceiling. As she shook her head, moaning from the sensation, Grant began to massage his erection as it returned to its full glory.

Taking him in her mouth once again, Kamara began to massage his balls with her fingertips. Lifting her head to face him, she asked, "Are you ready for this?"

Grant nodded, his smile bright, even in the darkness. "Hell, yes!"

As he approached her, she lifted one leg high, holding it up near her ear.

"Damn, you're flexible," he said, positioning himself over her. She smiled.

He entered her slowly, savoring every inch of his manhood entering her soaking wet walls. His triceps tightened as he held himself above her, allowing her to rock back and forth into him. As she enveloped and released him, he cursed himself silently for having never made a move on her before tonight.

Slowly, Kamara began to lower her leg onto Grant's shoulder, lifting her other leg onto his other shoulder. He cupped her soft, round ass in his palms and began to raise and lower her body so that he entered her in repetition.

"You feel so good," he uttered.

"Say that shit again. This time louder," she said, surprising him.

"You feel so good!"

"Yeah, baby," she responded, stretching out her legs. "I want you to hit it from the back, G."

Not wanting to lose a moment of her warmth massaging him, he lowered one of her legs and grabbed the other, turning her slowly onto her stomach. As she began to work her way to her knees, he ran his hands along her side, gradually resting them on her full hips. As she rocked back into him, he plowed into her until he heard her gasp.

"Fuck me," she moaned, as he thrust himself into her, his hands gripping her voluptuous ass.

He wanted nothing more than to stay inside her indefinitely, but as sweat trickled down his chest, he wondered how much longer he could last. He leaned over her, planting kisses along her back, as she rotated her hips in small circles.

"No, don't do that," he whispered breathlessly. "It feels too good."

"I want you to cum for me, baby."

He lifted himself so that his body was fully erect, and as she shifted, he withdrew, releasing himself onto her lower back while she moaned, her ass still moving, sliding lazily beneath his spent erection.

Barely able to feel his legs, Grant said, "Don't move. I'll be right back." He struggled to his feet and walked into the bathroom, returning with a few squares of paper towel. Kneeling down beside Kamara, he began to gently wipe her skin. When he finished, she lay down on her side, facing him while he reclined, propping himself up on his elbows.

"So what now?" she asked.

"I don't know. I'll be leaving in the morning. I wish I could take you with me."

She smiled. "You know what? You're a sweet guy. You're gonna make some woman very lucky."

Grant's brow furrowed as he watched her begin to dress. "You're leaving?"

"Yeah."

"I was hoping you'd stay the night."

"Close your eyes," Kamara said, kissing him gently on the lips. "Dream of me."

Grant followed her to the door, the air conditioner beginning to cool his nude body. He watched her leave as quietly as she had come, and as her car backed out of the parking lot, he realized that of all the things he'd miss about Atlanta, he would miss her most.

After Dark

Niyah Moore

Pigalle Palace was a notorious hot spot, an epicenter of sizzling sex shops, erotic peep shows, and dazzling strip clubs. It was an adults-only, X-rated, pleasurable adventure for the more risqué crowd and home to one of Paris's most famous cabarets, Moulin Rouge. After my first few weeks of studying abroad, I was ready to find out what really happened there after dark.

My roommate and I squeezed into the backseat of a tiny taxi to go bar-hopping one Friday night.

Once the door was closed, I asked, "Have you ever been to the red light district?"

She responded in her thick, French accent, "Pig Alley?"

"Pig Alley?" I repeated with a confused look on my face. "I'm talking about where all the freaky things happen. You know, topless bars? Nude strip clubs . . ."

"*Oui*. Pig Alley," she said, and laughed in her cute, girlish manner.

"Why do you call it Pig Alley?" I asked with a scowl.

"A lot of pigs tend to wallow in all the filthy diversions."

The fire inside of my curiosity grew wilder. "Let's go. How far is it from here?"

"Not too far." She shrugged while lighting a cigarette. "Are you sure you want to go?" She rolled down the small window to blow out a lungful of smoke.

"Positive. I won't rest until I know."

"What will you do once there?" She raised her eyebrow with a sleek grin appearing on her face.

I thought about that and, honestly, I had no idea what I would do.

"I don't know what to expect. I'm just going as a tourist."

Colette nodded and then smiled before taking another drag from her cancer stick. "Take us to the infamous club on the Boulevard de Clichy," she said to the taxi driver. "I have a spot in mind first and then, from there, we'll explore."

A sly, naughty grin appeared on the driver's pale face. With rose-colored cheeks, he knew exactly what spot she had in mind and had a hard time trying to conceal his discomfort, but he didn't say a word or yield a warning. Pulling away from the curb, the taxi drove through the wet streets toward the north side of a town called Montmartre.

Once in the red light district, I wiggled in my seat like a five-year-old kid going to McDonald's. From the taxi window, I stared out at all the colorful lights reflecting off the raindrops that remained on the car after the rain. In red and blue lights I read: DVDS, PEEP SHOWS, NUDE, NEW GIRLS, and SEX. I was in adult playland. Electric excitement filled me completely and I could feel my toes tingling in anticipation. I crossed my legs to stop myself from squirming.

"Reminds me of San Francisco," I noted aloud.

"Do you miss home?" Colette asked.

"I do, but studying in Paris has always been a dream of mine."

The taxi stopped in front of one of the clubs along the strip of a dark, unlit alley. The line to get inside stretched down the street.

"This joint is off the hook, huh?" I asked, placing my cold

hands in the pockets of my peacoat as soon as we were out of the cab.

Colette laughed and nodded her head. "*Oui.* It is very popular."

There were diverse groups of people waiting in line. Some smoked cigarettes and others chatted while the line moved quickly.

After tossing her cigarette on the ground, Colette stepped on it, sprayed her favorite peach-smelling perfume from her purse—something she did every time she smoked—and then adjusted her black bikini top underneath her coat to prevent her breasts from popping out.

I stared down the dark, foggy alley we came through. There was no way I would be able to walk down that alley alone. It was definitely too dark and scary, plus the smell of the soggy sewer left an unsettling feeling in my gut.

I moved my eyes up to the club's vivid flashing red sign above our heads.

"*Vaisseau,*" I read aloud. "Nice . . ." *Vaisseau* meant "vessel" in French. "Does this spot crack?"

Colette laughed at me again. "The American slang is so strange. What does *crack* mean?"

"You know, jumpin', like is this where people have a great time?"

"I like this place. The drinks are superb and there is plenty of yummy eye candy."

My pussy pounded. I was looking for some fun, ending with me having a few orgasms before the night was over. We walked to the end of the line with our three-inch boots clicking against the wet pavement, causing small puddles to splash away from us.

Lightning lit up the gloomy sky, which caused me to jump a little. A roaring thunder accompanied the shortened sparks of quickened light. I was glad we'd worn our coats to protect us, in case it started raining again.

The line moved so fast that we were at Vaisseau's entrance in a matter of minutes.

The bouncer immediately caught my eye. "Wow," I said to Colette. "He's nice . . ."

I couldn't see him from the alley as we'd walked up, but I was glad to know he was a fine, bald brother standing a little over six feet. His skin was the color of café au lait.

"*Oui,* he is one of the owner's sons. This is the only black-owned place in all of Pigalle."

"Welcome to Vaisseau," he uttered with his sultry, deep voice as he took my I.D. first. He looked at me to see if the picture matched. "Wow, all the way from United States? California? Your name is Essence?"

"Yes to all you just asked," I replied in a flirty manner. "What's your name, handsome?"

He smiled and bit on his lower lip. That's when I spotted the small but noticeable dimple in his right cheek. He was too ador-able for me not to swoon in front of him.

"Onyx," he stated proudly.

"Onyx? Like a precious black gem? That name fits you."

Laughing casually, he showed off his pearly whites. "Thank you. Enjoy your evening."

He took a look at Colette's identification and then removed the red rope from in front of the door.

As soon as we were inside the highly energized club, the music thumped through my chest like a strong heartbeat. The air inside was so crisp it caused me to shiver a little. Topless go-go dancers were in each corner of the dark club with red lights flashing all over them. The couches and chairs were red.

Even the bubbling water in a fountain behind the bar was red. All the red accents against the black walls gave the effect of blood pumping through the veins of the building.

"Bonsoir," a tall young woman with smoky eye shadow greeted us. "Nineteen euros."

I rummaged through my purse looking for euros, finding nothing but lipstick, old receipts, and American cash. "Colette, I left my euros in the room. What am I going to do?" I whined, waving my U.S. dollars in her face.

"Fifteen of your dollars," the woman interjected. "We welcome you. You can also check your coats and purses here."

I handed her the money and all of my belongings with a huge grin on my face. Bouncing to the beat, I took a ticket and hand stamp. I looked at the small black "V" that marked the top of my right hand before I placed the claim ticket in the back of my skintight jeans' pocket.

We made our way over to the bar through the howling dance crowd. Watching sweaty bodies pressed up against one another, ready to fuck, made my nipples harden. I bit on my lower lip to hide my arousal.

I nodded my head to the music and began to move my hips. The big fans flowing made the air blow, causing my wild curly hair to sway. I closed my eyes and imagined that I was a sexy video vixen waiting to dance with the hottest guy. I adjusted my halter top to make sure my boobs were pushed up just right.

My eyes immediately fell on the flashy bartender with long dreads who was spinning some bottles, juggling glasses, and engaging everyone around him. From the looks of it, he could have been another member of the family that owned the place.

"You weren't lying. The eye candy is unbelievable," I said to Colette. "Who's the sexy man behind the bar?"

"Oh, that's Legend."

"Legend looks like a god!"

Just when I thought I was in love with the muscular, dread-headed bartender, a taller, dark-skinned stud appeared from under the bar. His efficiently lined goatee and flawless haircut sent me over the edge. He looked a lot like a younger version of the actor Idris Elba.

"What can I get you ladies?" he asked as he leaned over the bar. Dimples in each cheek framed a perfect grin.

My heavy breathing halted as soon as I laid eyes on his shirtless, sculpted upper body. Sweet, honey brown eyes locked with mine and I clutched my heart because it skipped a beat.

Colette spoke up. "Can you give us two shots of vodka, *s'il vous plaît?*"

As he poured the liquor, Colette placed some money on the bar.

"Girl, I have a weakness for chocolate," I said into her ear, feeling my knees buckle.

I had to plant my feet firmly and lean up against a barstool to stop myself from fainting.

"Trés magnifique," she said.

He slid the two shot glasses in front of us with well-practiced fluidity, not wasting a single drop on the glass-topped bar.

"Bottoms up!" I yelled before downing my shot. Colette downed hers as well.

Before I could set the glass down, two more shots were in front of us.

"This one is on the house," he said with a wink before he made his way to the other end of the long bar.

The two bartenders worked so masterfully that I was entranced. All of the women were spellbound, fixated by the way they commanded all the attention in the room.

"Oh, my God!" I shouted, bouncing up and down, feeling the music propel through me. "What is Mr. Chocolate's name?"

Colette grinned widely as if she knew I would ask. She let me hang on to her silence for a moment before she said, "Rain."

"His name is Rain? Like from the sky? Okay, what's up with their names?"

"Onyx, Legend, and Rain are brothers."

"I take it their mother doesn't like traditional names."

Colette giggled and raised her hand to order another drink. "I'm ready to get drunk."

"Me too." I couldn't keep my eyes off Rain. I wanted him. "Do you think I can have Mr. Rain tonight?"

"I don't know . . ." Colette's glossy eyes glanced over in his direction to find that he was stealing stares at me. "From the looks of it . . . you might do just that, Madame Essence."

Rain was back in front of us after he mixed more drinks for the other thirsty ladies farther down the bar. Legend covered him by taking over the end he'd abandoned.

"Encore du vodka, mademoiselles," he said with his left eyebrow raised.

"Give me one with cranberry juice," I replied.

"Encore!" Colette exclaimed as she shook her ass to the music.

Rain poured the drinks, smiling, as I admired his well-manicured fingernails. Everything about his appearance was perfect. He licked his lips before asking, "Do you like what you see?"

"I do," I admitted timidly.

When he smiled wider, I felt my skin grow hot from the inside.

"I've never seen you here before. Are you new to the city?" Rain questioned.

"I've been here for a few weeks. Maybe you can show me around sometime," I flirted, afraid he would reject me.

"I would love to."

"Hopefully, you can show me more than just the city," I hinted, leaning on the bar.

He smiled broadly, staring at me with those honey brown eyes before hopping from the other side of the bar easily and gracefully like a gazelle. There was no bar between us anymore. Once I cleared my tightened throat, I felt myself get even hotter.

"And your name is?" Rain asked.

Swallowing the hard lump in my throat, I replied, "Essence."

"Essence," he said easily. "I like that. Come with me."

As Colette flirted with some guy who was whispering in her ear with his hand easing inside her bikini top, she flashed me a cunning wink and devilish smirk.

I didn't know if it was the liquor that had me feeling dazed or if I was under his hypnosis, but I let him take my hand while I followed him through the club to an elevator.

"Where are we going?"

"Do you trust me?"

I wanted to say I barely knew him, but for some reason, I felt so safe with him. "I trust you."

He smiled as the golden elevator opened. We went up to the third floor. Holding my hand, Rain took slow steps backward out of the elevator. I got the feeling he'd done this many times before, yet I didn't care.

We went down a long, dark hallway that was illuminated by red, pulsating lights. He pressed his body on mine so I could rest against one of the many doors in the hallway. My mind wondered what kind of freakiness went on behind them. The mere thought made my clit throb in anticipation of finding out.

Rain leaned in closer to me before I let him take me into a passionate kiss with his soft tongue.

"You taste so good," he whispered against my lips.

Both of his hands were in my curly hair before he gently moved my head to the side so he could kiss my neck.

I closed my eyes, feeling him sucking me hungrily. As if he had performed magic, the door I was resting against swiftly opened up on its own. His hands were on the small of my back to catch me before I could fall. I gasped, turning around to see that we were entering a bedroom.

Once we were inside the candlelit room, the door closed on its own.

"Pretty cool doors," I murmured.

I took a look around the room. Five narrow windows surrounded us. Behind each window, there was a peep show going on. A woman behind each window danced erotically, dressed in barely anything except masks to cover her eyes. Porn was playing on a high-definition flat screen behind the round bed in the center of the room. Goose bumps covered both of my arms.

"Tell me something about you," I said, trying to break the ice.

He whirled me back around to him so he could put his lips to my ear. He whispered sweetly, "I am the unspoken passion women secretly desire. You wonder about the mystery behind my eyes, don't you?"

"Yes," I whispered back.

"I am sex, upright and poised. I am the lover you dream of."

I shuddered underneath his touch, enthralled by every word that came from his thick lips. Every inch of my skin crawled as I moved my hands all over his body. Smooth, unblemished, dark skin looked as if it had been kissed by the ideal amount of sun. His chiseled chest, ripped abs, and defined, lean arms had my mouth watering lustfully.

"Rain . . ."

"Yes?"

Lifting me off my feet, he carried me to the plush bed covered in a golden silk comforter and laid me down gently.

"I want you to have me," I stated with assertiveness, feeling my panties beginning to soak.

He placed his index finger over my lips. "Shhhh . . . Not another word."

For some reason, I couldn't utter another word. It was like he had taken my voice from me. I couldn't make sense of the way I was feeling as my breathing intensified. My clit throbbed harder, causing me to rock back and forth.

Removing my halter top, jeans, lace panties, and bra, he took off his black jeans, and slowly removed his boxers to reveal his ample package. As his hands caressed me, I quivered.

Rain's lips found my nipples and they tingled once his tongue roamed.

"A storm is on its way," he uttered before flicking his tongue back and forth.

His fingers played around my clit, slipping through my crevasses, and finding my soft wet spot, fingering me slowly. As I closed my eyes, I felt a sensation I'd never felt before. How could he make me feel this way with just his fingers?

Moving my hands to his dick, I was more than ready to feel him inside me. I stroked him and he moaned. I guided him to my sweet center, and he inched his way inside my juicy walls. I gasped as he filled me to capacity, skillfully moving in and out of me.

As my juices trickled between my legs, he kissed my lips and kept at his steady pace. He moaned louder against my lips, feeling powerful and intense with each pounding stroke, his rhythm far from timid. Knowing exactly how he wanted to please me, he had no problem handling me. He lifted one of my legs and rested it on his shoulder as he clutched my ass with both of his hands. Deeper he went.

I closed my eyes and wrapped my arms around him, never wanting to take my eyes off his handsome face, but I couldn't help it. Only for a few more seconds, just in case I would never see him again, I opened my eyes. Rain was riding me, biting on his lower lip with a look of delight all over his face.

His brown eyes unexpectedly changed from that sweet honey brown to a blazing rouge. I was mesmerized by the fire in them. Suddenly, my body stiffened completely and my arms dropped limply to my sides.

My heart raced and fear struck me. Why couldn't I move my hands or feet? I tried to move, but I couldn't. He caressed the side of my face with his fingertips, turning my head slightly to the right and placing his lips on my neck.

The blood pumped through my veins against his lips. I could feel his warm breathing become thicker. He quickly removed his lips from my skin as if he was hesitant, but then kissed my neck softly again, this time opening his mouth to bite me.

What was supposed to be a sensual nibble evolved into something else as he actually pierced my skin. The first taste of my warm blood caused him to moan instantly. He sucked while my blood drained down his parched throat.

I closed my eyes to fight the pain, taking deep breaths. The bite made tears come to my eyes, yet there was a shocking intimacy to it. Even though I could feel the pulls he was taking on my vein, Rain's warm body against my own didn't feel so weird.

When he stopped, Rain gazed at me while my blood oozed from the sides of his mouth. He licked the blood completely off as if I tasted like a succulent mango. I could clearly see fangs that hadn't been there before.

My eyes widened, but underneath his spell, I lost the fight within myself to try to break free. It was too late. The worst had already been done.

"Relax," he said easily and calmly as he read my lost and dazed expression.

He thrust his hips into me. An orgasm was coming as he rocked inside me, deeper, faster, and then harder. All I could do was feel my body go through this tremendous quake until I couldn't contain the explosion.

The temporary immobility wore off as if he snapped his fingers. I moved my hands to my neck to feel the spot where he'd bitten me. It was completely smooth, as if the bite had never taken place.

"Where's Colette?" I shrieked. My voice had finally returned.

The fire that was just there in his eyes was gone. "She's one of us . . . She brought you to me."

I gasped. "So, what does this mean?"

"It means you are mine for eternity."

He kissed me with such a fiery passion, lowering his kisses from my chin down to the center of my belly button. Rain spread my legs wider as he buried himself between my thighs to distract me from the transformation. My body shook. Though the pain was excruciating, I felt ecstasy. I bit down on my lower lip to contain my scream. When I tasted my own blood, I knew it was almost done. I licked my teeth and felt small, sharp fangs emerging.

Destiny

Camille Blue

He walks naked into my bedroom, my dream lover who haunts me every night. The moonlight hits his body, illuminating the tattoo of Chinese characters on his right shoulder. I lay waiting for him to come to me. As he moves over me, I embrace his hard body with my arms and legs. We kiss like longtime lovers. We touch with impatient passion, as we make love once, twice, then again. After hours pass, he kisses my shoulder, before moving toward the edge of the bed. I reach for him, but he vanishes.

I jolt awake. My breathing sounded harsh. My sweat-drenched nightgown clung to me, making me shiver in the coolness of my bedroom. I headed to the kitchen for something to drink. The quietness of the house still unnerved me. Until a month ago, my twin sisters had kept the house buzzing with their activities. Now they were at Howard University living their lives. I felt so proud of my sisters, but I missed them so much.

After I poured myself a glass of ice water, I pressed the cold glass against my hot chest. My mind imagined meeting a real man who could stimulate me as much as my dream lover did.

"I want to lose my virginity. I need your help," I said to my best friend at dinner the next night.

Uli did not look surprised by my request. Little surprised

a woman who owned a sex empire that included a male escort service and an adult film production company.

"You've held on to your golden nugget this long, why not wait for Mr. Right?" Uli asked.

Uli's conservative attitude mystified me. She had been in a relationship with two men and a woman for three years. A *ménage à trois et moi* was what she liked to call her unique relationships.

"I'm too busy with my practice to find Mr. Right," I said. "I just want to . . ."

Uli lifted one perfectly arched eyebrow. "Fuck?"

"I wouldn't have put it quite like that, but yes," I said.

"So tell me, Dr. Kincaid, what kind of man are you interested in?" Uli asked.

"I want someone smart enough for good conversation," I said. "Nice looking. Confident, but not too cocky. He should be a really good lover; that is the point of all this, after all."

Uli nodded in understanding, and then sipped her lychee martini. "You want a cerebral Boy Next Door who fucks like Casanova," Uli said. "Anything else?"

I glanced around to see if anyone had heard Uli. No one seemed to be paying us any attention.

"No," I said. "I think you've got the idea."

"I know *the* place for your sex odyssey," Uli said. "New Orleans. That city will blast you out of your comfort zone, and bring out your sensual side."

"New Orleans," I said.

I nodded and smiled. I liked that idea a lot. I could not think of a sexier place. Uli and I spent the next several minutes settling all the details of my sexy weekend. We parted with a hug and a promise to have a long talk when I returned from New Orleans.

• • •

Later that night, I dried myself off after my bath. I took the time to really look at my body. My breasts were full, as were my hips, but my waist was small. I was a fit size twelve. I had few hangups about my body. When you care for sick people who would give anything for a healthy body, it makes carrying a few extra pounds insignificant.

I slipped into a lavender satin nightshirt and spritzed myself with my favorite perfume, Bulgari. I felt in a New Orleans frame of mind. So, I put on some Wynton Marsalis, made myself a Hurricane, and danced for the first time in years.

Two weeks later, the sultry scent of New Orleans infiltrated my body like a spirit massage. I checked into my hotel in the French Quarter, then went to my suite to get ready for my evening. After a cool shower, I dressed in an off-the-shoulder black dress and five-inch black stilettos. I carefully applied my new makeup. I smiled at my handiwork. I looked pretty damned good.

I felt eager about the evening ahead as I prepared to meet my three prospective lovers. My chauffeur drove me to a historic restaurant that Uli had suggested in the gorgeous Garden District. I selected a table near the entrance and waited for the show to begin.

A man who resembled Idris Elba entered, and looked to be searching for someone. I hoped he was searching for me. My heart skipped in excitement when he walked to my table. He frowned when he looked at me.

"You were waiting for me, weren't you?" he asked.

"Yes, I'm Destiny Kincaid," I said. I extended my hand to him. "Hello . . ."

"Adrian Martin," he said. "You're definitely not what I was expecting."

I decided to let that suspect comment go. "You're exactly what I was expecting. You're gorgeous."

Adrian looked bored by my compliment. He sat down at the table and ordered Grey Goose on the rocks. I tried to draw Adrian into conversation, but he answered me with curt, one-word answers. His obvious disinterest in me sapped the sexy right out of our encounter.

A green-eyed blonde in a tight red dress walked past our table. Adrian gave her a sexy smile that I wished he would have directed at me. The woman returned Adrian's look with a welcoming smile and a wink. I felt like I was intruding on their evening. Five minutes later, Adrian announced that he had to leave because of an emergency. He walked out without saying good-bye.

I looked out the window just in time to see Adrian and the lady in red getting into a taxi together. I felt humiliated by Adrian's behavior, but not enough to relinquish my evening. I ordered a Sazerac and hoped my luck would change with my next date.

Fifteen minutes later, I caught the eye of a guy in a navy suit with dark, framed glasses. He was handsome in a Clark Kent kind of way. I was looking for Superman, so maybe this would work out. I stood up as he made his way toward my table. We exchanged brief introductions. Guy Number Two, Niko Larsen's, gaze felt vulgar on me. He patted my ass. Then he kissed me like I was a hooker that he had rented for only fifteen minutes. My inner voice told me to leave then, but I was stupid and ignored it.

Niko sat down across from me. He grinned at me.

"I hope you've got muscle relaxants and Red Bull, girl," Niko said. "Tonight is going to be a long-ass night!"

Niko slithered one hand between my legs and cupped my

vagina. Before I realized it, I'd punched him between *his* legs. He yelped like a Pomeranian and cupped his crotch with both hands.

"You fuckin' bitch!" he roared. Shocked silence fell across the restaurant as several people stared at our table. Niko shot me a dirty look before he limped out of the restaurant.

I drained my drink, then glanced at my watch. I had twenty minutes before Guy Number Three would arrive.

I'm getting the hell out of here!

I was in the foyer of the restaurant when I felt a light touch at my waist.

"Destiny Kincaid?" a deep voice asked.

"Yes," I said. I felt a sexual jolt when I looked at him. With his confident smile and dimples, this man was everything implied by *tall, dark, and handsome*. He looked like a walking Armani billboard.

"I'm Nadir O'Neal," he said. "I'm here to meet you."

I scrubbed my forehead and sighed. "Look, this was a really bad idea. I've already run off two guys tonight."

"You don't scare me, beautiful," he said.

"All right, don't say I didn't warn you," I said.

Nadir laughed, low and genuine. I smiled in appreciation of him.

"Let's have dinner," he said.

I led the way back to the table. Nadir's hand on my waist felt nice. He pulled the chair out for me. After I sat down, Nadir leaned in and kissed me on the cheek.

"I couldn't resist," he said.

Pleasure spread over me as I relaxed in the company of a true gentleman. Over a dinner of seafood étouffée, I learned that Nadir was a thirty-two-year-old architect who specialized in historic restorations. He had never been married and had no children.

"Tell me about you," Nadir said.

I was hesitant about telling Nadir about myself. I did not want sympathy. My life story always inspired that emotion. I wanted Nadir to desire me as much as I desired him. So I told him an edited version of me. Nadir listened as if my every word fascinated him.

After our dinner, we lingered over coffee.

"We're the last ones here," I said.

"I hadn't noticed," Nadir said. "I've been enjoying you." He reached for my hand across the table. My fingers curved around his.

"Tonight was a wonderful night," I said. "Thank you. But I think we should leave so the staff can go home."

We held hands as we strolled to my car.

"Have breakfast with me tomorrow?" Nadir asked.

I felt disappointed that Nadir did not want to see me later that night, but I hid it well. "Sure, what time?"

"We can decide after we wake in your bed," he said against my ear. "Am I presuming too much?"

"No," I said. "I want this . . . with you."

Nadir cupped my face. Our kiss was too sexy for a public place. Still, I didn't resist when Nadir coaxed me into another steamy kiss. After several seconds, I ended the kiss and leaned against him.

The chauffeur opened the car door for us. Nadir helped me into the car and got in beside me. We held hands throughout the trip, but we did not speak. I kept my gaze focused on the lush scenery that passed my window. *This was really about to happen.* I could hear my heart pounding in my ears like booming bass in an Escalade.

As soon as we reached my hotel, we went straight to my room. I closed the door behind us. Nadir pressed me against the door with a firm hand on my stomach. He dragged the zipper down the side of my dress. I let my dress slip to the floor. My bra soon followed. I felt his tenderness and experience as he explored my sensitive breasts with his hands and his lips. Lower he went, until I drew in a deep breath as his lips moved across my stomach. I closed my eyes as Nadir slowly drew my panties down my legs, and then tossed them on the floor. When he made no move to touch me, I opened my eyes. He smiled at me, before kneeling in front of me. As I leaned against the wall, he lifted one of my legs over his shoulder.

Nadir kissed my left hip before turning his attention to the valley between my thighs. He breathed in my moist inner perfume. He tasted me. His tongue felt cool and soothing inside. At first I could not watch as he pleased me. Then I found that I could not look away; my body tightened with a delicious ache deep inside before a thumping release seized me. I couldn't move, but then I did not have to. Nadir lowered me to the Turkish rug. He lay beside me. He kissed me in a soothing way as my body still shook from my release.

"This next part will hurt you," Nadir said. "At least in the beginning."

"I know the mechanics of sex," I said. "I need you to teach me the pleasure."

He nodded, and then he took off his jacket and shirt. I gasped as I saw the tattoo on his shoulder, just like the man in my dreams. I traced the outline of the tattoo. He kissed my fingers.

"What do these symbols mean?" I asked.

His smile held a secret. "I will tell you in the morning, but you won't believe me."

We watched each other as he slowly stepped out of the rest of his clothes. His muscles were in peak condition, from his six-pack stomach, to his tight butt, down to his hard thighs and legs.

"Are you real?" I asked.

"Touch me," he said.

I traced the V-pattern of muscles, starting from his waist, down to where the muscles encased his flat stomach. I always found that part of a man's body so sexy. His body moved over mine. He touched me everywhere. Then he kissed all the places he'd touched. The hard press of his body felt foreign. His intense male scent overwhelmed my senses. My hands and lips explored Nadir's body with a boldness that surprised me. I needed to be a part of him. I felt two of his fingers slipping inside my vagina. I smelled my essence on his fingers when he withdrew them.

"Your body is ready for me," he said in satisfaction.

"Yes, come here," I said.

I handed Nadir a condom from the nightstand. I watched in fascination as he slipped the condom on.

Nadir leaned over me. My legs widened to welcome him. A tender look entered his eyes as he joined our bodies. I felt the hot sting of his entry into my body while I tasted the saltiness of the skin on his neck. My legs draped around his hard thighs as he rocked me with his strong body. He dominated me from the skin in. I relished giving up control for once.

I loved seeing the sharpness of his desire as it moved from his mouth, to his cheekbones, to the intensity blazing through his eyes. I gripped him under his arms. My legs gripped his waist. I bit him when another orgasm burst over my body.

• • •

I did not know how much time had passed when I woke up alone in bed. I sat up, then I saw Nadir sitting naked in a wingback chair, watching me. His smile held a bit of cockiness; he had earned that right. After the way he'd pleasured my body, I would never be the same.

"Come to me," he said.

I stood beside the bed. My muscles felt warm and loose, like after a deep-tissue massage. When I reached Nadir, he guided me to sit across his lap. I leaned against his chest. He kissed the top of my head.

"Tell me your real story," Nadir said.

Once Nadir gave me permission, I opened my heart. I told Nadir about my parents' dying within six months of each other. I told Nadir how terrified I felt that I could not fulfill my parents' expectations for my sisters and me. I told him that before tonight, no man had so much as kissed me in ten years.

I went silent. Nadir wiped the tears from my eyes. I kissed him, hard and needy. He kissed me, gentle and comforting. Our lovemaking met between those extremes. Afterward, I fell asleep to the rhythm of Nadir's heartbeat.

My cell phone rang early the next morning. I reached for it.

"Hey, sleepyhead," Uli said. "I'm sorry Niko and Adrian didn't work out. I'm sure Dmitri will be the one! I was so pissed when he missed his flight yesterday. He should be there by noon. So how did you spend your night?"

"With Nadir," I croaked out. I glanced over at Nadir. He still slept beside me.

"Who the hell is Nadir?" Uli asked.

"Don't tease me, Uli; you know you sent him to me," I whispered.

"Honey, I don't know anybody named Nadir," Uli said. "Get the hell out of there! Do you hear me?"

"I can handle this," I said.

I hung up the phone and tried to remain calm. I had almost made it out of bed when Nadir's right arm clamped around my waist. Nadir gave me a serious look. I drew myself up against the headboard. Nadir followed my movements as if we were dancing an ancient dance together.

"Who are you?" I demanded.

"It doesn't matter," Nadir said. He leaned in and kissed me, trying to manipulate me with the memories of our hot night together. My body wanted to betray me by giving in, but my mind refused to let me.

"It matters a hell of a lot," I said. "I just spent the night with a stranger!"

"You were all set to do that before you met me, baby," Nadir said.

"Don't you turn this around on me! I thought Uli chose you for me!"

I shoved at his arm, but his grip did not loosen. I panicked as I struggled against him.

"Calm down, Destiny," Nadir said.

"Get your damned hands off me! My God, what have I done?"

"I knew you before this weekend," Nadir said.

I went instantly still. "You're lying! We've never met!"

"No, but I know you," Nadir said. "We belong to the same gym. You take the treadmill farthest from anyone. You run with your headphones in your ears, looking straight ahead, never interacting with anyone."

When I tried to sit up, Nadir allowed me to, but he watched me with caution, as if he expected me to run screaming out of the room like any sane woman would.

"I sit five rows behind you in church," Nadir continued. "But you've never noticed me, or any other man. You keep yourself so shut off from the world."

I felt exposed by the truth in his observations. I had lived my life as a series of tasks to be checked off, when I should have been living to create unforgettable life experiences. I shoved my self-analysis aside and focused on the issue at hand with Nadir.

"How did you know my plans for this weekend?"

"I was sitting behind you in the restaurant when you and your friend were discussing it."

"Why would you do this?" I asked.

"I knew you were ready for a man in your life," he said. "I needed that man to be me."

"You had better be gone by the time I get out of my shower!" I hopped out of bed and hurried into the bathroom. I slammed the bathroom door behind me.

I drenched myself from head to toe under the warm spray of the shower. Nadir had entered my life under false pretenses. That really pissed me off. Still, Nadir had made losing my virginity the most pleasurable event of my life. I would always cherish our night together. I did not know what the hell to think about Nadir, or myself.

Nadir opened the shower door. He stood there naked, looking unsure of his welcome. "May I come in?"

I grunted. "You've already been inside a place more intimate than my shower," I said. "Come on in."

He stepped into the shower and pulled me into his arms.

"I know I got you in a shady way," Nadir said. "Still, I wouldn't change anything I did to get you. Being with you was exquisite."

He'd admitted that his actions were wrong, but he did not regret the outcome. I found that oddly noble under these messed-up circumstances.

"When we get home, I want to see you again," Nadir said.

"You don't have to say that to me," I said.

"I do," Nadir said. "I want to be with you in our real lives."

I mulled over Nadir's words. I had no plans for a lover after this weekend. I did not think I had room in my life for a relationship. But this weekend had made me realize just how much I needed a personal life.

"All right," I said. "But no sex for thirty days."

He frowned, in wry acceptance. "Agreed, on one condition?"

"What's that?"

"That our celibacy starts after this weekend."

"Hecky yeah!" I intended to drain every drop of pleasure during our time in New Orleans.

We laughed together. It felt so sweet and natural. Nadir nuzzled my neck. I cupped his head in my hands. I felt such tenderness for this man, whom I had known less than twenty-four hours. I kissed the tattoo on his shoulder.

"You said you would tell me what your tattoo means," I said.

"Claim Your Destiny," he said.

Nadir had claimed my body last night, but was he my destiny? Could I be his? Maybe the two of us could figure that out.

In the Dark

SA Brown

I woke to the stillness of our 3,500-square-foot home. I waved my hand over the spot where he should've been, but all I found was a note and one long-stemmed red rose. I caressed my face with one hand and gathered my rose and note with the other. The sweet essence from its bud woke me more. The note smelled of I Am King cologne, which reminded me that he could not have gone far.

Happy anniversary to the most beautiful and wonderful wife known to man. I am so grateful for the twenty years you've given me and pray for twenty more. I am going to show you the time of your life. Tonight, fantasies become realities. Get ready . . .

I hopped out of bed and took a quick shower. I bounced around the house in erotic anticipation of what my husband had planned for the evening. Once outfitted in powder blue jeans and a red cami, I grabbed my cell phone to find out what he was up to.

My husband answered on the first ring. "Hello, my sweetness. How's your morning going?"

"Boring because you aren't here with me. Where are you?"

There was a long silence before he answered.

"Don't be mad, baby. I had to shake and bake before we began our celebration. I'll catch up with you right after lunch."

"Gavin, we promised, no business this weekend. Just you and me. How could you?"

"Calm down, my queen." As always, his voice soothed me. "I need a few hours to close this deal and then 'I'll be working my way back to you, babe.'" He sang as if he was one of the Four Tops. "I've got something very special planned for you. You just wait and see."

"But we said no business this weekend—this one weekend. No cell phones. No hospital shifts. No business deals."

"I know, baby, but will you please trust your man. Be ready to go by eleven o'clock and pack an overnight bag. I gotta go."

Gavin hung up before I could respond. An overnight bag? What did this man have planned this time? There wasn't much he and I did not share with each other. The key to our relationship was communication. We were open and honest about everything. In our twenty years together, we had forgiven each other for past indiscretions and there had been plenty. Some might say we had an open marriage. But the truth was we discussed what we wanted. While we had enough love for each other for each of us to make sacrifices for the other's happiness, I guess there were some sacrifices a man simply could not surrender. I had bent over backward for him—literally and figuratively. Yet, there was this one thing I wanted, but Gavin said he would never do. I respected his wishes.

As I prepared for this big surprise Gavin had planned, someone knocked on the front door. When I opened it, the most handsome face greeted me. His pearly whites complemented his dark chocolate, clean-shaven face. He stood at least six foot three in his black double-breasted suit, with a hat tucked underneath his left arm.

"Good morning, ma'am. Are you Dr. Malorie Cummings?"

I stared at this Adonis before me. I licked my lips as I imagined his toned pectorals beneath his suit. "Yes, I'm Dr. Cummings."

"My name's Malcolm and I'm your driver for today." He stepped to his left to allow full view of a 1968 two-toned classic Daimler Princess parked at the curb.

I whispered, "That damn Gavin." Once I regained my focus, I asked, "And where will the driver be taking me today?"

He reached for my hand, lifted it, and gently pecked its back. His lips were so soft to the touch. "My only instructions are to give the lady whatever she would like."

If I had my way, I would've had a big bite of him, but I had to remain a lady. We'd just met. I turned to walk back upstairs and get my bag. When I returned, Malcolm had not moved one inch. The Atlanta sun beamed down on his bald, chocolate head. I handed him my bag and he escorted me to the car. The smooth leather hugged my round bottom. Malcolm offered me a glass of champagne, which I gladly accepted, as we pulled away from my Dunwoody home.

"Ma'am, before we begin your day, I was told to check you into the Four Seasons. Once there, you can decide where we go and what we do." Malcolm let up the partition.

If only he knew . . .

Once we arrived at the Four Seasons, I checked into the luxury suite Gavin had booked. The room was fresh and elegant with sunshine beaming through the windows that looked out on the panoramic view of midtown Atlanta. The concierge explained to me that my husband had a spa reservation for me if I desired to use those services. I was so glad I did. After the fifty-minute, deep-tissue massage, I indulged in a vanilla coffee scrub, a facial, and a peaches-and-cream manicure and pedicure. I returned to the suite feeling like a new woman. I was draped across the bed when Gavin came in. He was wearing plaid shorts and a blue polo shirt, his typical golf gear.

"A business deal, eh?" I asked as I looked him up and down.

He stretched out beside me on the bed. His I Am King scent was just as strong as it was on the note this morning. "Now, you know I do my best wheelin' and dealin' on the golf course. Besides, you're supposed to be out shopping or something. I got a driver and car to supply your every need."

I rolled on top of him. "All I need is you."

His strong hands explored underneath my terrycloth robe. They found their favorite place as he cupped and squeezed my plump behind. We kissed and I slid down his body, but he stopped me.

"Not right now, baby. You'll spoil my surprise."

I pouted. "I don't want your surprise. I want you inside me. This instant."

He laughed. He sat up and placed me beside him. "No, ma'am. You'll have to wait until tonight. I need to shower and get a massage of my own. We have dinner reservations for seven-thirty."

"Dinner reservations? I didn't bring anything to wear for dinner."

Gavin stood up and began undressing for his shower. "Then go and buy something. Your driver and chariot await."

I dressed and went downstairs. Malcolm was sitting in the lobby, reading a magazine. When he noticed me, his eyes explored every inch of my five-foot-eight-inch frame that fit snugly into my lavender sundress. My matching heels handled my freshly pedicured feet, which led to my well-defined calves and thighs. Suddenly he stopped at my 38Ds. They normally got all of the attention, so I was used to it.

I snapped my fingers. "Are we going somewhere or not?"

He cleared his throat. "Where shall I take you?"

"Anywhere you damn well please. I'm always ready for a good ride."

Malcolm blushed and walked me to the car. I told him I needed a dress for my anniversary dinner. He suggested Nordstrom's and off we rode. We exchanged small talk along the way. I learned he was twenty-five and chauffeuring to pay his way through law school. He was single and had no kids—a rarity in this day and age. I shared with him that I was a professor at Emory University and my husband was a commercial land developer. I talked about how we'd met while he was at Morehouse and I was at Spelman and how we'd managed to stay together for twenty years. When we arrived at the store, Malcolm waited for me at the car. I didn't take long, as the time for the reservation was approaching. I wore the silver, off-the-shoulder dress I'd purchased out of the store. We drove back to the hotel and picked up Gavin.

That husband of mine! He had reserved a private dining experience at the 103 West in Buckhead. After dinner we went back to the room. He'd had room service light candles everywhere and cover the entire room with rose petals. We danced to John Coltrane awhile and then Gavin drew a warm bath for me. He washed and dried my entire body. We held each other as the moon provided the only light. He caressed my naked body with oils and hummed with the music in my ear. Our groove was interrupted by a knock on our suite door.

Gavin nudged my shoulder. "Why don't you get that? It's probably room service." He handed me my robe and walked into the bathroom.

I walked through the living room and over to the door. I asked who it was and the voice replied, "Room service." There was a hint of familiarity in that voice.

Imagine my surprise when I saw Malcolm standing behind a cart, which was draped with a white cloth and held a large silver platter and matching carrier with champagne chilling inside.

"I thought you drove cars for a living."

He pushed the cart inside the room. "Like I said earlier, I was instructed to give the lady anything she wants."

Malcolm grabbed me and tore off my robe. He ravished my body with hot and moist kisses. We fell onto the sofa where his barrage of touching and licking continued.

I had barely heard the showerheads turn off when Gavin asked, "Who was that at the door, baby?"

At that moment, I remembered my husband was in the very next room. This was our anniversary. I pushed Malcolm off me and helped him adjust his clothes. His slacks did a poor job of masking his massive manhood. Its head jumped at the zipper.

"It was room service, just like you said." I gathered my robe and covered my body with it. As I finger-raked my hair, I thought my heart would beat out of my chest.

Just then, Gavin came out of the bathroom with towels around his waist and neck. He walked over to the tray, examined it, and thanked the server for bringing everything he ordered.

I stood frozen. I didn't know what to expect. Gavin simply handed Malcolm the towel from around his neck and told him, "Let's give the lady what she wants."

Malcolm did as he was told and undressed as he walked into the bathroom. Gavin walked behind me and rubbed my shoulders.

He whispered, "Anything you want, I can give it to you."

Gavin spun me around and tongued me for what seemed like an hour. He led me to the bedroom and removed my robe. He laid me upon the bed and made me promise to let him control this evening. Just before he covered my eyes with a red satin scarf, I watched Malcolm come out of the bathroom. His naked body still glistened from the shower. His semi-erect tool danced with each step that he took.

"Gavin, what is all this?"

"This is about your pleasure." Gavin teased my nipple with his tongue. "Well, baby, I know you've given me everything I've ever wanted—sexually. You've allowed me another woman; you've been with another woman and allowed me to watch, in public places, in the rain. Whatever I wanted, you granted. All you ever asked for was one thing. So tonight, I return the favor. Me and another man completely focused on pleasuring you."

Gavin kissed my lips and tightened the scarf. He warned me that if I peeked, I would be reprimanded. I heard them moving about. Suddenly, a pair of hands caressed my breasts. I could not tell if they were Gavin's or Malcolm's. Maybe it was both of them. At that point, I didn't care. The touch was sensual and erotic. My nipples tightened as they became erect, showed their approval.

Next, a moist tongue tickled my inner thigh. I squirmed. I needed to see this. I reached for the blindfold and a hand slapped it away. A firm hand landed on my left outer thigh. The sting enticed my arousal.

"I told you, no peeking," Gavin reprimanded. I could hear Malcolm laughing. "Don't make me tie your hands up, too."

One of them sucked on my big left toe. "Nice color," I heard Malcolm say.

I could hear the cart moving. Then a cold liquid splashed on my firm tummy. Someone's tongue licked it all up. Firm lips planted moist kisses all over my face before landing on my lips. The tongue did a sensual dance with my mouth. I thought I would swallow it whole. At the same time, another tongue was exploring my inner thighs. I thought I would explode. I didn't know who was doing what and it turned me on. I had never been so hot.

"Open your mouth," Gavin instructed. One of them placed a piece of kiwi inside and when I bit down, the juices ran down the sides of my mouth and my neck. Someone was there to lick up the excess. Another piece. This time it was mango.

"Tilt your head back." Malcolm was more pleasant than Gavin with his commands. Next, I tasted cold Moët as it washed my teeth and gums. Before I could swallow, one of them kissed me and jacked me for most of my drink. Our exotic buffet continued until . . .

"Turn over," they said together.

What felt like eight pairs of hands covered my entire backside. No skin was untouched. Then I felt more tongue than one woman should be allowed. They licked everywhere. And I do mean everywhere.

One of them flipped me over and buried his head in my mound. I didn't have time to figure out which one. Since they were both bald and clean-shaven, I would probably never know. Whoever it was had to be the champion of oral sex because he left no area unattended. He kissed my outer lips, rimmed my inner lips, and plunged his thick tongue into me like it was his penis. I came so hard I almost flipped over. The other one grabbed me and showed what he could do. My body never had a chance to recover from the first orgasm. I contorted and convulsed. He grabbed my thighs and held me down until I could feel my juices flowing down my thighs. And he devoured it all.

I reached for the blindfold. This wasn't fair. I should be able to see this. One of them grabbed my hand and began sucking on my fingers. The other lifted me by my legs and placed a pillow underneath the small of my back. He rested my legs on his shoulders and slowly rocked his tool inside me. I had felt this pleasure so many times before. Gavin penetrated me harder with each thrust while Malcolm's hands and mouth explored my breasts and stomach. I howled through my orgasm as Gavin turned me on all fours. He slid underneath me and I could feel Malcolm entering me from behind.

Malcolm was so gentle. I had to have this my way. I moved away from him and told him, "Don't play with it. Make it yours."

He grabbed my hips. "As you wish." He rammed me from behind and each pump provided just the right amount of pleasure and pain. Gavin sucked my breasts as if there was nourishment in them. I collapsed into a heap of sweating flesh on the bed as my body shuddered uncontrollably.

They only gave me a few minutes to compose myself as they moved around. Still blindfolded, I felt one of them caress my lower back and separate my cheeks. I felt a head insert itself as whoever he was laid me on my side. One was behind me, loving me anally, while the other was in front of me, loving me vaginally. After a few tries, they were both inside me and had found a rhythm. One was in while the other pulled out. We were making beautiful music together.

Gavin moaned. Malcolm whispered obscenities. Suddenly, they both released me, but I assumed Malcolm had more to give. He placed me on top of him and I rode him until his hands bruised my thighs from their tight grip.

All three of us lay in complete ecstasy, panting and moaning. I was nearly asleep when I heard Gavin whisper, "Happy anniversary, baby." I kissed him and fell asleep with my blindfold still on.

I woke to the stillness of our 1,000-square-foot luxury suite. I waved my hand over the spot where he should've been, but found nothing. As I removed the blindfold, I saw that the room was illuminated only by the moon inking through the drapes. Soft hums led me to the living area of the suite. Once my mind finally grasped the image before me, my heart sank.

Was my new lover's forehead really bobbing up and down on my husband's abs?

Surely, this was a dream—a nightmare. I want to believe I screamed, but all I heard was a whisper.

"Gavin."

The men must have heard me because they disconnected. Gavin walked over to me with his aroused manhood bouncing in the air.

He asked, "Who told you to take off your blindfold?"

The Other Side of Midnight

Elissa Gabrielle

"Your walls are imploring me to have my way with them, I just know it. Because no one knows that pussy the way I do. And no one satisfies it the way that I can."

~Tre'

HER . . .

The bane of my existence once again speaks an all-too-familiar tune to me. Actually, it shouts, sings, and tugs at my heartstrings. I constantly struggle with rhyme and sound reason, knowing that he must know that my love is so much deeper than hers could ever possibly be. I can't believe the love of my life is married.

"Married," I whisper, sadly, under my breath, ashamed, I whisper, "he's married."

Toasted vanilla votive candles give light to a seductively dim, chic upscale bistro in the heart of New York City on this March night. An unusually windy night for this time of year—where the weather almost kisses spring, but keeps one foot planted in the dead of winter—it is confused; just like me.

I've loved this man for what appears to be centuries. He says we're married in eternity, throughout galaxies, and former lifetimes. I believe him. My heart and body won't allow me to believe otherwise.

As clichéd as the term *soul mate* may be to some, I know with no uncertainty that Tre' is mine. My soul mate. My man. My king in this lifetime, the next, the one prior—throughout eternity.

He's married. But not to me.

And my love is so much sweeter than hers. *Lucky bitch.*

My eyes follow his chiseled jawline, around his sweetheart chocolate lips, and I take a voyage to his perfectly trimmed goatee. Tre's luscious lips part to reveal a majestic set of piano keys, pure white, pristine, like ivory straight from the Congo—the motherland. Yes, he was born of royal seed. Brought in my existence from Ghana, this man, amazingly splendid in physical beauty, adeptly regal in physical supremacy, commands all attention when he enters a room. His swagger is undeniable.

"What are you staring at?" he questions as he takes a sip of his Crown Royal.

"You," I reply, as I take a sip of the chilled drink in front of me, in hopes of slowing down our time together. Stammering over my thoughts, trying to find something to say that won't make me sound like either a complete fool or a slut. Whatever comes out of my mouth will only reveal the truth; I'm his forever, a faithful concubine.

"It's almost midnight. Getting late," he tells me as he takes a spoonful of his dessert; white chocolate bread pudding.

Leaning into the center of our quaint table, the votive candle illuminating my face, I whisper, "Then, we should get going."

He grabs my hand. "I'm not ready." His voice is seductive as he draws circles in the palm of my hand with his fingertip. Although he's not ready, the words he really wants to utter are, "Please don't leave me."

Staring into his eyes, I reveal, "We eventually have to go home, Tre'."

"I am home." He smiles. His fingertip slowly runs up the side of my arm.

The cocoa-colored silk shirt lays over his firm chest softly. The two top buttons are undone. He knows that drives me wild. He's fucking with me and I like it. The smell of his cologne penetrates all my senses and as I inhale his pheromones, my pussy gushes and releases in anticipation of him. A sticky wetness announces its presence.

"Still hungry?" he asks as he places a spoon of white chocolate into my mouth, dangling the spoon around my lips, making me smile as I try to capture it.

"Let me see your tongue," he commands.

I obey.

As my tongue parts my lips once more, I reach for what he has to offer. As I place the pudding on the tip of my tongue, the sweet sensation arouses my senses. I lick my lips, wanting more.

"Lick it slowly," he tells me.

Once again, I obey.

"Good girl. You like the way it tastes, don't you?" His eyes watch my lips with envy.

"I do."

"More where that came from." Lust lingers in the air as he licks the spoon behind me, showing a bit of his skill.

I want to fuck the shit out of him.

"I know."

I smile. Missing the smell of his day's work. The smell of his erection then eventual release.

"So, why did you marry her?"

HIM . . .

In a seductive upsweep, long curls of wavy jet black hair adorn her crown. There's a whole lot I'd like her to do with those big, juicy lips of hers—namely, use them to meet and greet every inch of my body. Thoughts of the warmth of her mouth around my dick make me slightly hard. The discomfort is inviting.

Damn, I want her in the worst way.

I keep reminding myself every ten minutes or so that I'm not here to kiss those pretty, luscious, crimson-stained lips; and that reminder has me going crazy inside. Unapologetically, she's built. Cornbread fed, thick, like she grew up eating shrimp and grits. Truth be told, I have no business being here: dim lights, candles all around, close to midnight, in the corner of a restaurant that has been our place of reconnection over the years. In a strange way, it is home—our own private, secluded place in the universe where she is mine and I am hers, alone. *Our home,* I think, our place of refuge where everything that is so wrong about our love affair is so unequivocally right.

But I have every damn right to be here with my woman, my lady, my heart, my life, the love of my life . . . but she's not my wife.

Sitting alluringly, she crosses one long, curvaceous leg over the other and softly feathers a loose curl from her brow.

With the boldness of a cobra, I believe, in my world full of fantasies, that she is all mine and that during this lifetime, we just never got on the same page at the same time. We each somehow ended up on the opposite sides of the tracks.

I fucked up, and I know it. She moved on. I grew up. She was gone. I fell in love again. Newly married now. I'm happy. I love my wife.

But Tia is my soul mate.

She laughs when I use those words. But it's the truth. Her heart sings the same song as mine. Our hearts beat to the tune of the same drum. Richly appealing to the senses and my mind, she is without a doubt the best lover I've ever had.

"I married her because you were already taken." I smile as I lean in to watch those lips of hers go to work on this spoonful of white chocolate bread pudding.

"Right."

A look of sarcasm comes over her face and the writing is once again on the wall.

"Well, you are, aren't you?"

"What?"

"Taken, Tia."

"Yes."

"So . . ."

"Tre', I've always been yours."

"I know I fucked up."

"You did."

"I love you, Tia."

"I love you too, always."

"Be with me."

"I'd have to murder you, Tre'." She smirks and is fully aware of what that does to me.

Bowing my head in shame, I smile, and at the same time she rubs her foot across my leg.

My eyes gaze down at her leg—big, thick, juicy, sweet, caramel-coated piece of heavenly perfection. And those shoes. Those come-fuck-me-daddy heels, with the peep toe and cherry-red painted nails making an entrance, force me into temporary psychosis as I try to regain my composure. The blood rushes to my dick and I'm solid, like the Rock of Gibraltar. She knows it. She knows this dick so well since she was the one who'd trained it. I miss the stickiness of her nectar.

Smiling as she wickedly rubs my leg with hers, she tells me to touch.

"Go ahead. Touch it." Authority dictates her words.

"Touch what?"

"Whatever you want, Tre'."

I'm going straight to hell after tonight.

"You look so damn good tonight, baby."

I want that good ole feeling. The sensation of our bodies as we arrive together. Need that like I need this air I'm breathing.

"Talking like that will get your dick sucked."

Straight to hell I go, but not until I get knee-deep in that pussy that's been drowning me so good for the last two decades.

"So, how's the family?"

HER . . .

The walls of my pussy are set on fire just by the pure thought of him. Sensing the heat on my body, I feel his eyes pierce through to the depths of my soul. I know he's watching, scoping, observing all of the lumps, bumps, curves, peaks, and valleys better known as me these days.

I'm remembering nights of unbridled passion. I was his godless bride, who sinfully, yet delightfully, received a plethora of deep dick—so deep, I breathed for him.

My favorite nightmare. In my dreams, he is my reality. In my reality, he is all I've ever dreamed of. Even in those places and times where our souls collided, and then made love, in this lifetime, in the here and now, and eternities past, over decades, through our ancestors, and beyond; every time I close my eyes, he's been right there. He says we've been married in every life we've ever known. I believe him.

When I'm in his arms, I feel free. I've fallen, head over heels, for two decades with this man, in this lifetime, others, and throughout eternity.

I remember him . . .

A decade ago, we met once again. Our souls cried to the heavens, shouted aloud to soft clouds; our spirits yearned for the comfort of each other's pillow. Our bodies, riddled with uncontrollable desire, anxiously waited long enough, too long, for the chance to rekindle, reconnect—to love, to suck, to feel, to fuck, over and over again. Limbs and fingertips, hot skin, weak and weary flesh called, our spirits yearned, our souls begged; we put the call out into the universe, she heard our pleas, and placed "us" into the midst of each other, once again, to put closure to a love of the past; a stubborn lust, infatuation, dependency, a rare love, a delightful combination of fire and desire that, over time, became impossible to extinguish.

We met in the parking lot of a mall that we had fucked in, in every crevice and corner allowed. That mall parking lot had seen my ass in the air in the back of a Grand Cherokee. Same mall became privy to a long, thick, chocolate-coated staff that delved into a hot, wet cave that had his name engraved on its sweltering flesh.

He opened the door to his Infiniti and I hopped in. We gazed into each other's eyes for an eternity, and as his foot pressed the pedal to the floor, we woke up, and cruised down Route 1 and 9. Small talk ensued, and the comfort level that had laid a foundation of love soared through the air, until those words parted from his lips, "I'll always love you."

A raging, untamable, hot, wet pussy screamed his name, and I crossed my legs to shut her the fuck up. His right hand rubbed up and down my thigh and landed on my love; he covered it with his hand, felt my heat, he smiled; I turned red, embarrassed. "That pussy is hot for me, already, Tia. I'm pulling over."

I had no words for him. He was and still is the boss. I exhaled. He switched lanes. Ninety miles per hour. He drove to the nearest exit. I leaned in to kiss him. Gave him my tongue. He received it, gave me his in return. Nipples hardened. I planted my hand on his crotch. Rock solid, beautiful dick of a gorgeous black man, made me release. I exhaled in his mouth.

My face found its way to an unfastened zipper. I kissed the bulbous head of a dick that only arrived into my life straight from the motherland. Kissed it. Licked it. Sucked it. Loved it.

Parking lot. Corner space. Couldn't get into the backseat soon enough. My legs wrapped around his neck and landed on his shoulders where they belonged. His hands ran up my thighs, hiked up my skirt. Pulled my panties to the side. Deep dick he gave me. He cried out as he entered me. We fucked each other like we were mad, happy, sad. We made love like we owed each other something. He stroked me like he was teaching me a lesson. I gave him back those glorious thrusts like I had to do it. Like a goddamn gun was pointed to my head, I fucked him, well, because he deserved it. He fucked me like I was his whore. Made love to me like I was his wife. Kissed me like I was the love of his life.

Damn, I remember the days . . .

"You are my family."

"I know that, but you know what I meant, Tia."

"I'm here with you. Savor the moment."

"I am. It's bittersweet. You'll go to another once we've renewed our vows tonight," he tells me as he smiles. It's a nervous grin. I know he's hurting.

"I'll always belong to you."

"Promise?"

"Promise, baby. Besides, no one can take you to flight like I can. I know you better than you know yourself."

I stare in his eyes.

"You have fans in that corner over there." He leans his head to the right, where there are two women, presumably lesbians from the way they're curled up with each other in that booth.

"Is that right?" I ask, blushing from ear to ear. I saw them jocking earlier but gave it no energy.

"See, you turn everyone on."

I smile, raise my martini glass to acknowledge them.

"Stop," he demands, grabs my hand.

"Why?"

"I don't want anyone loving you but me."

"Have me any way you want to."

"Word?"

"Yes."

"I've thought about you all night. Dick gets so hard, just thinking about seeing you again."

I smile. "I miss the sound of your footsteps as you walk toward my bed."

"Your walls are imploring me to have my way with them, I just know it. Because no one knows that pussy the way I do. And no one satisfies it the way I can."

I look to my right. My eyes meet with his thighs, and every ounce of me wants to lick those pretty, brown, muscular, strong thighs. As my eyes peer upward, the bulge sits fat and firm in between his thighs, awaiting my lips to suck it from root to tip and back again. Delicious, delectable, delightful dick, dares me to make its acquaintance once more; it wants and needs my undying and undivided attention.

Sweet cum pours from succulent and swollen pussy lips and fluidly flows onto my thighs. If he only knew how badly I wanted him to drink what I poureth, as my cup runneth over with a savory and slick, wet mess for him to devour.

"We're on the other side of midnight, Tre'. Now what?"

HIM . . .

The warmth of her touch, the shadow of her smile, and the bounce in her stride made her my daily feast throughout history where we'd invade each other's worlds and universe in this life and any other lives. I have loved her throughout time and I'm convinced she is all of me, infinitely, all the time; it's a neverending journey with her. She's my life, my lover, and my wife in all of my lives. Night after night, I yearned for a drop of her time and a piece of her mind, and just like that I was in ecstasy. Tender, tempting, touching, made for tantalizing, thunderous taunts that led to sultry, sweltering, scintillating sex. Making love to Tia every night, without inhibition, is what has fed this monster over decades, across states, even after other lovers dissipate. To let her get away was crazy. My picture in life would not be the same if she were absent from my world.

"The other side of midnight is where we go into a dangerous place. That place where neither of us needs to be, yet we belong here," I tell her as she reaches for her drink.

My hand covers hers, and I see her leg start to tremble. She taught me how to love. What I've given in return is the best love she's ever had. The kind of love that has her pussy twitching for days; the kind of loving she wants over and over, the kind of love only I can provide. The kind of love that has her sugar walls trained to my command.

"You really wear the hell out of that shirt," she tells me. She smiles, trying to ease the tension.

"I thought you would like it."

"I love it, Tre'."

"I love you, Tia."

"I need to get home, Tre'."

"I need you."

"Don't do this."

"Why did you come, Tia?"

"B . . . b . . . because . . ."

"Because you need me, just as much as I need you." Taking her hand in mine, I tell her, "I need you so bad. Please don't leave me."

"You have a wife."

"You have a husband."

"I'm gonna go," she says as she gets up to leave.

"Not yet. Please."

"What do you want from me?"

"You, Tia. I want you; all of you. I don't want to share. I'm getting too old to play this twenty-plus-year-old game. I need you. I want you. Now."

"I need to use the ladies' room."

The waitress walks toward us. Her presence is welcomed as it will give us a much-needed time out.

"Another drink?"

"Yes," I reply. "We'll have another round."

With the grace of a ballerina, Tia stands and her statuesque, five-foot-eleven-inch frame glides graciously across the room.

Instinct gets the better of me and I follow, walking in beat to her rhythm.

The sight of Tia's ass swaying confidently and magically from side to side, up and down, as her hips coincide with perfection, makes the tip of my manhood as solid as a rock. She is wearing the hell, shit, and damn out of that black dress. She is a sin and a shame in human form. As she takes the first step of a small flight of stairs to the ladies' room, I trace the curvature of her thick thighs with my eyes; I imagine them wrapped securely and seductively around my waist and with each blow, my manhood delves deeper into her righteousness, further into her faithfulness, and takes my breath away. Her pretty, pulsating pussy would give way to every one of my bold, blunt blows.

She looks back at me, as the hair around her sweet face dances a beautiful jig down her jaw. Knowing that look has the power to drop me to my knees, she does it again and smirks the second time around. She is carrying that extra forty pounds like it's a million damn dollars. Every time she bounces, I feel like I may bust.

We reach the ladies' room. Her hand reaches for the doorknob, but I open the door instead.

Looking back at me, she asks, "Does this make any sense to you, Tre'?"

"Doesn't have to make sense, it's who we are. I don't want to wake up again and know that you could be gone forever. Been there, done that; don't want to do it again."

We enter the ladies' room. The marble sink and cleverly decorated small space are both sexy and inviting. Boasting earth tones and rich purples, the bathroom could be a backdrop to something magnificent.

"Will you ever leave her for me?"

HER . . .

Experience trumps assumption every time. Knowing this man the way I do makes me an expert in the field of everything Tre'. Still, I wonder why he chose her. I often contemplate what things would be like if we had met in a different time and space.

"I already belong to you, Tia."

"Right."

He locks the door behind us. Taking my hands in his, he moves in close and that glazed look of euphoria covers him completely. Pressing me against the wall, he places his lips right on mine, but doesn't kiss me. He makes me beg for it—and he knows I will.

"Kiss me," he says as his tongue licks my lips.

"Touch me," he commands as he places my hands on his erection.

"Love me," he tells me as his long, piano-player fingers wrap around my waist.

My tongue dances with the devil and his mouth tastes like the sweetest sin. Like water for chocolate—he is divine.

"Let me eat your pussy from the back. Bend over."

Have mercy.

His wish is my command. I bend over, to the point that I can touch my toes.

"Good girl. Now, spread your legs."

As if on a mission he parts my legs and his hands travel the length of my thighs until he reaches the point of no return. Uncontrollably, my thighs surrender to his fingers as he inserts them one by one inside me, releasing a precursor of my nectar.

"No panties, huh?" he whispers.

"Just get in the way," I exhale.

Skillfully, he burrows his head in the land of milk and honey and devours me so good. His tongue tries to calm my hot flesh. I try not to flinch at every caress and instinctively I pinch at my hardened nipples. As he grabs my cheeks, forcing them to clap, the volcano set ablaze inside me ruptures.

"Oooh," I coo. He loves to hear me make the sound.

"Don't leave me this way . . ."

HIM . . .

I place a single finger over her lips and pull her toward me. My tongue slithers out of my mouth and enters her with force and determination. My hunger gets the best of me. I lick and suck with a fierceness, satisfying my craving, ensuring I don't miss a drop.

"Damn, I've missed the taste of your pretty lips, baby. Please don't keep this away from me." I kiss her cheek, lingering for a moment, enjoying the feeling of being at home within the sweet walls of her flesh.

As the tears fill her eyes, one begins to stream and I take my thumb and wipe it away.

"But . . ."

"Shhhh. Just let me love you."

Kissing me softly on the lips, the seductress has once again come out to play.

"I've been dreaming of being your whore, Tre'."

Those tantalizing words ooze from her mouth and enter my psyche, shooting orgasmic pulses through my entire being, finally landing at the tip of my length, where it releases my juices as I hunger for her even more.

"Let me see that pretty pussy, please, baby."

Tia lies down on her back, and the fine hairs are just starting to grow back on her pussy, and her lips, now swollen with desire, beg silently for me.

"Spread it real nasty for me."

Like Moses parted the Red Sea, so does she, for me. The sweetest thing I've ever known.

"Oh, Tre'. Baby, I have to . . ."

HER . . .

He interrupts by placing his tongue in my mouth. I can still smell my pussy on his breath. With sticky, cum-stained lips, he nibbles my lips gently and licks and bites my neck. Grabbing a deliciously treacherous hold of my breast, Tre' sucks on my nipple, tugging at it until it reaches its firmness.

I'm almost afraid of what he has planned next, but my fear is overcome by the thought of him having his way with me, again. Tre' licks his lips and reaches down to his manhood. He strokes it with his hand, but not for long. He needs to be inside me and I need him to be there as well. Stepping back, he lines his dick up for the perfect position to enter me and with one forceful thrust he gives it all to me deeply. Deliciously. Divinely.

I can almost hear the sound of my cherry popping once more when I go back in time, when he was my first, and I was his. The origin of our dance. The root of this beautiful evil.

"Tia, oh baby, damn, your pussy is so sweet." Tre' keeps his eyes glued on his erection sliding in and out of me and the more he watches his body in motion, the slower he goes. With each thrust, he gets deeper and deeper inside of me. He pins me to the floor. I can't move. I don't want to. It hurts so good. He's got me wide open, dripping wet, and about to cum all over him. I feel as if I am going to explode, if I don't go crazy first.

Trying to hold it all in for fear that someone may hear the sounds of our lovemaking, I bite my lip. I don't want to arouse him any further. Tre' comes in closer to my ear. "Tia, don't give this pussy to anybody else. This is my pussy. You belong to me, Tia."

I exhale deeply, preparing to respond, hoping that the words will come out of my mouth. "I'm all yours, Tre'." He picks up speed, still watching as he goes in and out of me. He's talking that good shit to me, moaning and sucking any and every thing he can get his mouth on. With one hand he caresses my nipples; the other hand slithers down to my ass elevating me slightly from the waist down. He grabs hold of my ass cheek and squeezes it firmly as he pounds into me harder and deeper. I can't help myself, I'm there, I'm seconds from cumming and he knows it. I guess he knows *his* pussy so well.

"Ahh, Tia, yes, that's a good girl; cum all over *your* dick. This is *your* dick, Tia, cum all over it, baby."

Without warning, and yet on cue, I cry out to Tre' as he gives me the hardest climax, matched with the deepest dick pounding I've ever had in my life. With one of his final blows, he delves into me, and whispers,

"I love you, Tia."

As a single tear emerges from Tre's eye, I feel exactly what lies deep in his heart; that we've come to the end of our favorite nightmare on the other side of midnight.

"Just close your eyes and I'll always be right there."

Tammy's Seminar

Jeremy Edwards

If I hadn't paused to glance at the headlines on the house copy of the *Miami Herald,* I wouldn't have seen Ellen Sanderson walk by the deli.

I hadn't set eyes on her since she'd entered a doctoral program up north. And it looked like Boston had been kind to Ellen. She seemed more self-assured, more radiantly intellectual, and more sexually desirable than ever. Her skin looked smooth as silk, and the peach-colored shorts she'd chosen to wear begged a comparison with the aforementioned fruit. She looked, in a word, delectable.

There'd been a time, not that long before, when I knew almost everybody in the friendly little African-American neighborhood that was my heritage. But I'd been living most of the past few years around the university, and these days I noticed new faces whenever I came back to this part of town. Still, it was surprising to see Ellen here, of all places. I knew for a fact that her family lived in a similar neighborhood, but all the way on the other side of the metropolis.

She stopped temporarily at the corner, still in view, where she waited for the light to change. The day was already warming up and, my imagination being one of my strong points, I imagined the thermal energy of Ellen's pussy sizzling in her little shorts as she walked around in the Miami heat. And I could also readily visualize her pulling her shorts and panties down later, in the air-conditioned cool of some private space. The nested garments, I decided, would descend in one piece, and Ellen would reach in to feel her sticky-sweet juncture, letting the aroma of her frisky honey filter into the room.

She moved on, and I forced myself out of the reverie, which I knew I'd return to in time. I permitted my incipient erection to stagnate, then dwindle, leaving me with a characteristic drop of precum to stain my briefs and lick at my skin. It was a sensation I always relished, in part because it made me feel I was tasting a hint of what a woman feels when she's horny and holds the thought . . . gliding through the next phase of her day with a bit of clingy wetness as a reminder. Letting her juice bookmark her appetite. I reflexively imagined Ellen experiencing all of that, and my cock re-hardened a notch before I successfully focused my attention on the newspaper.

With headlines scanned and peach now long out of frame, I turned toward the cash register.

The bratty-cute breakfast wrangler behind the counter smirked at me. She wore it well. Perhaps it was just my general randiness that morning, but I couldn't help thinking that if this had been midnight at the nu-jazz club rather than nine a.m. in an empty, brightly lit eatery, I might have had something to say for myself.

"What would you like? Besides *her,* I mean."

Despite having been forewarned by the impish affect, I was taken aback. But I did my best to play it cool, feigning polite confusion. "Her?"

"Gonna make me spell it, huh?" The imp nodded toward the window. "That tall woman with the nice ass."

Ellen was, in fact, tall. But this seemed like an unnecessarily boring adjective to apply to her, with so many others available. By contrast, I could fully understand an allusion to the niceness of Ellen's ass, which was a very apt description—in spite of my surprise at hearing a stranger direct it at me so pointedly.

"Do I know you?" I asked, peering through my glasses for a clue.

"No. Do you know *her?*"

"Actually," I confessed, "I do know Ellen. Or I did."

"Aha," said my foil. "So, did it feel as good as it looks?"

"I beg your pardon?"

"The *ass,* dude. In your hands. When you squeezed it."

This dialogue, I noted, had quickly taken a surreal turn, even by my tolerant standards as a modernist literary scholar. "What makes you infer that Ms. Sanderson and I were . . . intimate?" I ventured.

The woman laughed. Her black curls fluttered around her mirthful cheeks, and her generous breasts jiggled under her striped, flour-streaked T-shirt. The laughter rippled through her with an overtly sexual sensuality, suggesting some Renaissance painter's depiction of pleasure.

And when she turned her back on me briefly to attend to the stove, I saw that even her broad, attractive derriere appeared to be enlivened by the hilarity.

"Why are you laughing at me?"

"I'm not laughing at *you,*" she claimed, turning back to face me. "I'm laughing at the way you talk. You know, I've been to college, too, but I don't give seminars at the deli counter."

I decided I had nothing to lose by engaging with this personality on her own terms. "Okay, then . . . what *do* you give at the deli counter?"

"Point to you, professor," she said, still chuckling. "That's more like it."

"I'm not a professor yet," I replied. My obligatory humility was denatured, I feared, by my poorly concealed delight at the ad hoc promotion. "I'm still a graduate student."

"Uh-huh. Well, I can't imagine how stuffy you're going to be when you're a full-on professor, then." Her smirk returned, bolder than before. And I had a suspicion she'd chosen the term *full-on* specifically so as to evoke *hard-on*. I was intrigued by her attitude.

"I'd like to talk to you," I said quietly.

"You *are* talking to me. Or maybe you thought this was a cardboard cutout."

"No. Not with that beauty of a behind." I considered a wink, but elected instead to raise an eyebrow.

"I thought you said you liked Ellen Sandelman's behind."

"Sanderson. And I didn't say that—you did."

"But it's true."

"Yes, it's true. But Ellen Sanderson's behind is neither here nor there."

"It has to be somewhere. An ass like that can't just vanish into thin air."

Should I vanish into thin air myself, I wondered, rather than get drawn any further into this unpredictable interaction? No, I concluded.

"What's your name?" I demanded cordially.

"Tammy." She shrugged as if I'd asked an irrelevant question. By my calculations, this was the first straight answer I'd had from her. And it might well be the last.

"I'd like a pancake," I informed Tammy, playing for time.

The establishment had a special way of serving its signature pancakes: a single flapjack was lubed up with butter, then folded like a taco and stuffed into an elongated variation on the classic paper french-fry carrier, in which posture its yearning edges were drizzled with syrup. In due course, and with Tammy watching me, I brought the soft, sticky pancake to my mouth.

After a few bites, I was ready to resume the negotiations. "Tell me, Tammy . . . are you fascinated by my erotic interest in Ellen, or are you fascinated by Ellen herself?"

"Who says I have to choose?"

"Yes, I suppose the two possibilities aren't mutually exclusive."

"That's what I just said."

"Are you bisexual?"

"Duh."

I nourished myself with another mouthful of pancake before proceeding. "All right. If you must know, Ellen and I only dated a couple of times. We didn't click that well, and we broke it off before anything much developed."

"You *did* at least grab that ass of hers once or twice on the dance floor, right? Don't be disappointing me now, professor."

I studied my shoes, embarrassed but strangely flattered. "I did. That was about the extent of it . . . but, well, I'm not knocking it."

"Good man. That's the spirit I like to see in my guy."

I laughed. "Since when am I *your guy*?"

"Since you started eating my pancakes."

I was attracted by her logic—such as it was—and yet I felt compelled to challenge it, if only on principle. "A lot of people must come in here and eat your pancakes."

"I'm not talking about them. I'm talking about you. Mind your own business. Anyway, I didn't say it was cause and effect. You asked 'since when?' and I was trying to give you a time frame."

Before I could consider this, the bell over the door jingled.

"Now you're in trouble," said Tammy.

I spun around.

"We were just talking about you," Tammy volunteered matter-of-factly, as Ellen Sanderson walked in.

"Tammy!" I sputtered.

Ellen was scrutinizing her. "Do I know you?"

"It's no use," I averred. "I tried that."

Ellen managed to recover enough to smile at me, which I thought quite admirable, under the circumstances. "How the hell are you, Elliot?"

This was turning into a strange—no, a *stranger*—dream.

"I'm home for the week," Ellen explained, "and as usual I'm stuck running errands for the folks. But I wound up over here too early, so I thought I'd treat myself to breakfast."

In addition to the peach shorts, she was wearing a ribbed, off-white halter top that hugged her nipples, a hand-strung bead necklace, and a chic, wide-brimmed hat that flattened her auburn locks down around her elegant ears.

We made small talk while she waited for the egg and muffin that Tammy was cooking her, both of us ignoring the elephant in the room—namely, that I had noticed her walking by a few minutes earlier, and had been discussing her with Tammy. Ellen was gracious, and she pretended nothing had happened. I rattled off my recent academic triumphs, nodded with interest at hers, and temporarily suppressed my simmering thoughts about her warm, moist panties and her squeezable buttocks.

At last, Tammy handed over Ellen's breakfast.

"Elliot, it was great running into you," Ellen said with decisive finality. She looked out the window, then back at me. "I'm going to sit outside with this, I guess." I wasn't invited, and I took no offense: as I'd told Tammy, Ellen and I had never really clicked that well.

After leaving me with another reserved smile and Tammy with a sidelong glance, Ellen walked her gorgeous derriere out the door and made herself comfortable at the eatery's only café table—which put her in easy view of anyone inside. Soon she was absorbed in her breakfast and her paperback.

"Come here."

I turned around once again to face the counter. Tammy was lifting the chain and beckoning me in.

"Back there?"

"Quick," said Tammy. "We're gonna watch her together."

Before the unusual scene playing out earlier had been interrupted by Ellen's arrival, I'd been hoping I might rendezvous with Tammy somewhere sexy after work—as absurd as the prospect seemed to my more rational self. But I certainly hadn't planned on teaming up with her at breakfast time to salivate over my poor ex-girlfriend.

Yet, at that moment, it didn't occur to me *not* to do what Tammy asked. And so, an instant later, I stood just to her left in the narrow area between the counter and the unseen hinterland of the deli's stockroom.

"Her tits aren't bad, either," Tammy promptly observed. "Don't you think your Ellen Sanderson has nice, soft-looking tits, professor?"

She was being very casual about unbuttoning my fly. And then she was equally casual about placing her hand inside my trousers. She began to pet my cock through my shorts, as if absentmindedly.

I, on the other hand, did not feel remotely calm or collected. My face was hot, and I was squirming involuntarily, though pleasantly. I felt dirty, but undeniably aroused.

"Yes, she does," I hissed.

And so she did. However, I'd noticed that Tammy had lovely breasts, too; and I turned my head now to admire the way they'd begun heaving while she stroked me. I gave myself an extended moment to appreciate this sight, conscious of the paradoxical transgression of cheating on Tammy by looking at her instead of at Ellen.

Then I turned back to the picturesque spectacle of Ellen, book, and breakfast in profile, backlit by the Miami sun. I couldn't see below Ellen's waist—and yet below her waist, as before, was where my mind settled.

"Say it," said Tammy, her eyes never leaving the window.

"Say . . . what?"

"What you're thinking about her. Now's your chance to use those seminar words, professor. I want to hear what's going through that big academic brain of yours."

"I—"

"And, by the way, what happened to your hands? Don't you want to smooth the seat of my jeans, professor? Don't you want to slap my ass or something? I hope I didn't waste your time by inviting you back here."

The unfurling flesh beneath her left palm was my reply— followed, a moment later, by a playful, vigorous slap on the right cheek of her out-thrust bottom, where my own right hand subsequently remained.

"Yeah!" said Tammy. "Now give me some subtitles for this movie we're watching."

And so, as Ellen nibbled her muffin, I plunged in. In essence, I was picking up where I'd left off when I ogled her earlier. That meditation, in retrospect, appeared to have been a rehearsal for my present effort.

I used my "seminar words" for Tammy, and my most polished

public-speaking voice. "I'd like to suggest, Tammy, that Ellen is pressing her thighs together under the table. Her libido has been engaged by something. We might suppose, for example, that she's reading an erotic passage in that book."

I took a deep breath. I was quite accustomed to talking in front of a group, and quite accustomed to indulging in sexual fantasies—but I was not at all accustomed to combining the two.

"Keep it coming." Tammy was definitely an appreciative audience when I gave her what she wanted.

"Yes," I continued, "Ellen is horny this morning—as horny as we are." I didn't necessarily believe this, but it was the narrative that we were both depending on. "Her luxurious pussy is so slippery, so tingly."

Tammy growled like a velvet-coated motor as I rubbed her rear pocket. Out of the corner of my eye, I saw her rip open the top button of her jeans.

"I believe that Ellen won't be able to relax—be able even to sit still—until she's awarded herself a vivid orgasm."

"'Vivid,'" Tammy repeated. "That's nice." Her free hand buried itself inside her fly, popping additional buttons on the way in.

"So as soon as Ellen has finished her breakfast, she's going to face the inevitable, Tammy. She'll postpone her parents' errands and hasten home."

Tammy chortled. "No one says 'hasten.'" But her fingers continued to grow more insistent in my pants.

"She'll lock the door to her room and draw the curtains."

I paused again, my head reeling from the delirious chemistry of the scenario I was creating about Ellen and the sensations of having Tammy's hand on my cock, and my hand on Tammy's bottom. Furthermore, while Tammy's left hand had been busy fondling me, her right hand had evidently found its treasured place within her panties. Her hips were shimmying, and her jeans brushed my thigh with each gyration, nudging me further into arousal. I started kneading fistfuls of her ass, my hand hungry for more of her.

"Go on," she breathed. "Go the fuck on, already."

My speech came more haltingly—though my enthusiasm was waxing, my control was waning. "She'll . . . yank her pretty underwear . . . down to her knees. It's . . . it's . . . her favorite moment of the day."

"Oh, fuck," said Tammy. The arc of her grinding pattern increased.

I seemed to have run out of recherché vocabulary. "She'll . . . cup . . . one of her breasts . . . under her top, and . . . tw-twist her own nipple."

Oblivious to my words—and yet it was as if she'd somehow been affected by them—Ellen shifted sensuously in her chair while turning the page in her novel. A tremor ran through all the nerves of my cock, reverberating against Tammy's fingers.

In a series of swift, sudden motions, Tammy ejected her other hand from her jeans, snatched my hand off her rear, and relocated my itchy fingers to the front of her body, practically shoving them inside the damp panties her own hand had just vacated. "Touch me, professor. Touch me like she's going to touch herself."

Reciprocating, I moved Tammy's left hand from the outside to the inside of my briefs so that she was clasping my nakedness as I fingered hers. The parallel feasts were overwhelming: Here was her deft touch all over my tensing hardness, while there was her slick, dribbling softness engulfing my digits.

We began to sway in sync, left to right to left, doing a grotesquely beautiful dance of mutual masturbation.

And when Ellen got up and walked away, it didn't matter. The fantasy had already done its job . . . but much more important,

I realized in that moment, was the fact that Tammy had become far sexier to me than the estimable Ellen Sanderson.

She was writhing on my palm, and the raw smell of her excitement was filling the small space we shared. I pivoted away from the window now to glue myself to Tammy, turning her toward me so we could meld, front to front. I rocketed my free arm up her syrup-stained T-shirt to tickle her warm breasts, fucking her in earnest now with the hand stationed below—grazing her clit with the heel while the fingers burrowed and wiggled. My cock, drunk and bloated with pleasure, twitched in time with her strokes, and I knew that both of us were going to come soon.

Ellen might have been a peach that morning, but Tammy in climax was a fruit far more succulent. As her cunt pulsed around my fingers, her fresh-squeezed juice soaked me. She pumped and trickled longer than I'd ever known a woman to do, washing me in shuddering spoonfuls of her sauce. The wet heat in her pants made me manic with lust, and I clamped her breast hard as my morning's worth of male desire spurted impassioned streams all over her clutching fingertips.

Our lurching, spastic dance gradually slowed. Finally we were still, and we each reclaimed our hands, leaving the other's dampened underpants in privacy. We stood there for a minute, laughing, breathing hard, then laughing some more.

"So, professor, it's a shame you didn't click with Ellen Sanderson," said Tammy.

I shrugged.

"Are you gonna click with me?"

"I think I already did," I replied.

"Good man," said Tammy.

So Much for Rules

W. Biddle Street

I still don't know why I went to Jerome's house that day. I had a decent boyfriend who was just a few months away from asking me to marry him. Yet there I was, driving over to Jerome's place knowing that he wanted to fuck me. And I'd kind of given him signals that I might finally let him. Which doesn't make sense because I had always been a one-man-at-a-time woman.

I'd known Jerome since Michael Jackson was black. He was with me through kindergarten and grade school. He was with me from my homely girl stage right up through becoming homecoming queen back when it was still cool to be an HC queen. I was with him through his geek stage. He was always a good friend, just not my type.

I had a brand-new black teddy in my bag just in case I couldn't come up with a way to get out of letting him do me. He had invited me over on the pretense of a home-cooked meal and a little wine before he left for Tennessee. He had a job in Memphis and was leaving Baltimore for good.

True to his word, just like the gentleman that he was, he had a fine meal waiting for me when I arrived. We ate and made small talk. He talked about getting to live in the city where Stax Records was born. The city that was home to Carla Thomas, Otis Redding, Booker T. & the MG's, Sam & Dave, Isaac Hayes, and many lesser-known stars. He said he was excited about the chance to see the newly renovated Stax recording studio museum. He was excited all right, but I don't think it was about going to Memphis. His dick was hard. I could see it doubling up in his crouch.

I wanted to give him some but didn't know if I should, so I started talking off-the-wall shit about being a campaign manager for a state house candidate and how much fun it was being involved in elective politics. We were not really talking to each other. We were just sending words into the air, trying to buy time and avoid the obvious. Neither one of us wanted to make first contact.

I was trying to wait him out in the hope that, even though I was leaning toward kinda wanting to give him some, I would not have to have his dick in me. That is, until I stood up from the table to go to the couch. I felt wetness I had never experienced in his presence before. And it had nothing to do with whether Stax or Motown was the best music company of the sixties. It had everything to do with how his bulge was hanging to the left as he poured me a glass of German Liebfraumilch wine. That bulge just kept on bulging.

I made sure that he got a good look down my blouse when I leaned forward to pick up my glass. He took a good look. Did not even attempt to be sly, no pretense at all. Then, just as casually, he started talking about Al Green, Hi Records, and Willie Mitchell's influence on Memphis soul music of the seventies.

I listened to him ramble on through two glasses of the German table wine. It was an inexpensive wine he drank as a private in the army stationed in Geissen, in what was then West Germany. It was the only decent wine he could afford. A retired army buddy of his would periodically supply him with a few bottles from the army/air force exchange store at Fort Meade.

I interrupted his rendition of Al Green's "For the Good Times" by telling him I had to pee. Without waiting for his acknowledgment I grabbed my bag and headed for his bathroom. Sitting on the toilet with a nice buzz and a wet tingling between my legs, I had to make a decision. It was now or never. I didn't want to fuck him, but I didn't not want to fuck him, either. A wet pussy on a single girl, involved or not, is a terrible thing to waste. I often had sex with my fiancé without being wet when we started, but we would make up for it by the time we finished. But here I was in Jerome's apartment, getting turned on, enjoying and hating it at the same time. I'd often heard my brother say that a hard dick has no conscience. Well, a throbbing wet pussy is a lonely hunter, but of course I would never say that to my brother. (If he knew what went through the mind of his little sister when she had a wet pussy, he would be shocked beyond belief. The thought of me having a wet pussy probably never crossed his mind.)

It's hard for me to pee when I'm already horny. I decided to put on the black teddy. Besides, with my panties already down around my ankles, I was already halfway there. And no way was I putting that sticky wet material back between my legs. I decided to hang them on his towel rack. Leave him a little souvenir of his conquest. Some men may think it's gross, some like freaky stuff like that. And since this was a one-shot deal, I really didn't care. I hung them on the towel rack above his sink. "Shave and savor, sweetheart," I said to myself.

None of my girlfriends talk about looking at themselves naked. But I just love to look at my body. Perfect tits, perfect hips, strong black thighs, beautiful ass, and very pretty face. Hell, I'd fuck me in a heartbeat. I thought about covering myself with some of the baby oil he had in his medicine cabinet, spraying some water on my body from the flower sprayer sitting in his window, and walking out there stark naked, wet inside and wet outside. But that would telegraph the fact that I was too horny to turn back, that it was either fuck me or cut off your dick. What if I had read his signals wrong? What if he was gay and that was a banana in his pants! Yeah, right! But, just to be safe, I put on the teddy and went back out to meet my fate.

That was no banana! Nor should I have worried about him being gay. He was sitting on the sofa with nothing on but a pair of blue University of Memphis basketball shorts. Were my horns that obvious or did the boy just want to make sure he got this good pussy? For a former geek, Jerome had a fine body. He had a hairy chest. Not that common in black men and a first for me. This would be a nice little treat for my tits. Treat for my tits, treat for my tits. That would make a good hip-hop song title.

The time for indecision, being coy, or whatever, was over. We were going to fuck. That was that. I was not about to let all of this juice running down my leg go to waste. And I'm sure Jerome planned to stick his dick somewhere tonight besides in his hand.

I sat down next to him on the couch. As I did, he stood up, took me by the shoulders, and laid me back. My tits separated under the flimsy material, moving to either side of my chest. The movement of the fabric across my nipples turned them into hard, rubbery points of sensation. My nipples sent a signal to my pussy, checking to see if it was interested in playing. Which was just as well, because without much fanfare, Jerome used two of his fingers and slowly inserted them into my pussy until the heel of his hand was resting against my bushy box. He used his thumb to rub my clitoris. I came for the first time. Then I grabbed his wrist to stop what he was doing without taking his fingers out of me.

"Talk time, first. Okay," I said. "Let's lay down the rules of engagement. Kissing—no tongue. You can kiss me on the lips, and I really like being kissed on the neck, but putting your tongue down my throat is off limits. I want to keep that for my boyfriend. When he does it, it gets me really wet. But since I already have a miniature Niagara Falls going on between my legs, it's not necessary.

"Sucking dick is off limits, too. My boyfriend's dick is just the right length. I can get his whole dick in my mouth without having to gag. He likes to grab me by the head and fuck my mouth like it's a pussy. And I swallow. The first time I let him come down my throat it freaked him out so bad I think he would have married me on the spot if I had asked him.

"The last restriction is the asshole. Boy, do I have a sensitive asshole. If you want to score brownie points, then pull my cheeks open and stick your tongue as far up my asshole as it will go. It doesn't hurt if you lick my brown slit for a while, either. Also, if you want to take me doggie style, you can smack my ass as hard as you want and you can even stick your thumb up my ass if you need to hold on to something, but no dick head in the butt. Digits only.

"Now just because I'm not giving up any head does not mean you can't. Feel free to lick and suck as much as you want. When you get to the clit, I prefer that you put your whole mouth on the little knob, create some suction, and tickle it with your tongue until my butt starts bouncing on the bed. My orgasm won't be far behind.

"That leaves the pussy, which I assume is what you are after, after all. You can do anything to the pussy you want. You can use your fingers, tongue, thumb, nose. If you have a dildo you want to put in my pussy while you suck my clit, I'm game. Or, if you want to watch phallic vegetables or small fruits going in and out of my pussy, that's okay, too, as long as they are clean and you can get them out. I don't know how freaky you are when it comes to sex and most of this pussy stuff I have never tried, but I have always been interested in it, and since you are leaving for good, I won't have to worry about hearing about what a freak I am, and I won't have to worry about doing it again. I don't even trust my boyfriend with this side of me.

"Now that we have gotten the fucktials out of the way, how about taking off those shorts and using me for your fuck lust."

I didn't have to ask him twice. He took his fingers out of my pussy, stood up, pulled off his shorts, and walked back toward me with the longest, thickest, meanest-looking dick I have ever seen in my life.

"My god! Jerome," I said, staring at his thick-veined dick, not looking at his face. "I had no earthly idea that you were packing this much meat."

"Would you have let me fuck you any sooner?" he asked, half-laughing.

"I don't know, but I wouldn't have wasted all that time think-ing about sugar and spice and everything nice."

"Well, here's to snakes, snails, and puppy dog tails; mostly snakes." He laughed again.

I had to touch it. In all my years of fucking, I don't remember touching a dick just to touch it. I've grabbed a few to stick in my pussy when my lover couldn't find the hole and I didn't want to wait. But to take a dick in my hand just to play with it—this was a first. I used my left hand to lightly cup his balls, which made my boyfriend's balls look like raisins. I used my right hand to push the skin back, to fully expose the head, and stuffed his dick into my mouth. So much for rules.

As I enjoyed the sensation of his dick in my mouth I became excited, if a bit afraid. A big dick was new, it was challenging; I was afraid for my throat and my butt hole. As the head filled my mouth my pussy tightened, my butt hole loosened—spreading, winking, waiting, hoping. Everything that I'd said was off limits was now in play.

With his hands on my ears he pushed forward, and I could feel the head inching toward my throat. I knew I should stop because I had to sing a solo on Sunday. The last Saturday night my boyfriend had his dick in my throat my soprano was nowhere to be found the next day. Fortunately I didn't have to solo that day. I hadn't missed a solo since singing in the junior choir. If I didn't sing tomorrow, I would have some explaining to do to our choir director.

Of course, if I were true to my Christian values, I wouldn't be down on my knees, in the house of a man other than my boyfriend, with a dick in my mouth. I would have to figure this shit out tomorrow because sin and lust had me in their grip and I was loving losing the battle.

Jerome saved me from the dick-throat dilemma. In one fluid motion he was out of my mouth and I was on my back, wet, willing, and wide open. He was inside me so fast and so deep that I didn't have a chance to experience anything but pleasure. My mind stopped processing. My senses of sight, sound, smell, and hearing turned off as he slowly slid into my body. I forgot to breathe until he stuck his tongue in my mouth, grabbed a tit in each hand, and tried to bottom out. That shit was not happening. My pussy was not built for a dick like his. Mine was a nice-girl pussy, built for normal-sized dicks doing normal stuff. He had reached the limits of what I had to give, I thought. He put those basketball hands on my ample butt, pulled me close, and found new territory inside my body. In my mind's eye I could see his dick slowly entering my womb at the same time I felt him digging me a new hole. All my senses kicked back in. I opened my eyes, groaned really hard; I smelled his peppermint breath as he softly said, "I love you."

When I stopped coming I started crying. I was coming here to give a good friend some pussy. I didn't mind getting laid, but had not planned on getting stuffed. I didn't mind giving him some pussy, but had not planned on giving him my body. I wasn't sure exactly how I felt about our relationship beyond twenty years of friendship. I had even started out setting down rules to govern our lust, only to have lust turn into love.

I held him as he kissed me. As he slid all the way to the back of my pussy, my tears kept falling. I knew that snot was running from my nose, but Jerome didn't seem to mind. He was in the zone now, taking what I had come to give him, giving me what I had come for. Giving me more than I had come for in feelings and in dick.

Jerome was a one-of-a-kind friend. I would never see him again. Even though it was the best sex I ever had, I got over it. I got married. I have lived happily ever after. You think?

A Soldier for Cupcake

Shaniqua Holt

My legal name is Connie Johnson, but everyone calls me Cupcake because I am a chef. I relish working in the culinary field. Occasionally, I also work as a plus-sized model. I find that lifestyle extremely appealing. I'm confident about my curves and succulent dark skin. Many men regard me as a "dime-piece."

A few weeks ago I caught wind of an announcement that auditions were taking place for the May issue of a hip-hop magazine. Even though they did not specify plus-sized models, I decided to audition. Considering that my body is on point, I figured I wouldn't have any problems.

The audition was going smoothly until the time arrived for the actual shoot. When it came time to take my pictures, a thin, ass-less model vigorously complained. She believed I was *too large* to be allowed at the audition and that I was breaking some kind of an unwritten fat-model code or rule. She complained so much that I was politely asked to step aside and leave.

Darrin, my hero in more ways than one, came to my defense. He chastised the other photographers and the model. He told the other photographers that he would take my pictures for the magazine.

During the shoot, I made sure I showed off every curve, posing seductively in a sexy black bra and panty set. I was convinced that I looked better than anyone else; my curves only enhanced my sex appeal.

Darrin seemed to love taking my pictures. I posed exclusively for him. I caught some of the other photographers talking among each other and watching my body with desperation in their eyes. I imagined they were whispering, "Damn . . . I want to fuck you to death."

Darrin continued to snap pictures and even accumulated significantly more shots than the other photographers. Every few minutes, he paused and scanned my body as he held on to his camera. I would tease him and pout my lips, pretending to be naughty.

After the shoot, Darrin informed me that chances were slim that my pictures would be included in the magazine. He informed me that the model who had complained was remarkably good at getting her way with the other photographers, if I understood what he meant. He smiled a sad, but extremely sexy, smile that sent quakes down my spine and then he winked. It was then that I noticed the cane he was grasping in one hand. He blessed me with his business card and told me that if I ever needed him, give him a call.

The next day I told my friend Star, also a model, about the fallout at the shoot and how kind Darrin had been. She acknowledged his good deed, but warned me to stay away from him. She claimed that he had a terrible reputation within the model pool because he seemed to disregard everyone. Whenever someone tried to get close to him, he generally pushed them away. She then proceeded to tell me all about his past.

Darrin Sullivan had been stationed in Afghanistan two years earlier and was gravely injured, which resulted in the loss of both legs from the knees down. He had been honorably discharged, then had returned to the States and had a brief stay at a veterans' hospital where he underwent physical therapy and learned to walk again using prosthetic legs. He had recuperated at home after that.

Sadly, during that time, he had also discovered his fiancée cheating on him with another man. My friend told me that the breakup had devastated him more than the loss of his legs. He decided to return to college and immersed himself in his studies. He excelled in college and earned a masters in fine arts. Presently, he was working full-time as an art teacher and artist. He occasionally worked as a photographer for the hip-hop magazine.

I listened to her information and critical judgment of Darrin, but despite her warning, I decided to contact him.

I waited until Friday of that same week to call. I was stunned that he remembered me since there were so many girls at the shoot. He assumed that I needed him for model work. I needed him, but not in the way that he imagined. I told him that I never had the opportunity to thank him for saving me from an embarrassing situation. After all, he did not have to intervene when he did. I offered to cook him dinner that night. He quickly declined at first, but I insisted and, with some persuasion, he eventually gave in.

He arrived at my house a few minutes early, almost as if it were intentional so he could also depart early. I noticed that he was wearing loose-fitting denim jeans and a white tee. His eyes looked me over as a familiar smile formed on his face. I was sporting black stilettos, skinny dark denim jeans, and a green shirt that enhanced my bosom. I had made sure that my clothes would enhance my curves. I escorted him in and pointed in the direction of the dining room. Once inside, Darrin complimented my décor decisions.

He followed me into the dining room. The prepared food, a miniature feast with extra servings, was already on the table, allowing it to cool.

"Everything looks delicious. Can I help myself?" he asked.

"Yes, pick your seat, sit down, and dig in. I hope everything is prepared to your liking."

He grabbed a plate and quickly loaded it with a large helping of everything on the table. Then he sat down in the nearest chair.

"It all smells so good and tastes wonderful."

"Good . . . I didn't know what you might like to eat so I cooked a variety of foods. That's why there's so much of it."

"Well, you're definitely a great cook," he complimented me.

He beamed as he loaded his plate with more food. I smiled as I loaded a plate and then I took a seat across from him. Before I took a bite, I watched his lips take a mouthful of food. He didn't realize how much it turned me on.

I cooked him dinner every Friday and Sunday for the next four weeks. The more time we met and talked, the more attracted we became to each other. I found out that we had a lot in common, like a taste for the same foods. I also discovered that we had similar pet peeves. We both enjoyed watching the same sports. We admired the same athletes. We each told a few confessions. One time, he confessed that he enjoyed painting more than photography. I confessed that I enjoyed eating fast food more than gourmet cuisine. Each time we met, we seemed to hit it off even more. I hoped that it was only a matter of time before we took it to the next level. The last time we had hooked up, I noticed some standoffish behavior. When he left that Sunday, I sensed that our meetings were in danger of being nonexistent. I had asked him if he sketched nudes. At first, he didn't reply but then admitted to drawing his ex-fiancée in the nude. The memories seemed to sadden him, almost ruining the evening. He smiled his sweet-sad smile before finishing his meal. I noticed that he didn't decline to draw me nude.

It was obvious that he was attracted to me in every way possible. But it was also apparent that he feared becoming too involved. He didn't trust all too well because of his past relationship. I was determined to have him in my life, and in my bed. I was convinced that we were made for each other. I had come too far to let him leave. I made up my mind to fight for him.

On Friday of the fifth week, I decided to make a move. Darrin arrived on time. Dinner consisted of cheese pizza and beer. He let me feed him slices of pizza. After dinner, I asked him to join me in the basement for dessert.

I left the dining room to put on a silky red robe before returning. This time I insisted that Darrin follow me to the basement. He followed me down the steps to a scene created specifically for him. I had persuaded my antiquarian friend to locate a vintage couch for me. She located a beautiful one, and bought a red crushed velvet slipcover that looked like something Freud would have utilized. In front of the couch was a table with a large porcelain bowl of fruit near a wine bottle with two glasses. There was a tablet with a pencil on the table. I poured him some wine and handed him the glass along with the tablet and pencil. He took them both and grinned.

I discarded my robe, allowing it to plunge to the floor. I wanted him to appreciate my breasts and beautiful curves. I sauntered slowly over to the piece of antique furniture and then bent over it slowly so he could gaze at my pink pussy before I sat down.

I told him to draw me and I watched as he drained the glass of wine in two gulps. I imagined that it had been awhile since he'd had any sex, so I was determined to ignite his flame.

It seemed like he was sketching me faster than I had expected. I got up to see the drawing and was impressed by his talents. I asked him if I could draw him nude. He laughed but I insisted until he slowly removed his clothes.

I was pleasantly surprised at the length of his deliciously dark dick. The sight of it drenched my pussy and I couldn't wait any longer. He sat down on the couch in the same spot. I walked over to him seductively, my breasts moving with each step, and sat beside him.

I kissed his lips and ran my fingers through his hair. Then I kissed him again. He gazed at me with a stunned look before he returned the kiss.

I quickly clutched his dick. Before he could protest, I placed him in my mouth and sucked on him for dear life. I continued to suck while he twisted above my head. I watched his stomach move and he seemed slowly to lose control. I sucked harder, circling his dick with my tongue. I pulled it out and licked on his balls in an upward motion like one would do an ice cream cone, before returning his dick to my mouth. I felt the head of his dick swell and realized that he was about to cum.

I sat on the couch and spread my legs wide for him. He grabbed them as he got on his knees and then plunged three fingers into my wet pussy. He slipped his warm mouth over my clit. He sucked and finger fucked me until I started shaking. After a while, he removed his fingers and started licking the juices from my pussy. He licked my pussy and sucked on my clit once again. Slurping sounds filled the room. I cried out and moaned as loud as I could. He sat on the couch beside me and sucked both of my hard nipples. He sucked and licked them while rubbing my clit.

"Fuck my pussy; fuck my pussy now."

"Damn, you're soaking wet."

I turned around, facing the wall behind the couch with my ass in the air. He licked my soaking wet walls again before he entered my pussy. This time around, sloppy wet sounds filled the basement. I moaned and my pulse quickened as his hard dick moved in and out of me. My body started shaking as he fucked me. I insisted that he fuck deeper inside my pussy and he did, working my entire body. He had to grip my breasts to steady his footing.

"I can't take any more!" I shouted.

I screamed as loud as I could as I climaxed and then squirted everywhere. He pulled out at the same time, ejaculated, and then dropped to his knees and licked the juices off my pussy. I turned around on the couch to face him.

Afterward, we both had a glass of wine while sitting on the couch. We were both exhausted. We talked a little and he confessed that he still desired for me to draw him in the nude. He also opened up about how lonely he had been. We agreed to see each other more often. That day was the beginning of a beautiful relationship. We are perfect for each other. We are exactly what we need in each other's lives.

Club Head

Gemini Blaque

I love everything about clubbin'. From the moment I step out of my Infiniti QX56, sashaying through the parking lot on my six-inch stilettos, rocking my hips back and forth to the rhythm of the bass that rises from the asphalt as I make way toward the door to enter VIP; until the time I roll out a little tipsy, still holding my own, flipping niggas to the left as they make their pathetic last attempts to get at me, I feel like I'm in heaven. You know that song by Ludacris? Yeah, he wrote that about me, 'cause this chick right here is bad, and yes, I'm a little hood, and you better believe I do shit that any average chick wish she could; all the while doing it up champagne-style with my two besties.

When my girls and I walk up into the hot spot on any particular night, it's like we're on the red carpet. All eyes are on us. Tonight, we're at Madame Montage's downtown. My ex, Shay, is working security and tipped me off that some celebrities are supposed to saunter in a little later. She wouldn't say who; she just said roll through. That place usually isn't for me, but I said fuck it, called my girls, smoked some kush, and kicked back a double shot of Hennessy and let it ride.

Buzz Buzz "Tri-na calling, Tri-na calling," the automated lady on my phone announces. Trina and Diamond pulled up just in time to hit the second blunt I had finished rolling. She must be driving her girlfriend's Charger 'cause I can hear the rev of the engine as well as the bass all the way on the fourth floor of my apartment building. Sure enough, I spy the slick, black and red two-toned, chromed-out Dodge Charger on twenty-fours idling in my complex's parking lot. I can also see the illuminating glow of the two screens in the headrest and one in the dash, looping porn in an endless eyeful of tits, ass, pussy, and straps.

I shake my head and lick my lips. Every time we ride in this car, I end up having some crazy-ass sexcapade. I guess it's the addition of the neverending porn on top of my inebriated state that leads me to these crazy adventures, or it could be the type of women I attract when I ride in it. I really don't know what it is, but whatever the case, tonight I'm ready for it.

My girls are looking on point, as usual. Trina is looking like some damn cayenne pepper in the driver's seat and just as hot in them red booty shorts and tube top. I always like the way red looks against her high-yellow complexion, like it is vibrating against her skin. Diamond has on a sexy navy halter dress that contrasts beautifully against her flawless redbone complexion. Since her name is Diamond, she feels like she always has to have some bling on, so of course she's rocking her white gold bangles with the infinity diamonds, two-carat diamond earrings, and her platinum anklet that rests right above her silver Manolo Blahniks.

This bitch must have went to Mr. Andre's without me. Her strawberry blond sew-in is on point and she's got a fresh mani-cure. It's cool, I'm feeling too good right now to care. I'll get in that ass tomorrow, though. Plus, I'm looking like an eagle my-self, as fly as I am. I'm white hot tonight, literally. I swung by this little boutique downtown a couple of days ago and picked up a white strapless dress. I've been waiting to rock this mug since the moment I laid eyes on it and there was no better night than tonight. I feel like white lightning in this little number. Against my deep ebony skin, the dress looks like a star brightening up the night. Even though that trick went to Mr. Andre's without me, my mani/pedi is still on point and my butters are whipped into a perfect jet-black bob. I must be high as hell already 'cause I look at all of us together and start to crack up. They look at me as if I'm crazy and all I can say is we look like the sexiest American flag I've ever seen in our red, white, and blue. Trina shakes her head and slams on the gas.

As we ride toward downtown, I catch a glimpse of the Magnificent Mile. As many times as I've seen it, the Chicago skyline still takes my breath away and I feel at home. I moved to Louisiana after high school to go to Grambling, where I majored in computer engineering. I had a really good internship at this computer company, but after a year, I chose to transfer back to Chicago. Even though I hate being cold, this is my home and I can't see myself being away too long.

I sit back and listen to Diamond and Trina talk about stupid stuff and shake my head. I swear, for these two chicks to be college educated, they talk about the dumbest shit! Usually, I'd start banging on them hoes, but my mind is elsewhere tonight. I haven't had sex in months, unless you count B.O.B. Yeah, it does the trick, but I can only turn myself on so much. Ever since Shay and I called it quits, trying to find some decent sex has been a hassle. Even though she can be irritating, Shay could lay it down something fierce in the bedroom.

As we pull up, the searchlights are beaming, the velvet ropes are up, and security is posted deep. I guess Shay wasn't lying when she said it was going to be popping tonight. The crowd is super thick. We pull up to the front so Trina can give the car to the valet. I see Shay eyeing me as we walk up to the door. Any other night, this would irritate the hell out of me; tonight, it doesn't even matter. From the looks of things, she'll be busy all night and won't have time to run up behind me. I have to smile, though; watching her posted up in front of the door in all black with her arms crossed and her biceps flexing I-too-damn-cute. Even though her arms are crossed, I can still see the strain of her breasts against her shirt. I don't care whether you're a stud, femme, andro, whatever, I'm a titty freak and love to see a beautiful pair. You better believe Shay had some luscious boobies! Her braids are fresh as well and flow down her back like waterfalls. I can see the edge of her black stallion tattoo peeking out under her sleeve, and I want to lick it clean off.

I peek down at the bunny tattoo on my ankle and smile 'cause we got our tats at the same time. Even though we're broken up, we'll always have a connection. See, we're both in LGBT Greek-lettered organizations. Trina, Diamond, and I all are in KΛΛ, which is by far the elite sisterhood for professional, feminine lesbians, and Shay is in AΛZ, which caters to aggressive lesbians. Anyway, I met Shay at her probate a couple of years back when the two orgs were the KΛΛZ *phamily*. When I heard that they were probating, I figured I'd roll through and rep that pink, black, and pearl. We hit it off and after our first-year anniversary, we decided to go get our tats together as a gesture of our love for each other and for what had brought us together. So, even though the orgs and our relationship split, not to mention the fact that she works my last nerve, I'll *alwayz* have love for Shay. Man, I got to get it together! This trip down Memory Lane has got my mind buggin'. I'm not about to slip up after all this time.

"I.D., please, and the cover is twenty bucks each," Shay announces and smirks my way. Diamond and Trina roll their eyes and smack their lips as they walk past her. I follow suit and, right as I do, I feel her hands pull me back by my waist.

"Where you think you going, sexy?" she whispers in my ear.

My pussy starts twitching as soon as her lips brush against my ear. My smart mouth melts as soon as I realize she is strapped up and pressing it against my butt. All I can do is flash her a dirty look and snatch away. Before the door closes, I see her flashing them pearly whites and laughing. She realizes that I'm horny. Otherwise, I would've cussed her ass out. Damn, she smells good.

As we walk through the inside door, I can already hear one of my jams. It is wall-to-wall lesbos up in here. I feel like Charlie in the Chocolate Factory! It's so many scrum-diddly-umptious choices, I don't even know where to begin. So I go to the bar for a quick drink. My favorite bartender is behind the counter. As soon as she sees me, she grins and pours my signature drink: a Grey Goose Cosmo. I must say she is looking mighty fine tonight in her black lace bustier, shorts, and red heels. As I approach the counter, she tosses the bottle up in the air and catches it behind her back. She's trying to impress me. Little does she know, she doesn't have to do much; she caught my eye a while ago. I peeped that pretty brown skin and those big hazel green eyes a *looong* time ago, as well as them thick thighs and that phat ass. She thinks she's cute, leaning on the bar top, pushing up her cleavage and batting her eyelashes. Hell, she is cute and tonight, I have no problem telling her so.

"Hey, how you doing, Ms. Lex?" she oozes over her juicy lips.

"I'm good, Ava. You looking sexy as ever tonight," I quip as I devour her with my eyes.

She licks her lips and says, "Is that so? Well, maybe you should meet me upstairs a little later and I can show you how sexy I can get." At that, she hands me my drink.

I take a twenty out of my wallet and slide it in between her boobs, smile, and walk away.

I don't know how sexy she can get, but one thing I do know is that Ava can make one hell of a drink! Trina and Diamond are already in the middle of the dance floor, shaking their asses on some random chicks, so, of course, I have to go show them chicks how it's really done. So I finish the rest of my drink and head on over.

As I dance, the beat totally takes over. The beat is banging against my body like a hard dick, and I rotate and gyrate my hips like I'm trying to bust a nut. As good as I'm feeling, I might just go ahead and bust one. After a few minutes, I open my eyes to discover that my girls are nowhere to be found. Fuck it, I gotta pee anyway.

As I walk upstairs to the bathroom, I spot Shay down the hall, talking to somebody I can't see. I try and hurry up so she doesn't see me. I don't know why I feel like I have to avoid her; it ain't like she's some stranger. I just try and forget about it.

I'm finishing up and washing my hands when I hear someone come in. I must be tweaking 'cause I swear I heard a lock turn. I hear footsteps, but no one comes around the corner. As I rinse the silky, lavender-scented lather off my hands with warm water, I see a smooth, chestnut-colored hand extend toward me with a paper towel. I smile and take it as I look back into those hazel green eyes I'd admired earlier.

"Hello again, Ava. What you doing here? I've never seen you leave from behind the bar."

I know damn well what she is doing up here. But I figure I'll play along with this little game for a minute.

"Well . . ." She stretches the word like she's figuring out if she wants to let it go. "You forgot your change. We have a special tonight, five-dollar Cosmos. So I thought I'd bring it to you personally," she coos.

"I know how much it was. That's all for you, baby girl. Since you're my favorite bartender and all."

"Is that so?"

"Yeah, you know that."

"Well, there's one more thing that I wanted."

"Oh, yeah, and what's that?"

"Your sexy ass."

"Girl, stop playing!"

"I told you I wanted to show you how sexy I can get. You're a free agent now, right?"

"You've been knowin' that. Why you trying to act brand new?" I laugh.

She laughs, too, and tries to put me on Front Street. "Oh, I'm acting brand new? You're the one straight out the cellophane, acting like you don't be staring me down. I know you want me and hell, I've been wanting you."

She steps in closer and lifts her leg up to the sink. I can feel the heat of her snatch radiate through the fabric on her shorts. Without warning, she slips her tongue in my mouth and pins me against the sink. I grab two handfuls of all that ass she's got and pull her closer to me. Our tongues swirl back and forth in an ecstasy-filled dream. And at some point during this creamy bliss, she slips her fingers into my wetness.

"Security!!!" someone yells suddenly from the other side of the door while banging so hard it sounds like the door will split in two any second. *"Open up!"*

I quickly fix my clothes while Ava hurries to the nearest stall. This fool at the door is still pounding like they ain't got a lick of sense. I unlock the door and pull it open, as if nothing is going on, and who do I see with a grin slicker than the Cheshire Cat?

"Shay, what the fuck?!? Why are you beating this door down like it owes you money!" I yell at her, pissed, yet a little relieved.

She saunters in like she realizes what's up. "Where's Ava?"

"How the fuck am I supposed to know! Why you want to know, anyway?" I shoot back, a little irritated.

" 'Cause Big Roc sent me looking for her. He wanna know why she's not behind the bar. He needs her to do VIP." She's staring me down the entire time she is speaking.

"She's not in my damn mouth, so why the fuck you staring down it so hard?" She realizes I'm being a bitch for a reason.

She steps in closer so that her lips brush the tip of my ear. She says, low and sultry, "Shit, from what I heard from the other side of that door, sounds like she was well past your mouth and deep up in that pussy." *Damn, was I that loud?* "Let me watch," she asks in something just above a whisper.

"What? You stupid. Go on and get out of here."

She locks eyes with me, daring me to turn her down. *Damn, she smells so good.*

"Come on, let me at least watch. Shit, maybe I can even join in."

As I break her stare and try to push past her, Ava walks out of the stall butt-ass naked, except for them red pumps. She struts her way over to the two of us, grabs my face, kisses me again, and then turns to Shay, licks her lips, and grabs her crotch. As she fondles Shay, she starts to talk, and though she is looking at Shay, I know she's talking to me. "She can watch. Hell, she can even join in, but I want to be the only one to taste you." And with that, she presses so hard against my body, I swear I can feel her pulse.

This girl ain't wasting no time, and neither is Shay. I hear the snap of a rubber and I look over to see she's already pulled her shirt over her head and behind her neck so only her arms are sticking through. She's standing there, strap in hand, squirting a travel-size pack of lube on the tip of her dick. I swear, this muthafucka' thinks she's a nigga sometimes.

I'm so focused on the heavenly body in front of me that I don't even care what Shay's doing. I can feel the wetness soak through my panties and slide down my thighs. Ava is working my body over something tough. My dress gathers on my torso so that all my goodies are exposed. I lay back on the counter and Ava spreads my legs. She laps up the slickness on my thighs first and wetly makes her way to my center. Shay trots up behind Ava and slips her dick into her pussy faster than Quick Draw McGraw. Ava's muffled moans echo deep in my pussy, vibrating my walls, sending me into pure carnal pleasure. I steady myself and tangle my fingers into Ava's hair and shove her tongue deeper inside me. I tease my rock-hard nipples so that with each stroke of this girl's tongue, a jolt of pleasure shoots through my body.

Our bodies are one fluid movement as each of Shay's strokes blast through Ava and resonate through me. Out the corner of my eye, I see the sticky handprints I left on the mirror. Suddenly, Ava's hands loosen from around my waist and her palms slap hard against the marble counter. Her whole lower half begins to rise. Her long legs tie around Shay's waist and the red pumps twist into a perfect bow behind Shay's back. Shay's biceps flex and her whole body glistens as she goes into overdrive with Ava suspended in midair. Sweat gathers on her forehead and a little pool of sweat starts to form at her clavicle and dribbles down to her chest.

Seeing Ava's ass jiggle with each stroke Shay throws at her is enough to push me over the edge. I guess Shay feels the same way 'cause she pops Ava's ass over and over again until an apple red handprint lingers on Ava's ass cheek. I can tell Shay is about to cum. She sucks her breath in through her teeth and low guttural moans escape her throat. She yanks off her strap, unlatches Ava's grip, snatches her around, and pushes her down into her now exposed crotch. She turns slightly and slips her fingers into my slickness just the way I like it and, to send me over the edge, she uses her thumb to fondle my clit.

Ava's tongue and my velvety smoothness make Shay cum hard and low. She pulls Ava up and kisses both our juices off her lips. Ava stands in front of me masturbating while Shay stands behind her, kissing her neck and still stroking me. I'm ready to explode as I watch Ava's body flush and her face contort in sexual delight.

She leans over to my ear and whispers, "You ready to see how sexy I can really get?"

What the fuck, is she 'bout to bring out her bag now?

Ava lifts her leg up to the sink and I get an eagle's eyeful of her dripping wet pinkness. She leans back and announces that she is cumming and, at that moment, a stream of hot liquid arcs into the air and lands on my thigh. *Did this bitch just nut on me like a nigga!?! Did I just like it?* I must have because, at the same time, I bust the biggest nut I've ever had in my life!

We gather ourselves and exchange glances across the room. Before I leave I slip my number into Ava's pocket. I walk back to the dance floor, where Trina and Diamond spot me and immediately begin interrogating me.

"We've been looking all over for you! Where the fuck have you been?!"

I think back to what just happened and all I can say is, "Nuttin'," and start busting up laughing.

Once again they look at me like I've lost my mind. I just brush them heifers off and head over to the dance floor.

Hard Times

Lynn Lake

He gunned the car, tearing down the back road, stirring up a trail of thick dust that hung heavy in the breathless air. The temperature was a hundred and ten degrees, and the flat, barren land all around offered not a bit of shade. Soon, the engine of the '32 coupe gulped, and the car shuddered, steam billowing out from under the hood.

He nursed the overheated Ford to within a couple hundred yards of a dirt drive that led up to a small, white farmhouse, and then the vehicle expired with a final hiss of steam. Ted Stevens stepped out of the car into the searing sun. He pushed his straw hat back and mopped his face with a handkerchief. Then he set his hat and tie on straight and strode down the road and into the driveway of the farmhouse.

From behind the faded chintz curtains in the parlor, Ruby Garner watched the tall, lean man walk up onto the porch of her house. He had a rugged, handsome face, brown eyes and broad shoulders, wiry black hair peeking out from under his hat. Despite the stifling heat, she shivered when he knocked on the screen door.

"Hello, ma'am," Ted said, smiling and doffing his hat. "I've had some car trouble." He pointed up the road at the black vehicle baking under the hot summer sun. "I wonder if I might trouble you for some water for my radiator?"

She gazed at him through the flimsy screen, her hazel eyes narrowed. "You best let it cool down some, first. Why don't you come inside, have a glass of lemonade?"

"Why, thank you, ma'am! That would be fine. Sure is hot out."

He sat at the kitchen table, tall and straight, while she poured cool lemonade from a pitcher into a glass, set the glass down in front of him. She was wearing a plain white cotton dress, thin from washing, hugging to the curves of her dark body, and she could feel his glittering eyes appraising her.

He took a deep gulp of the lemonade. "Will you join me, ma'am?"

She held the pitcher against her stomach, the iced glass cooling her not a bit. "You just out for a drive?"

He laughed, staring at her rising and falling breasts pressing against the front of her dress. "No, ma'am. I'm out on business. I'm a crop adjuster for a large insurance concern."

He was wearing a brown pinstriped suit and white shirt, brown tie and shoes. He looked like he had a steady job. "Not much crop of any kind around here, these days," Ruby said, drawing a little closer. The man's musky cologne filled the stuffy kitchen. "Hasn't been since thirty-one."

"Times are tough." He nodded solemnly, glancing up, noticing how the woman's eyes were shining now. He took another swallow of lemonade, his Adam's apple bobbing powerfully. "Your, uh, husband is out in the fields?"

She wet her full lips with the tip of her pink tongue. "He's off on . . . business, himself. Has been for a while."

"Oh? Must get mighty lonely here all by yourself."

She stared at his deep-brown face, the sheen of perspiration on his broad forehead, his long, strong fingers gripping the glass and the table. It *was* lonely, had been for too long with no man around. Her young body swayed, her pretty face flushing. It was so very hot, the man so very close.

She crashed the pitcher of lemonade down on the table.

"Well, I suppose I'd better be——"

Ruby grabbed him by the shoulders, lowered her head, and mashed her mouth against his, unable to control herself. And she shivered with delight as she felt his long, strong arms catch her trembling body, his soft, wet lips move against hers.

He rose to his feet, their mouths locked together. The chair tumbled over to the floor. They clutched each other, Ted's hot, hard body melding into Ruby's hot, soft form, in the steamy heat of the kitchen. She grabbed at his hair and ran her fingers through the kinky curls, as his big hands swooped down her curved back and rounded onto her buttocks.

They broke apart only when they had to breathe. Then they glared at each other. Ted towered over Ruby, but the strength of her passion placed them on an equal footing.

She pushed him back against the wall, gasping. "It's been too long!" Not as an excuse, or an explanation, just a statement of fact. She pressed her mouth against his and darted her tongue in between his plush lips, searching for and finding his tongue, entwining.

They wildly frenched. Until Ted spun Ruby around and slammed her up against the wall. "Oh, God, yes!" she cried, letting him pull her arms up over her head and clasp them together at the wrists. Her breasts strained against the worn fabric of her dress, and she arched her back needfully.

Holding her wrists with one hand, he tore her dress down the middle with the other. Her breasts spilled out into the open, black and round and quivering, darker nipples pointing.

She gasped when he cupped a tit, screamed when he kissed the nipple.

Ted gripped one soft, warm breast and licked at the stiffened nipple, sucked on it. Then popped it shining out of his mouth and gripped the woman's other breast, sucked on her other nipple. Ruby writhed against the wall, feeling the heated tug of the man's wet mouth all through her shimmering body.

He bounced his head back and forth, tongue swirling, mouth sucking. She thrust out her breasts even more, giving herself up to him. He released her wrists and grasped both of her breasts, squeezing the ripe meat, sucking almost half of one of her tits into his mouth and pulling on it, then the other.

Until Ruby couldn't take any more. She jerked her arms down and dropped down out of his, onto her knees on the kitchen floor. She clawed the buttons of Ted's fly open. He barely had time to catch his breath, grab onto her soft, straightened black hair, before she had his cock out and in her mouth.

"Jesus!" he groaned, watching her, feeling her suck on his pulsating organ.

Ruby was a starving woman, frantically bobbing her head back and forth, lips sealed tight to meaty shaft and cheeks billowing with pressure, sucking and sucking on Ted's cock. She plunged down to his pubes and pulled back up again, consuming him over and over. His cock was smooth and clean-cut, and it filled her mouth and throat, satiating a small part of her pent-up appetite, but not nearly all of it.

He pulled her to her feet and shoved her back against the wall, reading her need, and reacting to his own. Ruby jumped up into his arms, coiling her own arms around his strong neck, her legs around his narrow waist. He shoved her dress up to her hips and stuck his slathered cock into her dripping wetness.

He went in deep and long, all the way, and they moaned into each other's mouths. Then kissed, frenched, Ted pumping his hips, pounding his cock into Ruby's tight, velvety tunnel, the wall and the woman shaking. They were bathed in sweat, burning with lust.

She caught his outstretched tongue between her teeth and urgently sucked on it, feeling every inch of him thrusting into her. He gripped her rippling breasts and pistoned her pussy, driving both of them over the edge.

Ruby desperately clung to the man, shuddering in his arms, biting into his tongue. Wet, wonderful orgasm burst out from between her churned loins and surged through her body and being. Just as Ted groaned and spasmed, blasting white-hot semen into Ruby's gushing pussy.

It didn't end there.

Ruby was a wild woman, on fire with desire. The sensations aroused from having another man's cock fucking her pussy, her own powerful orgasm as a result, served to inflame her passion still more. It was hot outside, scorching in the kitchen, an inferno in the bedroom.

Ruby grabbed up a small plate of butter and dragged Ted out of the kitchen, down the hall, and into her bedroom. She stared boldly and meaningfully into his eyes the entire way, and he tried to comprehend what she had in mind.

She put it into words, filthy words. "I want you to fuck me in the ass," she stated, amber eyes ablaze. "I want you to punish my ass."

He gaped, as she set the butter down on the nightstand and pushed the torn dress off her shoulders, then stood there naked before him. Her body shone with perspiration, glowing in the sunlight illuminating the chintz curtains, her breasts bobbing up and down on her heaving chest, pussy fur matted with her juices and his. Ted's cock rose up between his legs, even so soon after coming.

Ruby walked over to him, undressed him with quivering hands until he was as starkly naked as she was, his lean body glistening with moisture, long muscles drawn tight. Then she pushed him down onto the edge of the bed, and sprawled over his knees and cock.

"Spank me! Punish me for what I've done and will do!" she yelled.

He looked down at the heaped, dark mounds of her buttocks. He brought his big right hand up, brought it down.

The stifling room shuddered with the crack of each blow. Ruby jumped, butt cheeks singed and rippling wildly, blood rushing to her face, juice to her pussy. Ted smacked her again, and again, smashing the hard flat of his hand down onto her soft, upraised bottom.

His palm burned like his face, like the beautifully rounded buttocks in front of him. He'd never hit a woman; not that she'd liked it. But Ruby was liking it, loving it, trembling naked across his legs and whimpering pleasure with every heavy blow he laid down.

"Harder! Hit me harder!" she shrieked before clenching her teeth and fists, rocking with the impact of a brutal belt to her ass.

Ted's hand knifed through the air, flailing Ruby's bum. So fast that the sharp cracks came only split-seconds apart, Ruby's cheeks gyrating continuously. Her buttocks blazed, seared with sensation. Until, finally, they went almost numb under the end-

less onslaught, Ted's crushing palm striking pure pain and pleasure across her beaten bottom.

Ruby pushed herself upright, shaking uncontrollably. She
scooped up some of the butter with her fingers, smeared it onto
Ted's cock.

"Christ!" he groaned, getting to his feet, getting greased from
balls to hood, his erection coursing out full-length in Ruby's
rubbing hand.

"Now punish me with your cock!" she rasped.

She climbed onto the bed and positioned herself on all fours,
like an animal. Her blistered rump stuck up into the air. Ted
crawled in behind her, on his knees, clutching his slippery cock
and staring at her bum.

"You're sure—"

"Fuck me!"

He bit his lip and poked his gleaming cap in between Ruby's
battered cheeks, pressed against her sensitive asshole. Ruby
flung her hands back and grabbed onto her buttocks and tore
them apart, baring her pucker to the man. Her knuckles blazed
white on the coal-black flesh of her ass.

Ted grunted, pushing forward as Ruby pushed back.

His hood burst through her ring and sank into her anus,
followed by inches and inches of swollen, shining shaft. Ruby
moaned like an animal, Ted's cock stuffing her full of strange,
wicked feelings, bloating her bottom and dizzying her head.

He went in all the way, burying his cock in her chute. The
heat, the tightness, was incredible. He was gripped deep, his
balls pressing up against her cheeks. He grasped her thin waist
and pumped his hips, fucking her ass.

Ruby let go of her bum and clutched the bedspread, rocking with the rhythm of Ted's cock driving back and forth in her anus. Her mouth hung open, her pretty face twisted with raw, exquisite emotion. It felt so weird, so wild, so wonderful—a man fucking her ass.

Ted's thighs shivered against Ruby's buttocks as he pumped faster and faster. He knew he wouldn't, couldn't, last long under the suffocating, sucking pressure, so he wanted to get in every hard pounding stroke that he could. The crack of damp, heated flesh against flesh filled the gasping room again, along with the hot hiss of air steaming out of rigidly set mouths and flared nostrils.

Ruby, hair flying, body shunted violently to and fro, tore a hand off the bedspread and shoved it between her legs, onto her pussy. "Oh, God, have mercy!" she screamed, instantly jolted by orgasm, her clit engorged beyond belief. She spasmed the full length of her cock-racked body, again and again and again.

Ted growled, thrusting in a frenzy, smashing into Ruby's bum, reaming her chute. He threw his head back and roared, exploding inside her. His hot cum filled her trembling ass, as she came on the end of his spurting cock.

He pillow-talked the information out of her later on: the approximate time and date and place that Machine Gun Murray, midwestern bank robber, murderer, and local folk hero, would finally be stealing back into his home state to visit his lonely, abandoned wife. The overheated car had been a swell ruse, the hot-blooded woman's own desires used to success where all else had failed.

Ted dozed off in Ruby's arms, in Machine Gun's bed, intending to sneak out at dawn and report his findings.

Ruby watched the sleeping man, the smile of pure contentment on his face matching the one on hers. Then she slipped out of bed and picked up Ted's suit jacket and pants off the floor. She carried them out to the parlor, intent on ironing them for him before he woke up.

Something fell out of a jacket pocket—a leather billfold. She picked it up, flipped it open, stared at the gold badge inside: FBI.

From a distance, the small, white farmhouse appeared peaceful, slumbering in the warmth of the gray early dawn. But then, suddenly, a flash of white light lit up the bedroom window of the house. Followed quickly by another flash, and another. Then the sound of gunfire, thundering over the flat, barren, hostile land.

Dirty

Carla S. Pennington

I had avoided Preston long enough. He couldn't understand why, especially after I was the one who had pursued him. We'd gone out on a few dates in the two months since I'd approached him in the auto shop where we both were getting the oil changed in our cars. I'd taken a chance and stepped to him after we'd made eye contact a few times. His light, deep-set eyes tried to roam away from me, but they didn't stay away for long. My skinny jeans were fitting nice and tight on my perfectly round ass and I made sure that he saw it every time he glanced in my direction. The jeans were tucked snugly inside my black, thigh-high, four-inch Jessica Simpson boots that added a few extra inches to my short frame. My shoulder-length, chestnut brown hair was freshly relaxed so the slanted bob I was rocking swayed with every step I took. I was a five-star chick and he recognized it.

On his last glance at me, his eyes stayed locked. It was do or die and I did. I wasn't the type of woman who sat back and waited for a man to make the first move. I went after what I wanted and, as it usually did, my first move paid off.

I had my reasons for avoiding him, though. He was so damn sexy and I was trying to stop jumping in guys' beds soon after I met them. I figured that was the reason for always catching Mr. Right Now instead of Mr. Right. I had a high sex drive that I was trying to control, but Preston wouldn't let me. It definitely didn't help that he sounded like the singer Tank. I would imagine him singing "Sex Music" while stroking inside me. My numerous sex toys were beginning to play out. I needed the real thing, so when Preston asked me out again, I prayed, gave myself a pep talk, and then agreed to the date.

"Corrine, you can't grip the cue that hard, sweetie." Preston laughed as he adjusted the pool stick in my hand and between my fingers.

"Stop laughing." I pouted. "I'm doing the best I can. I'm not a pro at this like you are."

"Just relax." He laughed again. "Do you need me to help you?" he asked as he stepped behind me. Preston and I had been dating for nearly two months and hadn't gotten past first base, but the feel of his body against mine was quickly moving us to second. "Sweetie, you have to hold it like this," he instructed as he placed his hand over mine.

At that moment, I didn't give a damn about that pool stick or that solid yellow number seven ball that I was trying to hit, but I kept my grip on the stick, wishing that it was the one inside his lightly starched jeans. I quickly shook those naughty thoughts out of my head and turned my focus back to the table.

"Preston, I can't hit that ball," I whined as I glanced around the table, searching for the perfect position to strike.

"Corrine, you can't be afraid to use your body."

"Huh?" I questioned as I looked back at him.

"If you have to, get all up on this table and then do it." He chuckled. *To hell with that,* I said to myself. I took a deep breath when I felt his breath on my neck. "Sweetie, you've got to feel it in your bones," he whispered in my ear. "You're the one in control. Don't be afraid of the stick because it sure as hell ain't afraid of you."

That did it. I dropped the stick on the table and stepped away from him. He was making this too hard and that I Am King cologne he was wearing wasn't helping either.

"Are you okay?" He smiled.

"I'm okay," I lied. That smile was a sure sign that he realized what he was doing.

"Do you want me to get us another pitcher of beer?"

Hell naw! I was already staggering a little and didn't need anything else to make me completely drunk.

I smiled. "I'm good, Preston."

"Well, do you want to finish this game or what?"

"We can, since we have the table for twenty more minutes."

I retrieved the pool stick and he anxiously stood behind me.

"Don't put too much pressure on the stick," he breathed in my ear.

"I'm not."

"Yes, you are. Let me help you."

My body froze when he got all up on me. I wished he would've ordered that second pitcher of beer. The room was getting hot and I felt sweat building on my forehead and chest. He gave me a puzzled look when I dropped the stick on the table again. I couldn't take it anymore.

"I think we need to get out of here," I said when I turned around to him.

"Oh really?" He smiled devilishly.

I stepped up to him and threw my tongue down his throat. Who was I fooling? I wanted that man. Moments later, we were out the door and inside his jet black Magnum, which fit his chiseled running back's body to a tee. I couldn't tell if the leather seats were hot because of the weather or from the steam building between my legs. He hurriedly hopped on the interstate with his hand stroking the inside of my thigh. I naughtily pushed it farther up and he fingered me until we made it to his house. We raced out of the car and he anxiously lifted me around his waist. No doubt, we were hungry for each other.

I felt him thrusting his hammer on me while fumbling with the key in the door. If any of his neighbors were out, they were receiving an eyeful. He finally managed to get the door open and kicked it shut when we were inside. The kissing and fondling were intense. We made it to his sofa and he plopped down on it with me still in his lap.

"You just don't know how long I've been waiting for this," he panted while pushing my shirt up and over my head.

I hushed him with my mouth. He unbuttoned and unzipped his pants and whipped out a treat that my candy jar just couldn't resist. I lifted my skirt and hurriedly slid my panties to the side while he rolled on a Magnum condom. Within a matter of seconds, he was inside me. I matched his thrusts with my own. My vibrators and dildos had nothing on the real thing, especially his. He unbuttoned my bra, tossed it aside, and ravished my breasts like a hungry tiger. I threw my head back and enjoyed the moment. When he squeezed my ass, I raised his chin and disappeared under his neck.

"Damn, baby," he moaned. When I lifted my head, my body tensed. He noticed. "What's the matter?" he asked, never stopping his rhythm.

"N-nothing," I stuttered, never stopping my rhythm either.

In fact, I was a little bit more turned on than I'd been before. Preston's roommate had come out of his room and I watched him watching us. I should have informed Preston of his presence, but he gave me reason not to. I watched him whip out his third leg and then slowly and seductively knead it. I buried

Preston's face in my chest so that he couldn't see his roommate watching us or me watching him.

"Ooooh, Corrine, this pussy is so wet," he moaned into my chest.

If only he knew that his roommate had something to do with the extra secretions. My eyes remained fixated on the roommate while my geyser continued to gush out floods of juices I never knew it could hold. He was a stallion that I wanted to mount. He stood about six foot four with glossy, honeysuckle skin, a bald head, and sexy pecs that he revealed after removing his T-shirt. He was fine.

Preston gripped my waist to assist with my ride. I enjoyed it as well as the visual freak show I was viewing. I shook away thoughts of having him in my mouth while Preston was in my hot box trying to put out the fire, but looking at his roommate's shaft, I wanted to do a switch-a-roo. After seeing what he was packing, he should've been the one driving that Magnum.

"Corrine, throw this pussy on me," Preston moaned when he came up for air.

I followed his commands and did just that. I watched his roommate's strokes speed up and so did my thrusts.

"Oooohhh, Corrine! Yes! Yes! Give that pussy to me, baby!"

I rode him as hard and as fast as I could. I shoved his mouth on my breasts because his head was in the way of my visual tease. While the roommate worked his magic, he blew sensual kisses at me that I wished were on both sets of my lips.

We were wrong. Dead wrong. If Preston knew what was going on in front of him and behind him, he would've been extremely pissed. The roommate continued his strokes. His Hershey love stick was looking extremely scrumptious and enticing.

I wanted to climb off Preston and let his roommate take over, or let them both take turns pounding me in competition.

I quickly tossed those thoughts away after Preston spoke his next words. "Baby, let me hit this pussy from the back."

When his roommate heard those words, he slowly backed away.

"No!" I yelled to them both.

Preston stopped trying to flip me over and his roommate returned to his original position, with his stripper pole still in hand. I called it a stripper pole because I wanted to slide up and down it.

Preston and his roommate were sending me into an abyss that I didn't want to climb out of. I didn't know if it was merely my imagination but it looked as though the roommate's wand was getting longer and thicker with each stroke of his hand. I wanted him. I wanted to see what he was about. I wanted to see if he could stoke me like he was doing himself. Preston's thrusts grew harder and deeper as he watched me fondle my nipples. I was having a blast being pleasured by both men. All of a sudden, Preston gripped my shoulders and hungrily thrust inside me. I watched his roommate's body flinch. I knew he was about to cum, too. I wanted to join the both of them so I increased my speed and my bounce.

"Preston, harder," I moaned loudly, never taking my eyes off his roommate. I shoved my breast in Preston's mouth. "Yes! Yes!" Little did Preston know, I was cheering his roommate. I wanted him in me, too, whether it was in my man hole or my mouth. Part of me wanted to tell Preston that his friend was behind him and we needed to let him join us, but I was afraid of what he would say. If he agreed, that would be a first for me.

"Corrine! Corrine!"

Preston came. I came all over him and his friend came in his T-shirt. The moment was intense and satisfying. The roommate disappeared back into his room. I collapsed on Preston's shoulder and he politely lay me down on the sofa. He caught his breath, then stood up.

"Where's your bathroom?" I asked after catching my own breath.

He pointed me in the right direction. I went inside and freshened up. When I returned to the living room, I plopped down on the sofa and watched Preston zip up. He retrieved his keys off the table and I assumed he was about to take me home, but my assumption was wrong.

"Baby, I need to dash to the store and get some cigarettes. I'm out," he informed me as he patted his pockets. "You can stay here and chill if you want."

"W-what about your roommate?" I worried, but didn't.

"His car is not out there. He's probably with his girl."

"Oh." I smiled internally. "How long will you be gone?"

"About twenty minutes or so. If you're not comfortable being here alone, come and ride with me. I'm just not ready to take you home yet." He smiled devilishly.

And I'm not ready to go either.

"I'll be fine. Bring me back a Coke and some Doritos."

"Will do."

He left. The slut in me couldn't pass up the opportunity that was thrown in my face. I dashed to the roommate's door and tapped on it. "Can I come in?" I asked, trying to disguise the eagerness in my voice.

"Come on. It's open."

I slowly pushed the door open and felt my way through the

darkness as his deep voice guided me to him. When my knees hit the bed, I knew I had made it to the promised land.

"Preston went to get some cigarettes," I informed him.

"That's more than enough time to do what we gotta do, huh?" he asked but expected no answer.

"I-I-I shouldn't be in here," I stammered and trembled slightly.

"There are a lot of things we shouldn't do but we do 'em anyway, don't we?" I nodded slowly, forgetting that it was pitch black in the room and he couldn't see. "Come here." I did as I was ordered. I crawled onto the bed until I reached him. "You like what you saw out there?" he asked.

"I loved what I saw."

"How much did you love it?"

"I . . ."

"Don't tell me. Show me," he said after placing his finger on my lips to shush me. I liked where this was going. I gently grabbed his legs and smiled after realizing he had no pants on. I pushed them apart then lowered my head toward his hypnotic stick.

"Mmmmmmmmmm," he moaned while I flicked my tongue all around the head. I bobbed on his dick like it was the last thing I was supposed to do before I died. I was so into pleasuring him that I didn't hear Preston come inside. I jumped when I felt him climb onto the bed.

"Preston!" I gasped, knowing that it could only be him.

"Shhhh. Stay just like that. Don't move," he said softly after gripping my thighs.

"Don't stop what you were doing," the roommate spoke to me when I stopped sucking him off to gather myself at what was about to go down. I went back to my task while Preston removed my skirt and panties, then began sucking on my ass.

Is this shit really happening? I thought. Preston made me realize it wasn't a dream when he eased underneath me and began flicking his tongue on my precious.

"You picked a good one this time," the roommate addressed Preston.

Little did they know, I was scoping them both out at the auto shop. This was part of my plan all along. I let them think that it was all their doing. Mama always told me, "Baby, sometimes you gotta let a man think he's in control." I smiled and went back to bobbing and grinding. I guess Mr. Right was going to have to wait.

Lunch Break

T. Ariez

"Look, Carmen, as your friend, I gotta tell you, you need to get your shit together. Whatever it is you're going through at home, you're going to let it ruin your career if you don't pull it together. Now, as your boss, I'm telling you that I need you to have all the documents and the presentation to me by the end of the day. The meeting's first thing tomorrow morning and we have to close this deal!"

Erica patted me on my shoulder as she walked out of the bathroom and left me standing there. I stood in the mirror and fixed my suit. My black skirt had risen a bit because my ass was so big. I pulled it down and patted out the wrinkles on my navy blue blazer. Erica was my best friend and I loved working both with and for her, but damn, when she got into boss mode, she really meant business and our friendship went out the window. I still found it amazing how she could flip the script and be two different people all within the same breath.

Here it was nine o'clock in the morning and I hadn't even begun to put the presentation together. I had been allotted two weeks to get everything in order so that we could reel in this new client. We were one day away and I hadn't even started. Now, usually I was on my game and had clients eating out of the palm of my hand, but lately, Jarred and I had been fighting a lot and I couldn't seem to focus. I usually don't cry, but today my emotions had gotten the best of me, so I leaned my head back and dropped a couple drops of Clear Eyes into each pupil.

I needed to regain my composure before I stepped back outside. Hopefully, my red eyes would be clear again in a few moments. Jarred was the reason I'd been so emotional lately. He was my man and the father of my child. He was a good man and provided for both our child and me. His only problem was he couldn't keep his dick between him and me. He just had to go share it with the world, like it was God's gift to women or something.

I couldn't believe this fool had the nerve to tell me that I was lucky. He said, "All these other bitches just get to taste the dick, but you're the one I come home to."

Now what in the hell kind of shit was that? And I'll admit, for a while, my ass was dumb for taking it for as long as I have, but I could no longer do it. My son was three years old and I was tired of pretending that we had the perfect family. Jarred's ass was gonna have to straighten up, or he was gonna have to go. Period.

I ran my fingers through my loose curls and took one last look in the mirror before I left the bathroom. Image was everything to me, so I had to make sure that I looked good and was on point at all times. That's why I kept a bottle of Clear Eyes with me. I would say that my hazel eyes set against my slightly darker skin tone were my best asset. Besides that, I couldn't let these fools I worked with see me sweat. When I sat down at my desk, I stared at the computer screen, wishing the numbers would magically appear in front of my face. I opened PowerPoint and looked at a blank presentation, but I still couldn't concentrate. I had to really think about my situation for a moment.

Here I was, twenty-three years old. I'd just graduated magna cum laude, with degrees in marketing and management from an all-black university, and had landed a job with an almost all-white, non-diversified management consulting company. I worked my bag of tricks to get this job, and I wasn't about to lose it behind some personal matter that could have been taken care of a long time ago. It was hard enough for a sister to get a job in corporate America as it was. I was not about to let them regret hiring me and confirm the stereotype that black women weren't as good as their white counterparts. Shit, I was better.

So sitting back in my seat, I looked over at my nameplate for inspiration. It said proudly in big, bold, capital letters: CARMEN ROCKIFORD. That's right, I was Carmen Renee Rockiford. I was the first black woman to work for Smith Management Consultants. I had been here only a year and here they were looking for me to close the deal with a new client they were trying to bring on board. This would be one of our biggest clients, and the biggest power move of my career thus far.

If I were able to close it, this would likely bump me to partner in the firm, or at least junior partner. Now don't get me wrong, I was already doing big things as it was. I just wasn't doing them officially as partner. I made damn good money and really didn't need Jarred for anything. Well, almost anything; I needed that dick of his. But now that I think about it, just like him, I could get a nut from anywhere.

Jarred had his issues, but aside from his cheating habits, he really was a good man. I couldn't handle sharing my man with Lord knows how many other women, but I guess my battle was that I wasn't ready to run a "good man" off just yet. Hell, the only way this sixty grand I made a year could keep me warm at night was if I burned it. So, for now at least, I had to get my shit together and pull off this meeting, and then I could worry about Jarred.

I forced Jarred out of my mind and began clicking away at the computer. Before I knew it, it was 1:30 p.m., and I hadn't even taken lunch yet. I sat up in my chair and arched my back to stretch it a little. I slowly contemplated whether I should take lunch or just get through this as quickly as possible. Deciding to get it over with, I remained seated because I knew that if I fucked this up, as close as Erica and I had been, not even she would be able to save my job.

After I finished massaging my temples, I raised my hands again and stretched once more before getting back into my work. But as soon as I put my hand down and fixed my back into the upright position again, I felt a tingle at my center. I closed my eyes for a moment and tried not to think about it. I thought it subsided, but just as I was about to relax and start back working, that tingle turned into a spark and rattled aggressively up my spine.

It shook my entire body as if I were cold. Involuntarily, my legs squeezed tightly together and that was when I realized that it had been almost two months since I'd last had sex. I'd told Jarred that unless he could assure me that he would quit fucking around on me, he would never get another peek at this pussy. I stared at his picture on my desk and *God*—that million-dollar smile of his was making me hot.

Just one look at his picture, and my panties were soaked. I needed a fix right here and right now. I jumped out of my chair so quickly that I almost knocked it over. I ran out of my office and, in record time, I'd made my way to the main lobby. I passed by the security desk, and the two officers who were there smiled at me. I flashed a smile back and hurriedly made my way outside to the parking garage.

I parked on the sixth floor every day because, with no elevator in the parking garage, it forced me to walk those stairs. As I made my way up the stairs, I was hoping I wouldn't see Terry, one of the security guards, and thankfully, I didn't see him this time. I knew how worked up I usually got when I hadn't had sex, and I could only imagine the disgruntled look on my face.

Like I said, image was everything to me, and because I passed him three times a day—once in the morning when I got to work, once during my lunch hour, and once again on my way home—I didn't want Terry to see me, or my face, in a bad way. I probably could have scared a pit bull away with the look on my face alone. However, come to think of it, I didn't even see him this morning when I got to work.

I could tell that Terry liked me. I could see it in his eyes. I don't know what it was, but I had a thing about eyes. Anyway, Terry never really spoke to me, but he always smiled or winked at me when I passed by. I had to admit he was fine; I loved a tall, dark, and handsome-ass brother. I was faithful to my man, though, so I never paid too much attention to Terry. I was actually glad that I didn't see him, and maybe that meant I would have a moment alone in my car without interruption, if he wasn't on duty today.

Half-jogging, then half-walking, I finished my hike up the stairs, as it was part of my exercise regimen. I thought maybe if I jogged up and down the stairs a few times, I would be okay, and this sexual tension would go away. They say exercise helps relieve tension and that is what I was going for.

I looked down and then thought to myself, hmm no . . . *I needed a fix, and I needed it now*.

I could hear Usher sing in my ear, "There goes my baby" as I spotted my car. My black on black Explorer sat in the corner all by her lonesome. No one else parked on this floor and my car was parked all the way at the end. An idea popped in my head. Maybe I could handle my business real quick, calm my nerves, and then still have my presentation on Erica's desk by 5:30. I looked at my watch; it was 1:56.

I almost sprinted to the car. I sat in the driver's seat and reached over to the glove compartment. I always carried three things with me in my car: a duffel bag with a change of clothes and clean underwear in the backseat, and then a razor and a vibrator in my glove compartment.

I carried the razor for protection, just in case I had to stay late at work or if I was ever alone at night. And because Jarred and I were both freaks in the bedroom, I carried a vibrator for long trips. I never knew when I'd want to perform for him. I snatched the vibrator out of its baggie and then took a wet wipe to clean it.

I got out of the car and opened the back door. I climbed in so that I would have plenty of room. I hiked my skirt up, pulled my panties to the side, and inserted the vibrator. "Ahhh." Now this is what my body needed. Already I began to feel better.

Without even turning it on, I worked it in and out of my opening slowly so that I could work myself up. With my pointer finger on my left hand, I pressed the button once for the lowest vibration setting. In and out, in and out, slowly and methodically, I stroked my own pussy. I pressed the button again for the next level of vibrations.

It hit me harder and sent a moan from my gut upward and out of my mouth. I moved my right hand down to my honey pot and began to rub on my clit. With my eyes closed and the sensations from both the vibrator and my clit being stimulated, I was only a few minutes away from exploding.

I couldn't help myself as I arched my back, rocked my hips

back and forth, and then thrust myself into the vibrator. Moans began to escape me, and they turned into yelps and then screams of pleasure. My body jerked as I rode this wave, hoping I could get as high as the moon. My heart raced so fast and beat so loud, the pounding sounded like it was knocking on my window. I held the vibrator in place a few more moments to calm myself.

Now, I thought, I should be able to go finish my presentation. Slowly, I opened my eyes and I was startled at what stood in front of me. "Oh, my God, what are you doing?"

I was ashamed and quickly clamped my legs shut to cover myself. Terry, the security guard, was standing by my car door looking inside, staring at me with his mouth wide open. He immediately began to explain himself, "I am so sorry. I know that you always park up here so I came by to make sure your car hadn't been broken into or anything."

He put his hands up to show his innocence. "I saw something move inside the car and thought it was weird so I came to check it out. Then I heard muffled sounds like someone was being hurt and I ran to the car. When I got here, I saw you. I swear that I knocked on the window to let you know I was here, but I guess you didn't hear me and I *am* sorry. You're beautiful, I couldn't help myself; I had to watch."

My legs were shut, but the vibrator was still on and still inside me. I was too ashamed from getting caught to pull it out now, and with the exception of me clamping my legs together, I was frozen still. I looked into his eyes to see if he was telling the truth, and they told me that he was. I was about to say something when the vibrations from the vibrator started to hit my spot and got me started all over again.

Fuck it, I thought. I motioned for Terry to open the door, and he did just as he was told. As much as I wanted Jarred to be the one in between my legs, it was time for him to learn a lesson and realize that two could play that game. I spread my legs so Terry could see all of my glory. Using only my pussy muscles, slowly I pushed the vibrator out, inch by inch. The vibrator fell to the seat and then made a thud as it hit the floor of the car.

Not taking my eyes off Terry, I indicated that this was his pussy for the taking. Without having to be told, he immediately stuck his face between my legs. Now this was heaven; it had to be. Jarred's dick game was on point, but Terry, hmm, his mouth was much better than Jarred's.

I wriggled beneath him as he sucked, licked, and bit gently on my nether region. I grabbed his head and tried to ram it inside me. I had no idea if he had a woman at home or not, so I tried not to leave any marks on him, but then thought, *fuck it*. These other bitches didn't care if Jarred had a woman at home or not, so I stuck my nails deep into Terry's back and bucked him like I was a bull trying to get a cowboy off my back.

Terry was a pro at this shit, though; he was able to roll with the punches. Every time I moved, he was right there with me. He stuck his fingers inside me and I rode them until I couldn't ride any longer. Finally, I exploded. And like a real man, not afraid of pussy juices, Terry licked and sucked up all of my cum. I shivered and shuddered until I was no longer light-headed. I wanted to see what Terry's dick game was all about, but I remembered I had to head back into the office to get this presentation done.

This whole time Terry hadn't said a word, but once he was done, he smiled and said, "Thank you." He wiped his mouth with the back of his hand, said a few words in his walkie-talkie, and then headed back to work. I was proud to see my juices on his face. He looked full and satisfied. I was as well. I got out of the backseat, grabbed some of my wet wipes, and went back into the building to clean myself up.

I sat at my desk and struggled for a few more minutes, trying to regain my composure. After a few flashes of Terry's face wet with my pussy juices left my thoughts, I was finally able to focus on my computer screen and when I looked up again, it was 5:19. A click here to save, another click there to print, and ta da, I was done!

I walked proudly into Erica's office, my whole attitude changed and, for the first time in months, I was smiling. I guess a good lunch break can do that to you. "Here you are, Erica. Everything's done and I'll be ready for the meeting in the morning."

I walked behind her desk, gave her a hug and a sisterly kiss good-bye, and I walked out of her office, proud that I had been able to pull myself together—with Terry's help, of course. When I got back into my office, it was 5:30 exactly. I turned the lights off, locked my door, and headed toward the elevator.

When I walked past the security station, I asked if Terry was still working. I needed to tell him thank you, but I wasn't sure if I could let it happen again. Hell, well, maybe just maybe, I could give him one more round. You know, to find out what the dick was like. That would be my "Thank you. Now we are even, and I don't owe you anything else" good-bye sex.

This particular guard was new, and I didn't know him as well as the others yet. His name tag told me his name was John. Even if I didn't know it, I could guess that he was a newbie, because he was the only one that didn't flirt with every woman in the building.

"Hello, John, do you know if Terry is still working?"

"Well actually, she had an emergency, and had to leave early.

She should be back tomorrow, though. Should I leave her a message?" he answered.

"No, thank you," I said as I walked off to go home. Well, damn, I thought to myself as I took the long hike up the six flights of stairs, admittedly a little disappointed. I at least wanted to peek at him before I headed home. Oh well, I guess—*Wait a minute . . . she???*

The Dinner Party

Damian Lott

PART I

My day started off the same as usual so I had no reason to foresee anything out of the ordinary coming. I was up and dressed by eight a.m., boiling a pot of hot water, anticipating a dose of my morning java—a cup of Maxwell House with two tablespoons of sugar and a splash of low-fat milk. The sound of the Kenmore stainless steel toaster alerted me that my raisin bagels were toasted.

Taking a seat at the kitchen table, I noticed a note on top of my morning paper. I recognized the handwriting immediately. It was the gorgeous print of my wife of two years, Sandra. She made it her business to leave the paper on the table every morning before heading off to work. I reached into the chest pocket of my light blue, button-down Polo shirt, extracting my reading glasses. As I placed them on my shaven face over my dark brown eyes, I blushed as I thought about how sexy she always says I look in them. Unfolding the letter, I began to read:

Dear Brendan,

I would like you to meet me at the home of a friend tonight at seven o'clock sharp. I have a great surprise for you. Listed at the bottom are the directions and address to the home. Please don't

call me trying to figure out what's going on. I'm not going to
answer my phone.

Love, Sandra

I glanced over the address and directions to the home. I
sighed loudly and folded the paper, wondering why she had not
bothered to bring this up last night, probably knowing that I
would have declined. The last thing I wanted to do was have dinner with some colleagues of hers. I could think of a better way
to spend a Friday night. Lately, we were having dinner with different people at least three nights a week. It was always the same
thing over and over—unseasoned food and conversation about
dull current events. Most of the time, I found myself agreeing to
things I ordinarily would not.

My wife works for a prominent law firm that specializes in
criminal law in the city of Rochester, New York, a mid-sized city
in the western part of the state. I hate to brag, but she is one of
the best defense attorneys in the city and her main objective is to
become partner by any means necessary. So, I often find myself
supporting my lady even when I don't want to.

I buttered my bagel and sipped my hot coffee. I still had
about an hour before I was due in the classroom. I teach African-
American history at my alma mater, the University of Rochester. I graduated, along with my wife, in the class of 1993. We
dated all through college and grad school, deciding to get married after we established our careers, hoping to become successful and begin to raise a family. Your typical American dream, but
so far we haven't had any children.

I finished eating and headed out to my car, a black, 7-series
BMW that I had recently purchased. My daily newspaper almost
slipped from under my arm as I unlocked the door and noticed

what appeared to be a pair of women's panties wrapped around the gearshift. I looked around to see if someone was playing a cruel prank on me and the culprit would appear, laughing, but no one appeared except for my neighbor's dog barking through the white picket fence and wagging his tail briskly.

I entered the comfort of the black vehicle, smelling the pungent odor of the beige leather upholstery. I threw my burgundy leather briefcase, along with my newspaper, on the passenger seat while studying the black lace panties wrapped around the gearshift. Beside the women's undergarments, there was another folded note with my name on it.

I unbuttoned the bottom button of my navy blue blazer, reached into my pocket, and grabbed my spectacles again. I picked up the letter and began to read:

Dear Brendan,

This is not your typical dinner party. So please don't waste your time dreading this evening. I guarantee you will never say I'm not spontaneous or adventurous again in your life. The panties are just a sample.

Love, Sandra

I'm embarrassed to admit my dick grew a few inches rapidly. I grabbed the panties from the gearshift and stretched them apart to get a better look. There is something about women's lingerie that turns me on. I mean turning me on with a capital *T*. I examined them with a keen eye. My dick was throbbing and screaming for an orgasm. All in a matter of minutes, I was contemplating masturbation, something I enjoy a little too much.

I saw something move out of the corner of my eye, causing me to conceal the panties next to me. Turning around, I realized that it was just my neighbor to my right, carrying his trash to the front, so I picked the panties back up and continued to study them. They were silk and see-through, with lace running all around the outside of the fabric, and a black silk string was tied into a bow just above the crotch area. They were definitely an undergarment for an intimate setting. Bashfully, I put the crotch area to my nose and sniffed lightly, hoping to get a whiff of my lady's sweetness. I am sprung and not afraid to admit it. Besides my porno-watching addiction and my desire to relieve myself, Sandra is my all and all.

I snatched the panties away from my nose quickly. I knew that the scent did not belong to my wife. My big head came to life instantly, causing my little head to wonder if he should still remain erect. I was confused, and I knew I was not mistaken. My face had been in the place too much. I knew the fragrance of my wife's pussy from a mile away. I had sniffed her panties a thousand times. I suddenly realized they were not even my wife's size. These were another woman's underwear and she smelled delectable.

My mind was racing at a rapid pace. I was not sure how I was supposed to react. But, honestly, I was certainly aroused and craving to satisfy myself. My wife has caught me numerous times watching pornography and stroking my manhood. She believes that there is nothing wrong with satisfying yourself. Sandra is very open minded as well as free spirited. She just teases me a lot about all of the black women I seem to get off on. My wife is mulatto. She just seems to identify more with her white heritage.

I started my car, placed the panties in the inside pocket of my blazer, and headed off to work. I was convinced at that moment that my wife was simply toying with me, based on a discussion we'd had earlier this week. She caught me masturbating to an adult film starring two women in a lesbian scene. I really enjoy girl-on-girl footage. It seems to excite me more than anything else. But anyway, she asked me if I had ever experienced a threesome. I smiled, knowing she already knew the answer to her own question. I still answered out of respect, even though I wanted to say, "I wish." She then asked me, "Would you participate if given the chance?" I laughed, telling her yes if she was one of the women. She smiled and walked away, leaving me with my dick in my hand. I yelled after her, telling her she was not as spontaneous or adventurous as these porno stars and that was the reason why I loved her so much. Even though I was jacking off to them.

So, I knew this had to be a prank my lady was pulling on me. Obviously, she had acquired some woman's panties and sprayed a fragrance on them in an attempt to see how much she really meant to me. The games women play at times are hilarious. I knew that she was just trying to make me feel good about a boring dinner party this evening.

PART II

I arrived in front of a huge home located on the outskirts of the city, nestled in a cul-de-sac surrounded by a thick wooded area—a brick colonial with a two-car garage and a well-kept landscape. It looked extremely expensive.

I noticed my wife's gray Lexus parked beside a candy apple red Jaguar with custom plates that read Ms. Jones. I knew I had the right home.

My day had been long and exhausting to a certain degree. It

had taken all of my strength to not give my wife a call. I really was not up to your typical dinner party. But I was definitely famished and looking forward to eating. Hopefully, there was something that I could identify with on the dinner menu.

I exited my vehicle and walked toward the home, admiring the beauty of the numerous colors of lilies and daffodils on display. Reaching the heavy varnished oak door, I looked for the doorbell. To my surprise, there was another note taped just above the doorbell. I thought to myself, *What the fuck is going on?* Extracting my glasses from my shirt pocket, I began to read a list of directions, the first one telling me to come inside, the door was unlocked. I twisted the knob and stepped in cautiously. At this moment, I had no idea what was going on.

I walked into a dramatic, two-story foyer with two staircases opposite each other and a massive chandelier suspended from a cathedral-type ceiling. As I stood on the immaculate hardwood floors, I surveyed the opulence.

The next set of instructions led me into a cherry wood kitchen with a huge island and granite countertops. I was told to loosen my tie and have a drink to unwind. Fortunately, there was a bottle of Rémy Martin on the table along with two glasses and a bucket of ice. This was certainly my drink—I loved to drink cognac and chase it down with ice water. So, I fixed my stiff drink and looked around in the stillness of the home. Within a matter of twenty minutes, I was buzzing. I guzzled another full glass and noticed soft music coming from a distance.

The note directed me upstairs to what appeared to be the master bedroom. I walked inside to soft jazz and a hell of a layout. I'm talking about a bedroom fit for a king. The walls were painted eggshell white. The finish was extra smooth so I figured it to be the best money could buy. My burgundy loafers sank into the plush beige carpet as I eyed the cherry oak furnishings, including the king-size sleigh bed. To top it off, there was a flat screen television at least sixty-four to seventy-two inches wide against the wall in front of the bed, with an incredible entertainment system. I was apparently in the lap of luxury.

Draped across the bed was a man's black robe along with what appeared to be my personal initialed hygiene bag. I picked it up to verify the contents and confirmed that it was. Honestly, I felt a little better for some strange reason. It made me feel comfortable to know something belonged to me in this unfamiliar setting. All at once, I began to believe that this was a special rendezvous. Maybe some friend of my wife's owned this place and she was trying to spice up our sex game a bit by adding a little suspense to things. Between her schedule and mine, our love life was not what it should have been. But when it was, it was always great.

Adjacent to the bedroom was the master bathroom. The next set of instructions instructed me to shower thoroughly and await my surprise from the comfort of the bed. I showered and baby-oiled my body, paying close attention to my chest and legs. I'm in great condition, even though I don't work out as much as I used to. I rubbed my inner thighs and my private area, feeling a little stubble around my crotch. I shave my pubic hair all the time. It is something I don't care for. My wife teases me all the time about my feminine hygiene ways. I wished I would have shaved.

I stepped back into the bedroom, oiling my bald head and anticipating my surprise, wearing nothing except the robe that fit a little too loosely. As I took a seat on the bed, I noticed the television was on and the screen was blue. Then all of a sudden, it came to life and my wife was on the screen before me.

Sandra spoke, "Hello, baby. I hope you're comfortable and not irritated. I know you're wondering what this is all about and soon you will see. I just ask that you guide me through this process and let me know how far you would like me to go."

I watched my wife speak to me through the television. I was captivated by her beauty. Her light skin glistened underneath lights illuminating the room. She sat on what appeared to be a nice sized bed with her legs crossed Indian style, wearing just a pink T-shirt. She grinned sheepishly as if she wasn't sure of what was going on. Her shoulder-length black hair was pulled back, giving her a younger look. I was definitely turned on. I watched her slim face and hazel eyes as she explained to me that she could also see and hear me. I was astounded by what was going on.

She asked, "Would you like for me to begin?"

I nodded and answered yes. Watching as she reached behind her back and retrieved what appeared to be a vibrator in the shape of an erect penis, I smiled and licked my lips as she removed her T-shirt, revealing perfect-shaped breasts with deep purple nipples. She started the vibrator and ran it seductively over her chest as she parted her legs.

"Take off your robe," she whispered.

I removed it, never taking my eyes off the screen. I looked at her part her pretty pussy and bite her bottom lip. I could see her insides, thanks to high definition. She squirmed underneath the vibrator as she massaged her clitoris. My dick was as hard as Chinese arithmetic. I could feel myself beginning to perspire and to say I was horny would have been an understatement. I wanted to touch her. I asked, "Where are you? Come to me."

She continued to work the vibrator, making pleasurable noises, saying, "Not yet . . . Not yet, Brendan . . . but if you want me to spice it up, say yes."

I couldn't refuse, my hormones were jumping. I said, "Yes . . . please."

That was when she appeared, standing at least five feet six inches, a little taller than my wife. Her hair was cut low, revealing a round ebony face. She stood with her hands on her wide, child-bearing hips, peering into the camera with almond-shaped eyes. Her body was perfect, with her private parts covered by a matching silk bra and panty set the hue of lavender. She was sexy and I had never seen her before.

She spoke. "Do you mind if I help her out?"

I couldn't believe what was going on before my eyes. I stammered over my words, "Yeah . . . umm . . . go ahead . . . why not?"

She removed the vibrator from my wife's hand and kneeled in front of her, showing the thong between the cheeks of her round ass. She rubbed Sandra's thighs and played with her wet pussy while I watched. I was ecstatic to see my wife being turned on by another woman. Unknowingly, my hand was wrapped around my dick and I was stroking it slowly.

"I see you, Brendan . . . I see you," I heard Sandra say, pushing her hips toward the electronic stimulant. As the mysterious woman stopped all of a sudden, she took her underclothes off.

"Can I kiss her, Brendan?" she asked seductively.

I nodded in agreement, looking for the baby oil so I could lubricate my dick. Finding it, I squirted some on my right hand and went to work, watching as she held Sandra in her arms, tongue kissing her softly.

I watched my wife watching me, and then she asked, "Do you want me to go all the way with her?"

How could I refuse, being caught up in the moment? I gave her my nod of approval and watched as they went into action.

The mysterious woman straddled her and kissed her breasts, making her way toward her navel. Sandra blushed and shivered underneath her touch. As the woman parted Sandra's vulva and darted her tongue into her wetness, she gripped her ass and pulled her toward her face. The moans were enough to excite me, but the sight was sending me over the top.

I was stroking my manhood hard and massaging my balls at the same time, definitely holding back an orgasm.

They were in the sixty-nine position now, giving each other oral pleasure. With the mysterious woman on top, I could see the juices from her insides run down her legs. She was in a frenzy, bucking her hips against my wife's face and licking her moistness at the same time. Both were peeping into the camera from time to time, cheering me on as I masturbated.

I had never been so excited in my life and I wanted to join so bad. I asked, "Can I join you . . . ooh, baby . . . Can I join you?"

She screamed, "As soon as you cum, baby . . . as soon as you cum."

I was gripping my dick hard and stroking fast. I could feel the tingling sensation as it made its way from my balls up through my shaft to the head of my dick. I closed my eyes to the sexual noises and kept stroking. I jerked and caressed my balls while unloading my load all over the bed.

I was in a fog when I came to my senses. All I heard was my wife's voice. She was standing over me, speaking, yet I could not hear her.

"Brendan . . . wake up . . . wake up, Brendan."

Finally, I came to my senses and saw that Sandra was pointing at my stained boxers. It had all been a dream. Everything was just a dream. She shook her head and handed me a piece of paper. It was the directions to your typical dinner party.

She walked away saying, "Brendan, you should control yourself better. You were jacking off in your sleep."

One-Hour Proof

Asali

CHAPTER 1

I loved my job. Not that it was the most glamorous or prestigious work, but the people who came in were almost always in a good mood. Usually they had just come back from vacation, a family function, witnessing the birth of their newborn, or some type of memorable celebration. I helped them create tangible memories of those milestones in their lives. Here they could pick out frames, have photos matted, create cards, and receive their pictures in an hour. It wasn't hard work; computers performed the majority and I just packaged the items and assisted the customers with picking from available options. Most times they were in and out; everyone likes things done fast in this world. Sometimes they wanted life-sized cutouts or personalized gifts, which took a bit longer but customers were always grateful and satisfied with their purchases. For the occasional mishap with our machine or their camera, the customer always had the option not to buy the finished product. Happiness, one hundred percent guaranteed.

Cute kids, handsome couples, damage for insurance claims, sunny resorts, sexy shots taken for a love; I'd seen them all. I got to be a distant voyeur into the lives of other people. During the holiday season everyone wanted to have their memories from family events printed to share before leaving town, to print customized calendars for the upcoming year, or have Christmas gifts made using photos. So we were busy as heck and it had been a long day. I was on a double shift because someone called in sick *again*. If I had known I would be called for an extra shift, I wouldn't have spent my night clubbing into the early morning hours. My plan was to run outside to my car and nap during my hour-long lunch break. As sleepy as I was, I'm not sure which was worse, being tired or the lingering odor of cheap cologne left by my last customer. I'd been sneezing almost constantly for ten minutes since he'd left.

A beautiful black woman with long dreadlocks walked up to my counter as I wiped my nose for the hundredth time. She wore multiple layers of clothing but still hugged herself as if she were cold or trying to keep herself from falling apart. She wore no makeup on her clear, unblemished skin. That made her even more beautiful to stare at. Her perfectly arched brows, cute button nose, and flawlessly shaped full lips were the kind people paid for. At least five inches taller than me, she could have been a model if she hadn't been extra curvy in all the right places.

"Hello, how can I help you?" I asked, wearing my counter smile while stifling another sneeze.

She handed over a flash drive. "Can you print out the pictures on here for me?"

"Do you know the name of the folder that the images are in?" I attempted to look into her downcast eyes.

"They're the only files on there, so just print all of them, please." She stroked the tattoo on her left ring finger.

I gestured toward the media viewer. "How many prints of each image would you like, or would you rather look at the machine and pick your quantities and size based on the image?"

"No thanks, one of each will be all I need." Finally, she looked up and made eye contact; her eyes were filled with sadness and tears.

I immediately looked away and felt guilty for bothering her with pointless questions.

"Okay, can you fill out this sheet with your information? There are only a couple of quick jobs before yours and then I'll process your photos. It shouldn't take long."

I slid the blue order form across the counter to her.

With trembling hands, she filled out her information. I mentally took note of the name K. Miller written at the top of the form.

"Thank you," she said as she walked away with her arms tightly wrapped around her body again.

The temperature outside must have really dropped since I've been in here, I thought to myself while watching her walk out of the store. I straightened the counter, quickly put things back in place around the store, processed and packaged two print jobs, and then loaded the trembling woman's flash drive to print. Curious, I walked around the machine to the other side to see what the digital images revealed. Although the pictures were different, the frame and background were all the same, which piqued my curiosity even more. The developer shot out the pictures in rapid succession. The focal point of each frame was a large wooden sleigh bed with white bedding. On the wall above the bed the phrase TWO HEARTS, TWO LIVES, ONE LOVE was stenciled. On the left nightstand beside the bed sat a framed picture of K. Miller, but only a part of the picture showed. The other piece of the picture was out of view from the camera.

I could see the light in the room must have changed because at first the walls in the room appeared very light blue with rays of sunlight streaming in. As the pictures progressed it was as if I were watching time go by. I couldn't see the sunrays anymore and the walls appeared a darker blue.

Just as I'd begun to wonder why someone would want pictures of a room, a man and woman entered the frame. She had big loose curls in her auburn-colored hair and looked very short standing next to the tall man. I couldn't pinpoint her ethnicity—she could have been Hispanic, a light-complexioned African-American, or an olive-hued Caucasian, but he was definitely black. Now I could see that there was actually a bit of a time lapse between pictures. They were standing and kissing, then undressing while touching, then pulling the comforter and pillows from the bed, and then there was picture after picture of their bodies entwined in different positions. First she lay spread eagle with his head between her legs, then he stood at the side of the bed with her lying across it with her head upside down, out of the picture, but obviously feeding on his lingam. Next she was on top, then he was on top, and then he was behind her, and finally they lay spooning each other. The whole time I admired their bodies and watched the expressions on their faces, getting more and more turned on. I could see the beautiful mauve-colored areolas on her small, perky breasts, her curvy hips, and chin-length curls that seemed to move constantly. At times they were swept back off her face, at others they camouflaged one eye or the other eye, and a time or two they fell completely forward, covering her entire face.

He was ebony and covered with sinuous muscles. Completely bald with a neatly trimmed goatee, he bore a strong resemblance to the actor Morris Chestnut. He had a bright smile and seemed to get pleasure with every action. Right then, the store doors opened and my manager, Mr. Tim, walked in.

Quickly, I walked away from the processor to fill him in on the day's happenings and to conceal the fact that I'd been looking through a customer's pictures. Invading the customer's privacy was frowned upon; we were told to look only at the quality of the pictures, not the content. Afterward, I walked over to the machine and packaged the job for pickup. There were at least two hundred photos and I couldn't get the ones I'd seen out of my mind as I walked to my car, ready and anxious for my nap.

CHAPTER 2

Inside my car, I put my windshield sunshade in place to keep anyone passing by from staring at me. Wrapped in my Snuggie that I kept in my car specifically for this purpose, I was snug as a bug. It wasn't as cold as I thought but I wanted to be comfortable without needing to turn the car on to run the heater. I reclined my seat back as far as it would go and set the timer on my phone to wake me up. My Altima was a far cry from being in my comfortable bed at home, but it would have to do. It didn't take long for my heavy eyelids to fall and take me to dreamland.

It was as if I was in the room with them. She was standing next to him wearing only her black lace panties and bra, holding him around the waist. His massive hands were cupping her butt cheeks while he bent to kiss her. His colossal tool was barely concealed by the white boxer briefs he wore. It looked ready to jump and attack its victim at any second. They both lightly moaned as they kissed, taking pleasure in the contact and probably anticipating what was to come. I could smell their scent, like pheromones spreading in the air, arousing anyone who came in contact with it. My own nipples hardened against the fabric of my bra. They finished undressing, throwing their undergarments to the floor hurriedly.

They stared at each other's body in delight. Using their hands to outline their bodies, they each sporadically put kisses to their lover's flesh along the way. I watched them and began throbbing. She held his manhood between her petite hands and worked it up and down. Smiling all the while, he watched and moaned while she moved her hands in a quick rhythm. She bent to kiss the wet shiny tip and coated her lips with the juice.

"Get on the bed," he said, finally speaking.

"Wait a second; I want to pull these off. I'll just leave the fitted sheet on," she replied in her high-pitched voice.

He helped her yank the top layers of bedding hastily to the floor.

Cat-like, she climbed the wooden stepping stool onto the high sleigh bed, thrusting her ample derriere high in the air as she moved. Watching her movements, he licked his lips and kneeled onto the bed behind her, planting his face between her ass cheeks. Her giggles broke the silence as he shook his head from left to right, causing her cheeks to vibrate. In one quick move, he flipped her over onto her back and dove head first between her legs. The peaked tips of her mauve-colored nipples stood erect as she opened her legs wider, inviting him in closer. Her lover pushed her legs up to her chest and simultaneously grabbed both nipples between his fingertips. He pleasured her with his mouth and hands, licking, sucking, and lapping at her pink pearl. I could see his tongue flicking, circling and disappearing inside her. Wetness soaked my panties as I played Peeping Tom. Mercilessly, he tongue-fucked her to the point of her screaming and moaning from orgasmic sensations. Finally, done with his meal, he moved to the dessert, her nipples. He climbed over her body and took turns savoring each breast, alternating between licking and sucking. Meanwhile, she rubbed the head of his penis with the tip of her thumb, covered it in juice, and stuck the thumb in her mouth. Over and over she did this, sucking on the thumb like a pacifier. Her need for him was so great it seemed to fill the space and permeate the room with her lusty tang.

"I'm hungry, feed me," she purred.

Smiling, he crawled out of bed and pulled her body to the edge.

Whack, whack, he slapped his piece against the sides of her face. "Is this what you're hungry for?"

"Yes, please give it all to me. I miss it so much!"

"With pleasure," he said as she dropped her head over the side of the bed, slowly feeding his long penis into her mouth until the whole thing was in. I thought she would choke. She'd definitely mastered her gag reflex as she gave deep-throat head effortlessly. Slurping and sucking his dick in and out of her mouth, she drenched it with her saliva. In a constant rhythm she sucked him in halfway, to the tip, then to the base with her tongue, licking up and down the underside. My need to be more than a voyeur consumed me and I found myself masturbating while watching. The technique she used must have been very effective because her lover began to moan and cuss loudly.

"Oh no, you're not getting off that easy. I plan to pound your pussy and make you explode before you get it out of me. You have to work hard and earn it first."

She watched as he walked over to the dresser and retrieved a small, velvet pouch. A small, plastic bag fell into his open palm. Inside was a black, stay-hard cock ring. He fitted the silicone ring over his hefty cock and testicles and we all stared as it grew and became more engorged. I gasped. A wide smile appeared on his face as he gestured for her to mount him. She seemed hesitant as she moved closer to the large pendulum that moved up and down invitingly.

"It won't hurt you; it's just going to give you love and make you love it back."

Slowly, and with some caution, she eased down onto it until she reached the base. Immediately her body shuddered, as if that was all it needed to reach a climax. With his large hands on her hips, he pumped her body up and down until I could hear the smacking sound from his manhood and her innards separating. Finding her own tempo, she skillfully moved in circular and up-and-down motions. She rode his ditch digger like a madwoman, pounding her thighs against his waist. My own fingers worked wildly, stirring inside my honey pot. Sweat dripped from her chin to his chest. Suddenly, a quake erupted in her body and she began to spasm. Still flinching from her orgasm, he lifted her and lowered her onto her back. He entered her with a powerful thrust that made us both gasp. His back arched as he rocked his body into hers.

"Ah, fuck me, baby! Fuck me! Yes! Yes!" she screamed.

Smiling again, he entered her more forcefully. I could hear his thighs colliding with her body. I wondered if he had pushed the thing all the way up to her stomach. Her face contorted as she whispered the word *yes* over and over. Again, her climax came and made her limbs thrash wildly. With her toes curled, hairline sweaty, and eyes squeezed tight, she still begged for more. Putting his arm around her waist, he pulled her body as close to his as it would go and lay inside her. Deep.

"More, more, give me more."

Rigid penis leading the way, he got out of bed and retrieved two pairs of handcuffs from his dark blue pants.

"Touch your toes," he said as he helped her from the bed to her feet. Moving leisurely, she did as she was told. He fastened a set of cuffs around one wrist and an ankle and did the same on the other side. "Open your legs wide and brace yourself."

"I'm ready."

"Are you sure?"

"I'm ready, give me that dick," she yelled confidently.

With one hand on her waist, he steadied her body while he guided his length into her with the other. First, he worked himself in and out at a slow pace, then moved deep and fast, grinding into her. She tried to stand upright but couldn't because of the handcuffs.

"Hit it, hit it, hit it." It started as a scream but ended as a winded whisper. He drove his dick in harder, faster, and without mercy. At times he moved from side to side to hit it from an angle. She screamed to the top of her lungs and I came as she did. My fingers were covered in my sticky, sweet juice. I looked at the couple just as he began cumming, too. It shot all over her as he moved in and out of her, still maintaining his erection but allowing his penis to come all the way out to shower her with his jiz.

Delicately, he kissed her shoulders while freeing her from the cuffs. Spent, they both fell onto the bed in a spoon position. The warmth from their lovemaking blanketed their naked bodies.

CHAPTER 3

Knock knock! "Hey, wake up!"

I jerked my body up completely, unaware of my surroundings. Slowly, I opened my heavy eyelids and saw Mr. Tim's face pressed against my window. He wore a sly grin and an expression that made me think this was the highlight of his damn day. Just then, my alarm on my cell phone rang, a little too late to wake me.

Wow! I thought to myself, had I really just dreamed all of that while taking a short nap? Of course I had. The moisture I felt in the crotch of my work pants told me so as I made my way out of the car.

"Mr. Tim, can you give me five minutes? I need to take a bathroom break."

"Go ahead."

"Thanks."

Inside the restroom, I turned on the cold water at the sink. I cupped my hands and filled them with the water and splashed it on my face. I repeated this a few more times, then patted it dry with paper towels. Totally awake, I pulled a piece of mint gum from my purse and popped it into my mouth. The last thing I wanted to have was stale breath when standing close to a customer showing them their pictures on the viewer. I added on a layer of my favorite peach-stained lip gloss and opened the door.

As I entered the main store area, I could see K. Miller entering the store through the automated doors. I'd almost hoped to miss her. There was no doubt that what I'd seen on the pictures was not the outcome she'd hoped for. I sensed that from her body language.

"Just a minute, please, we'll be right with you," Tim said.

"No problem," K. Miller whispered as she tightened her arms about her waist and rocked from side to side. As Tim filled me in on what jobs had come in and gone out while I was on break, I watched K. Miller from my peripheral. She continued her self-hug rock dance but occasionally she would free her left hand and look at the tattoo.

After another minute, Tim said his good-byes.

"Sorry about that; he had to update me on orders before he left. I just returned from my break."

"So you didn't see my pictures?" The way I averted my eyes and the couple of seconds of hesitation must have given her an answer. "Were they making love? Tell me."

"Umm, we aren't supposed to look at the content of the pictures so I can't answer that question."

From somewhere, K. Miller seemed to draw strength and a boldness that made her even more beautiful. "Just be honest with me; right now I'd really appreciate a little honesty from someone."

"Yes! He made love to someone."

"He? He! What he?"

"The man in your pictures. That's who you're talking about, right?"

"The man? Wow!" she said as she hit her forehead with the palm of her hand. "I had a feeling she was cheating but I never would have thought it was with a man. I installed the nanny cam in our bedroom, planning to catch her with another woman. I never considered this. I can't and won't compete with this. She is not only a cheat, but a complete lie. She has made our life a lie. She said she's always only loved women and wanted to be with me always. We even had our own bonding ceremony," she said, thrusting that tattooed left hand at me. On closer inspection, I could see the name Jillian tattooed on her ring finger surrounded by filigree. Now I really dreaded what I had to do next.

Pulling the thick white envelope from the bin marked M, I slid it across the counter. She tore it open and fanned the pictures out. Immediately, she dropped to the floor and clutched her stomach.

Speedily, I made my way through the waist-high swinging doors to the other side of the counter. I bent over and lifted K. Miller from the floor and held her in my arms.

"I don't believe in mistakes or coincidences. You came here to me to get proof and so I could mend your heart. See, my name is Kia Miller, or K. Miller, just like yours, and I absolutely love loving women."

Me and Mr. Jones

Michelle Allen

Buzzzz . . . buzz . . . I could hear the sound of my phone vibrating in my clutch bag. I instantly knew that it was a text from him, and was very curious to see what the message said.

It was a simple: I want you.

I smiled to myself before texting my response: I know.

He replied quickly: Can I have you?

Here? Now? I asked.

Yes. I'm game if you are.

I had to admit I was intrigued: You know I always am. But where?

There's a black Escalade limo sitting outside right now. Wait five minutes, then go and get in it.

I only hesitated for about a half a second before I replied: See you in five.

I could feel the heat rising off my skin, not only from thinking about what I knew was going to happen, but also thinking about the shit storm that would ensue if we got caught. Though, I must admit, that actually turned me on even more.

I decided to use my five minutes wisely and took a quick trip to the ladies' room. I already wasn't wearing any underwear. Panty lines are not sexy, and my va-jay-jay is always bare as the day I was born; no worries there. So I checked my hair and makeup, and dabbed all the good spots with a little perfume, then sashayed back out the restroom door. The closer I got to the exit, the faster my heart beat, but I wasn't nervous, more like electrified with excitement. I was about two feet from the front door when I heard this loud voice.

"Vanessa Bradley, is that you?!"

I started to pretend I didn't hear him, but knowing the man behind the voice like I did, I figured he'd follow me outside if I didn't answer. So I turned quickly, trying to hide my irritation.

"Yes, it's me. Hello, Marcus."

I didn't ask how he was, because although I considered him a good friend, right now he was in my way. I was a woman on a mission.

He leaned in for a quick hug and said, "Girl, you look wonderful. You're definitely wearing the hell out of that dress."

I couldn't help but smile because, shit, I did look good. I was wearing my black, off-the-shoulder, Michael Kors draped goddess gown that accentuated my curves and had a nice, high, mid-thigh split that highlighted my long legs. I was not going to leave the house today without looking extra sexy; the occasion demanded it.

"Thank you, Marcus. You're looking pretty good yourself."

He stepped back and looked me over once more.

"V, I swear I don't know how my brother ever let you get away. I always said Mom dropped him on his head when he was born." He chuckled slightly.

"Well, Marcus, that's ancient history, and you know your brother and I are still very good friends. Besides, he seems to have done okay for himself, and I wish him well."

"Yeah, he's all right, but still not the same as he was with you."

I was beginning to get a little uncomfortable with this conversation, and I needed to get outside quickly anyway, so I would have to talk to Marcus later.

"Well, I need to run out to my car really quick, and get back inside before everything gets started. We'll talk afterward, okay?"

"Sure, V, I'll see you later."

It had been longer than five minutes, so I put a little pep in my step. I opened the door to stride out into the warm summer evening, and there was the black stretch Escalade. I held my breath and reached for the handle, but the door was locked. I pulled my hand back, and felt a flash of disappointment.

Then, just as I turned to walk back inside, I heard the window lower, and his deep, sexy baritone voice washed over me. "I guess you're on c.p. time today," he said, and then gave me that sexy smile.

I smiled back. "Well, I'm here now, so are you going to let me in, or not?"

He smiled again, and then the window went back up, and I heard the doors unlock. I looked around and then got inside.

"Hello, Vanessa," he said. "You look absolutely amazing."

"And you look very handsome yourself, Vincent." Actually, Vincent Michael Jones was looking better than handsome, he looked absolutely . . . delicious. I just had to stop for a second and take him all in: six feet, with dark, wavy hair, and smooth, brown skin the color of warm caramel. He also had the sexiest, piercing brown eyes that always seemed to see straight into my soul. Vincent was wearing a custom-made Dolce & Gabbana tux that fit him perfectly, showing off how well defined his beautiful body was, even through all the fabric; he was simply exquisite.

"V," he began, "I wanted to tell you what it means for you to be here for me today of all days . . . I know it must be hard. . . ." His voice trailed off, and I understood that he was genuinely hurting. But that's not what I wanted, I didn't want him to be in pain, and I definitely didn't want any sympathy. He began again. "V, you know . . . all you have to do is say the word. . . ."

I had to stop him right there; he was not going to put me in that position.

"Vincent, I know what you're saying, but you know I won't do that. So let's not make this any harder than it has to be . . . let's just enjoy the moment." I could see him searching my face for any sign of uncertainty, but there was none.

And just like that, he leaned in and kissed me, slowly and passionately. His lips felt so good, I swear they ignited every nerve in my body. I reached up and caressed the back of his head and pulled him in even closer, motivating him to kiss me harder. I could feel his hands searching my body, first at my neck, then down to my shoulders, where he slid off my dress, exposing my breasts. I could feel my pussy begin to throb faster and faster as he squeezed my dark brown nipples between his fingers, first one nipple, then both at the same time. He then traded his fingers for his mouth, taking his tongue and flicking it across my nipples and biting them gently. At this point I wanted him inside me so bad I could hardly stand it, but I knew Vincent, and he wouldn't penetrate me until he did what he does best. He must have been reading my mind, because the next thing I knew I was feeling his fingers massaging and tugging gently at my clit, preparing for what I knew would come next. Vincent then turned me around so I was sitting upright with my back against the seat, and kneeled down in front of me on the floor of the limo. He was still sucking on my nipples as he raised the bottom of my gown, exposing my pussy completely. He looked at me with those eyes of his and gave me a sly wink, and then lowered his head between my legs. I swear, I think I started cumming from the first flick of his tongue, the feeling was so intense. He alternated between licking and sucking gently on my clit, while sticking one, then two fingers inside me. This man knew my body so well, he knew what I liked, and what drove me crazy, and he always made sure he did it. I must've cum two or three times before I had to stop him, just so I could catch my breath. I could see him giving me that cocky smirk he always gave when he thought he'd had me beat, but oh, no . . . I was going to make sure he remembered who he was dealing with.

So I looked him dead in his eye and said, "Oh, so you think you're bad, huh, Mr. Jones? Well, trust and believe, you're nowhere near as bad as me."

Vincent raised his eyebrow, and replied, "Oh, really? Well, show me just how bad you are, Ms. Bradley."

I smiled and told him to lie back, and I would. He followed my directions eagerly because a brotha knew I would not disappoint. When I first pulled out his dick, I couldn't help but smile at it because it was the most beautiful one I'd ever seen. It was thick, and about nine inches; simply perfect. I took it in my hands and massaged it gently, and then swirled my tongue around the head, taking it into my mouth deeper and deeper. I could feel his body reacting to the sheer pleasure he was experiencing, and it only motivated me even more. I took every inch of him into my throat until his dick seemed to disappear, and then would pull back until my mouth was only covering the head. I did this repeatedly because it drove him crazy. I could feel his body tensing, so he was about to climax, which made me speed up my pace. I applied a little more pressure with my mouth, and that did it. Vincent convulsed slightly, and I felt him release his warm liquid into the back of my throat. Vincent tasted wonderful, I was so glad he took care of himself, and ate healthy. You can tell a lot about a man's diet by the way his semen tastes.

Now that I had done my duty properly, I looked up at Vincent and had to ask, "Now, who's the baddest?"

He looked back at me, and replied breathlessly, "You . . . definitely! . . . Damn, girl, I need a minute. . . ."

"Well, that's all you have." I looked at my watch. "Our time is very limited."

"Very true, so I'd guess I'd better get to work then."

And get to work he did. Vincent flipped me over so my knees were in the seat and I was facing the rear windshield of the limo, so he could hit it from the back; my second favorite position. When Vincent put his dick inside me, I had to gasp; he seemed to fill up every inch of me. He always said my pussy was made to fit him, and I was inclined to believe it. He moved himself all the way in, then all the way out, applying a little more force with every thrust. He gripped my ass and pulled me back onto him over and over, until I felt myself about to cum, but I didn't want to, not just yet. So I pulled myself off him, and turned around. I told him to sit down so I could climb on top of him; my very favorite position. My motto is "Somebody's gotta be on top, so it might as well be me," and I knew just how much Vincent loved me riding his dick. So I gave him the best ride of his life. I worked my hips back and forth, up and down, side to side, in circles, and some more shit. Vincent was in such ecstasy, he kept moaning my name over and over. The only thing that made him stop was me putting my breasts in his mouth, and he sucked on them like a starved newborn baby. The feel of his dick, his tongue on my nipples, his hands squeezing my ass, it was just all too overwhelming. I could feel the most intense orgasm beginning to surge through my body. I sped up my pace and Vincent and I climaxed together, which was always the way it seemed to happen with us. Our bodies were in sync that way.

Vincent looked at me and kissed me passionately, desperately even. Then he stared me straight in the eye and said, "Vanessa, I love you . . . more than I've ever loved anyone before, and in a way that I'll never love anyone else. Please? . . ."

As I looked into those gorgeous, pleading eyes, believe me, part of me wanted to give in, but I couldn't; it just wouldn't work. "Vincent, you know I love you, too, and I always will. But things are the way they have to be. Now I'm going to go freshen up, and I suggest you do the same. I'll see you soon."

I kissed him, straightened my dress, finger-combed my hair, and got out of the limo. As I headed back inside to go to the ladies' room, I thought about what had just happened, and what was about to happen, and I decided everything was as it needed to be. I went into the restroom and got myself all cleaned up, swirled around a little mouthwash, retouched the makeup, and I was good to go. I needed to get to my seat anyway, it was time to start.

I walked in and sat down, and it was then that I saw Vincent again. He was standing there all fixed up and looking wonderful, and staring straight at me. I smiled at him, and he smiled back, but only for a second, because he had to refocus on the woman standing in the back of the room. So I stood and turned to look at her, as did everyone else.

Winter Marie Henderson looked beautiful. She and I shared so many similarities; it was almost like looking in a mirror. We were both tall, with dark hair, fair skin, and brown eyes. But there was one major physical difference: the baby bump that was so subtly being hidden by the flowers in her hand. The other major difference was our personalities. She was quiet, demure, and the type of woman that would give up her entire career to be a stay-at-home mother and a housewife. Now don't get me wrong, to dedicate your life to your husband and child is admirable, but it wasn't for me. I'd worked entirely too hard to get where I was in my career to let it all go right then. And that was why she was the one in the white dress, and I was sitting among the guests.

I sat through Vincent's wedding and did question whether I had made the right decision, but I did what had to be done. Vincent wanted to marry me, but I couldn't be the type of wife he really wanted, so I set him free to find her, and find her he had.

I stood and clapped as they were pronounced husband and wife, and gave hugs and well wishes in the receiving line. I danced with Marcus at the reception, and watched as Vincent and his new bride fed each other cake. I even stood with everyone and threw birdseed as the newlyweds rode off together into the night in the very same limo that Vincent and I had made love in just hours earlier. What I'd done was wrong on so many levels, but I didn't regret it. I truly loved Vincent, he was my soul mate, but I had to let him go. So I resolved to do just that.

I was heading across the parking lot to get in my car when I felt my phone vibrate again. I pulled it out of my purse, wondering who it might be. To my surprise, it was a text from Vincent.

I have a business trip next month; I hope you'll be willing to join me. Please?

I was so conflicted. Sleeping with a married man was wrong, but I was beyond in love with Vincent.

So I sent my reply: E-mail me the details.

I got a simple ☺ as a response.

The decision I'd just made wasn't the smartest one. It could lead to all kinds of trouble. It was wrong, but then I thought about the old Luther Ingram lyrics, "If loving you is wrong . . . I don't wanna be right." So, with that decided, I got into my car and headed toward home, thinking about Vincent, my now-married lover.

Shadow Dancer

Landon Dixon

She was there again, third night in a row. I took a drag on my cigarette, staring at the window across the alley, at the silhouette of the naked woman dancing behind the lighted shade.

The bitch.

The building next door was a run-down hotel, like mine. But that body was the stuff of dreams.

I was in town on business, and every evening when I got back to my room, come midnight, the music went on and the woman started dancing. Exotic, erotic dancing, behind the lit-up shade. I'd added a few more stains to the threadbare carpeting, sucking down coffin nails like I was planning my own funeral, stroking dick like there was no tomorrow—watching her sway and undulate and writhe to the thumping music.

She was slim and curvy, agile, tits huge in profile, seductive hips in motion, legs long and slender. Her hair was loose, flying all over the place when the siren song burned hot, clutched in her hands and streaming through her fingers when it smoldered sultry.

I was there for the floor show every night, mesmerized, cigarette dangling from my dry lips, hard-on filling my damp hand. She cavorted in serpentine shadow for fifteen minutes or so. And then the lights would go out.

The curtain never rose, the shade staying down, despite my cursed begging.

I was ready to tear my cock out by the roots, tear that window covering to shreds. I *had* to do something more meaningful than jerk and jack. A man only gets such an opportunity once in a lifetime. I was a day overdue at my next stop already, but I wasn't about to hit the road until I'd seen for myself what was behind that shade—seen it and fucked it.

I crushed out my cigarette, did up my pants. I kicked my sample cases into the closet and locked it, exited the dingy room, testing the door lock on the way out. It was ten after midnight, and the dance was going full swing. Only tonight, the babe was going to have a partner.

I raced down the stairs and hustled along the sidewalk, punched through the door of the neighboring fleabag, and climbed those stairs three at a time. She was in 404. I knew that from hours of figuring and fantasizing. I knocked on the gray wooden door. It opened.

"Yes?"

She was naked, ten times as dark and delicious as she'd appeared behind the living window shade. "I've been watching you," I said, giving my eyes a free ride all over her lush, black velvet body.

She wetted her plush lips with the tip of her neon-pink tongue, and smiled. "You've seen me perform?"

"You could put it that way."

She had large, liquid brown eyes in a smooth, oval face, her hair dark and straight and long. Her tits hung plump and ripe off her chest, two-inch-wide areolas black as the night. Her waist was hands-spanningly narrow and her legs were shapely and shining, her pussy highlighted by a strip of fine, black fur.

It was too much too close for this sex-starved salesman. I grabbed the noir doll in my arms and mashed my hungry lips into hers, squeezing her big breasts against my chest, clutching her soft, hot, erotic body close. The nights of torment had turned me animal.

She sensed it, and welcomed it. Her lithe arms coiled around my neck and her lips moved against mine, body fitting mine like a heated glove. We only came up for air when some drunken bum staggered up the stairs and burped at us. Then I pushed the ebony goddess inside and kicked the door shut, my hands and mouth all over her.

Wildly kissing, I dove my paws down her silky, curved back and filled them full with the heavy, rounded meat of her butt, gripping and squeezing her bloated cheeks. She moaned into my mouth. The moan was followed by her tongue, spearing inside and wrapping around my tongue. Her hot, humid breath and body made my head spin, my heart pound.

I was way overdressed. I released her ass and tore my shirt open and off, kicked my shoes away, and shoved my pants and underwear down. She didn't let go of me for a second, clinging to my neck and snaking her tongue all around my lips and under my chin, squirming her body to the beat of my cock.

I pressed my erection into her belly, pumping skin-on-skin, gathering up her butt mounds again and lifting her right off the floor. I stuck my tongue out as far as it would go and let her suck on it, her pouty lips pulling hard.

She eased her head back, sliding her mouth off my tongue. "Where you seen me perform?"

I grinned, grinding my cock against her stomach. "Right across the alley. Through the shade."

She turned her head and looked at the window. "No shit? You can see through that?"

I didn't know who was shitting who, and didn't care. "Not like now," I said, moving my hands up between us and grabbing on to her luscious tits.

"Oooh!" she moaned. "Let's put on a real show—for anyone else watching."

It sounded like a plan—for getting into her pussy. There was probably more than one pervert peeping the late-night show, like I'd been doing. Now, they could see what happened when a man had the balls to act on his basic instincts.

We moved over next to the shaded window, in profile.

"I'm Monique, by the way."

I hefted her tits and dipped my head and painted her incredible areolas with my tongue. She shuddered, mambas jumping in my hands. They overflowed my mitts, huge and soft and hot, baby-smooth except for the aroused bumps on her areolas, where my tongue was spinning.

I swirled all around her engorged, licorice nipples, then spanked the jutters with my tongue, staring up into the woman's hooded eyes.

"Fuck, mama likes!" Monique groaned, her dragon nails biting into my bare shoulders.

I roughly massaged her breasts out to the tips and urgently sucked on her nipples, mouthing and tugging first one, then the other. The tangy-sweet scent of the vixen-in-heat filled my head, the taste and texture of her tits swelling my cock to the point of vibration.

Her turn.

She slid down out of my hands, landing on her knees on the

carpet, dick-high. She stared at my twitching rod, her eyes and tits shining. Then she laced her coal-black fingers around the pulsing tan organ, making me jump.

"Fuck!" I grunted, feeling the babe's warm, soft touch all through me.

She cupped my balls and stroked my cock, while looking up at me with her big brown eyes, her parted lips an inch away from my pearled cap.

Her mouth opened wider, engulfing my hood, wrapping me in wet, wicked warmth. I jerked, watching and feeling the woman slide her lips down my pulsating length, swallow my cock. I bucked when she hit the three-quarters mark, almost blasted when she kissed up against my balls.

What a show those pervs next door were getting, watching Monique fully inhale the rigid length of my dong. I was packed tight in her mouth and throat, cushioned in velvety wetness. The black bombshell gripped my trembling thighs and bobbed her head back and forth, sucking on my cock.

She absolutely wet-vacced my prick, lips sealed tight and tongue flowing, up and down, mouth and throat sensuously stretching to accommodate and envelop. She sucked fast, sucked slow, pulling me longer and harder, her cauldron of a mouth boiling my balls to the blow-off point.

My turn again. She smelled so wonderful, looked and felt and tasted so juicy, I just had to get the ultimate mouthful—in between her legs.

I picked her up by the waist, dropped down to my own knees on the carpet, pussy-level. She was sodden, dripping with moisture, lips swollen black and slick on the outside, pink and gleaming on the inside. I stuck out my tongue and touched her flaps with the tip.

"Jesus, yeah!" she gasped, jerking.

I slid my hands around her thighs and onto the twin, fleshy swells of her butt cheeks, digging my fingernails into the smooth, stretched skin. Then I licked up her slit from deep in between her legs to the top of her trimmed black fur, dragging her pussy in one long, hard, wet stroke.

"Oooh, baby!" she moaned, bum and body jumping in my hands.

She grabbed up her tits, squeezed them, staring down at me, trembling. I looked up at her and grinned, my lips glistening with the woman's dew. Then I licked her again, and again. I lapped her pussy, stroking her flaps with my tongue, scooping up her spicy juices and gulping them down.

Her long, lithe legs quivered out of control. She slid her hands forward on her tits and captured her jutting nipples between her fingers, rolled them, pulled them, as I tongued her repeatedly.

Finally, I jerked my head back and smacked my lips. Then I spread her plumped pussy lips wide with my fingers, exposing her shining pink still more, her swollen clit. I blew on her clit, making her shudder. I fashioned my tongue into a crimson wet blade and speared it inside her.

"Fuck!" she cried, jolted by the impact of my tongue in her slit.

I pistoned my head back and forth, pumping her, fucking her with my thrust-out sticker before burying it inside her and squirming it around, digging deep into her oiled twat. She bent over almost in two, grabbing onto my head, overcome with raw emotion.

I pulled my tongue out of her tunnel and dragged her flaps again. I tickled her clit. She groaned, staring glassy-eyed down at me. I flogged her hardened pink nub with my tongue.

"Suck it, baby! Please, suck on my clitty!" she gasped.

I kissed her clit, engulfed it with my lips, sucked on the swollen button. She bucked, her buttocks rippling under my grasping hands. I vacuum-sealed her clit, my cheeks billowing. Her trigger pulsed in my mouth, the babe quivering wickedly.

"Fuck! I'm gonna come!" she wailed.

Not yet, not solo. This was a shared dirty dance.

I spat out her clit and jumped to my feet, tried to push Monique onto the bed.

But she held her ground, gasping, gripping my throbbing cock. "Don't forget our audience," she said.

Then she spun around in front of me, and I grabbed onto her waist and my cock. I probed her pussy, and plunged inside. We both groaned.

Her twat was pure velvet heaven, juiced beyond succulent thanks to me, and her. I grasped her tits and rocked back and forth, fucking the babe. She leaned back into me, twisting her head around to squirm her tongue against my tongue.

Her booty bounced to my frantic thrusts, our bodies melded together with heat and sweat, cock and cunt. I fucked her ferociously, right in front of that lit-up window shade.

But before we both lost control, Monique bounced right off my rod, leaving me hanging and raging—temporarily. "Let's give 'em the full show, baby!" she rasped, bending forward and reaching back and spreading her thick, black buttocks.

I slapped her hands aside and grasped the twin dark moons, squeezing, kneading the taut flesh. She shimmied her ass in my hands, deliciously rippling her cheeks. She was built back there like up front, no question about it.

I smacked one of her cheeks, then the other, just to watch them gyrate. She whimpered, trembling. I clutched them again, sinking my fingers in deep, really working the pliable ass meat. Then I tore one hand away and grabbed on to my cock, split the babe's overblown mounds with my bloated hood. She pushed back, enveloping my knob in her hot cheeks. I played the slick tip of my dick up and down the smooth length of her ass cleavage, rubbing pre-cum and her own juices into her crack.

"Fuck my ass!" she hissed, reaching around again and tearing her butt open for business.

Her pucker blossomed like a night flower, just above my cap, right before my eyes. It was time to hit her ass, hardcore.

I scooped some juice from her pussy, slathered my already spit-slippery cock with it, then her crack. She jerked when I scrubbed her bum cleavage with my fingers, quivered when I hit her asshole with my cockhead.

Her fingertips burned white on her black buttocks, as I plowed my cap into her hole, popping ring, filling chute. She was oven-hot and vise-tight. I drove my dick so deep into her anus that my balls kissed up against her butt cheeks, buried.

"Jesus!" she moaned, rotating her plush bottom against my groin. "That feels sooo fuckin' nasty!"

It felt damn fine from my end, too, embedded in the woman's ass. I grasped her narrow waist, gritted my teeth, slowly pumped my hips, fucking her butt, gliding my glistening cock back and forth in her chute.

I surged with wicked heat, the babe's anus sucking on my cock as I plunged it. I quickly upped the tempo, pumping faster, banging my thighs into her back mounds, making them shudder, churning her chute.

She moaned low and long, pushing back against me in rhythm, splashing her cheeks against my body, consuming my pistoning cock with her ass. I hammered into her hole, my fingernails biting into the flesh of her waist. Her buttocks rippled nonstop with the brutal impact of my frantic thrusting. I was reaming the woman.

I pulled back, out, the both of us on the brink, almost over the edge. I hit her pussy again, going from her hole to her slit, spearing into the molten heat of the babe up to my nuts.

Monique arched her body upward, against me, flinging her arms back and around my neck, twisting her head around to flail her tongue against my tongue. I grabbed her jumping tits and pumped like a madman. We weren't long in coming, not after all that had gone on before.

I grunted, and jerked, my flapping balls boiling over. I bit into Monique's tongue and clamped down on her nipples, blasting inside the babe, spurting to the jolting rhythm of my orgasm. She shivered in my arms and screamed into my mouth, feeling every bit of what I was feeling in white-hot rushes.

Or maybe not.

Returning to my hotel room, I found the door ajar, the closet unlocked, my two sample cases full of pearls, diamonds, and gold jewelry gone. There was a scent of perfume in the air. I looked over at the window across the way—dark.

The shadow dancer had lured me away from my precious inventory so her girlfriend could rob me. Our triple-X tango behind the shade had merely been the signal for timing the heist.

But even the sneak-thief had still made time to leave behind a sticky squirt of her own enthusiasm on the carpet, no doubt after watching Monique's magnificent performance.

The bitches.

Keeping Him

Cynthia Marie

Dasia lay across her bed, exhausted. Another day had come to an end and the twins were sleeping soundly. Whoever said being a stay-at-home mother was easy and anyone who felt differently were truly fucked up in the head. Dasia was looking forward to her weekly outing tomorrow, just to get a break from her boring-ass life.

Once a popular news anchor for WSB-TV in Atlanta, Dasia met Stephen Anderson when he pulled her over for a speeding ticket. Afterward, they were inseparable and after two years of dating, they married at twenty-five. Their life was good until, nine months after their first anniversary, a set of twin boys made their debut. In an attempt to allow Dasia to be what she felt was a good mother, the couple decided it was best for her to quit her job and care for the kids until they were school-age.

Dasia missed the excitement of her life and career. She loved her boys, but neither she nor Stephen was prepared for the drastic change in their lives. No more weekend getaways, spontaneity, alone time, sleeping late, and no more bomb-ass sex. Dasia was self-conscious about her body. Not only were her breasts constantly leaking and her stomach was no longer taut, she was concerned that two seven-pound babies had stretched her pussy out and Stephen wouldn't be satisfied. She refused to let him see her naked for fear that he wouldn't see her the same way as before and it became a sore spot in their marriage. For the past four months, their lives revolved around the babies but neither wanted to address how *they* were feeling.

Dozing off, Dasia stirred when she heard her bedroom door close. Her eyes fluttered and her husband's body came into full view.

"Hey, bay," she greeted him, sitting up on her elbows and yawning.

"Hey." Stephen looked at his wife and saw that, as usual, she wore a pair of his sweats and her hair was wrapped.

"How was your day?" Dasia watched him remove his artillery and undress. Stephen's hard work had gotten him promoted to the fugitive recovery team and he always shared funny stories.

"Same ole, same ole. Ran up on a lot of folks tonight who missed their court dates. Had to remind them and put them in time out," he joked.

Dasia laughed.

"We even ran up on some hookers who were too busy working to go to court." He finished unfastening his bulletproof vest and flung it over the chair.

"Hookers, huh?"

"Yeah. You'd never believe the kind of shit they'd do to avoid going to jail."

"Did someone do something to you?" She glared at him, wondering if he'd tell her the truth.

He caught the sarcasm in his wife's voice but didn't feed into it. He didn't want to tell her that he was close to letting one of the chicks blow him as her get-out-of-jail-free card. She definitely wouldn't have understood. Things at home were tense and the couple hadn't been intimate since the twins were born. Stephen loved his wife but felt like she didn't have time for him.

Because he loved her, instead of cheating, he worked longer and harder.

"No, babe." Kicking off his shoes and pulling off his pants, he changed the subject because he knew where it would lead. "How was your day?"

"Besides changing diapers and being a human milk machine, I was able to make dinner for you. It's in the microwave."

"I ate earlier. I realize that you're busy so I didn't want you to do anything extra just for me."

"Stephen," she huffed, "I don't mind but you could have called."

Standing in front of her in his boxers, he looked at his wife. "I'm sorry and you're right. Well, maybe I can make it up to you."

Dasia looked at his crotch and saw an erection. "Hmm . . . maybe." She smiled. He still turned her on, and she wanted nothing more than to please her man, but was afraid of what he'd think.

Stephen knew that any chance of making love to his wife was damn near impossible, but he was going to try. With anticipation, he trotted off to the bathroom for a quick shower but his anticipation turned to frustration when he returned. His wife was curled up on her side of the bed, asleep.

The next morning, Dasia was awakened by a faint sound coming from their bathroom. Stephen wasn't in bed, but a light shone from underneath the door. She heard the noise again so she tiptoed to the door, pressed her ear against it, and heard muffled moans.

"Um . . . uh . . . uh . . . hmmm . . . ahhh . . ."

"What the——" She slowly turned the knob, peeked inside, and saw the outline of her husband, in the shower, jacking off.

Instantly, Dasia was hurt that he had chosen to get himself off instead of having sex with her.

Closing the door, Dasia sat on the bed, pissed. Within moments, the bathroom door opened and Stephen emerged.

"What's wrong with you?" he asked, seeing Dasia's twisted face. He dried off and put on a pair of underwear.

"Were you in the bathroom getting off?" She knew the answer but wanted to hear it from him.

Putting lotion on his body, Stephen answered bluntly, "Yep."

"Why do that when I'm right here?"

Stephen dressed but gathered his thoughts carefully. "When I wanted some last night, you were asleep. You're never in the mood. Either you're too tired or one of the kids is latched to you. Damn, I can't even feel a titty because you're slapping my hand away." He reached toward her and tried to touch one. As he expected, she slapped it away. "My point exactly."

"Stephen, I just had not one baby but two. What do you expect?"

He turned and looked at her. "Just had them? Dasia, it's been four months. Hell, one of them is getting teeth." Before he put the rest of his gear on, he hit her with an unexpected question. "Would you rather me get off at home or with another chick? I'm really trying not to step out on you because I love you, but damn, baby, it's hard."

If looks could have killed, Stephen would have been dead. Never in a million years would she have thought her husband would speak to her the way he had.

Before she could answer, a wail came through on the baby monitor. Heading to the nursery, Dasia heard the front door close and Stephen's car start. Her heart broke. She wondered how her husband could be so heartless.

It took Dasia two hours to get herself and the twins ready before she made it to the United Methodist Church in Dunwoody for her weekly outing.

She headed to Perimeter Mall with a group of other moms, where they window-shopped and talked about their kids. A display at Victoria's Secret caught her eye. She wanted to buy something, but she didn't want Stephen to be put off by her newfound appearance, so she passed.

Strolling to the food court, the women sat around at the Baja Bistro eating a variety of Mexican food until one of them became very quiet. "What's wrong, Stephanie?" Dasia asked. She noticed that she wasn't as talkative as she had been in the past, nor did she order any food.

"Michael wants a divorce," she confirmed. The women looked at her in shock. "He's been sleeping with someone else since I had the baby, and now he wants out."

Everybody tried to console Stephanie but Dasia thought back to what Stephen said a few hours ago. *Would you rather me get off at home or with another chick? I'm really trying not to step out on you because I love you, but damn, baby, it's hard.* She couldn't end up like Stephanie.

When Stephen arrived home that night, Dasia already had the kids down and wanted to talk to her husband.

"Hey, babe," he acknowledged, looking at his wife in his sweats and a head wrap. What he wouldn't give for her to get out of those just for one night. "I'm sorry about earlier. I was wrong for saying what I did."

"The way you said it, yes, but I understand." She looked at her handsome husband and reached her hand out toward him and through a stifled yawn, said, "I want to make love to you."

Stephen looked at her. "I'd like to but maybe another time."

• • •

Because of Stephen's reaction, Dasia's mind was busy and she was unable to sleep. The next morning, she called her mother because she needed someone to talk to.

"Hey, Ma," she spoke when her mother answered the phone.

"Hey, sweetheart! How are you? How're my grandbabies?" Dasia was silent. "Dasia. Honey, you there?"

Instantly, she began to cry. "Mom, I need your help. I think I'm losing Stephen. Things have changed since I had the twins. I . . . I don't know what to do anymore."

"I'll be right over." Her mother hung up the phone and within thirty minutes, she was at her daughter's door.

Dasia was thankful to see her mother and hugged her closely. "Mom, nobody said it would be this hard trying to take care of kids."

"Why do you think I only had you?" She laughed. "I wanted to give you everything and couldn't imagine sharing the love I have for you with someone else." She wiped her daughter's tears away.

Dasia spent the next hour telling her mother how she felt about Stephen and how things had changed with them.

"Look, honey, if you love your man, you have to keep him happy. That's first and foremost. The kids will fall into place. I'm not that far away, and I can always keep the kids; that's no problem. But the problem is, you've let yourself go."

"What do you mean?"

"Look at you." Her mother led her to a mirror. "You don't comb your hair and the sweats you always wear look like they stink." She looked at her. "What happened to the proud woman I raised? This isn't you, sweetheart."

Dasia looked at herself in the mirror and didn't like what she saw. She was once known as the sexiest anchor on television and ratings had spiked because of it. Now, she didn't know who she was.

"Now, get yourself together, do what you have to do, and keep your man."

Dasia's mother packed up her grandchildren for an overnight stay and left her daughter alone to get herself together. Dasia knew she was still the woman Stephen craved and she would show him.

Over the next three hours, Dasia pampered herself and picked up a few things from the mall. She knew Stephen would question the cost of her purchases but, in the end, he would be glad she'd bought them.

Driving home, she thought about Stephen and called him. "Hi, babe, I was just thinking about you."

"Really?" he spoke dryly. "Haven't heard that in a while."

"I know," she admitted. "What you doing?"

"Paperwork. What about you?"

"Just out. Had to pick up a few things. You in tonight?"

"For the most part, yes, but I'm working late."

"Really? Why?"

"Just a lot of work." A pregnant pause filled the air. "I gotta go." He hung up the phone.

She could tell he was fed up and she couldn't let things get any worse than they were. She bopped inside the house with a clear plan and all of her purchases in tow. After taking a shower, Dasia slid into the new navy push-up bra and matching high-cut bikinis she'd bought from Victoria's Secret. Looking at herself in the mirror, she couldn't believe what she saw. Although a little curvier, her body wasn't as bad as she'd thought it was. Yes, she had a few stretch marks here and there, and she wasn't as toned as she was before, but she still looked good.

She dressed in a mid-thigh–length, brown plaid skirt and tan silk blouse. The color contrast made her smile as it accentuated her skin color. Putting on her makeup, she looked in the mirror and realized that the woman who stood before her was someone she missed. That same person was still a mom but she was also still a wife, and was ready to be one again. Stepping into her stilettos, she went to reclaim her man.

"Hi. I'm looking for officer Stephen Anderson," Dasia said, walking into the precinct.

"What business do you have with him?" a female officer asked, glaring at her.

"The business a wife would have with her husband," Dasia told her, daring her to get crazy.

The woman pointed toward his office and Dasia walked ahead.

Standing at his door, she watched her husband dutifully at work. He looked so handsome. Quietly, she stepped into the small room and closed the door.

"Hey, you," she purred.

He looked up. "Whoa!" Stephen was shocked.

Turning toward the door, Dasia locked it and then looked back at her husband.

"What's all this?" He pointed.

"Your wife, baby, and I want you so bad."

Dasia unbuttoned her blouse as she walked toward him, and her breasts stood firm and full. Seeing his enormous erection, Dasia raised her skirt and straddled him. She put her hands on his face and whispered, "I've missed you."

Just then, the two began to kiss. First gently, and then with more passion. Stephen's hands palmed his wife's basketball-sized ass, kneading one cheek, then the other, then both at the same time.

Removing her blouse, she reached behind her and unbuttoned her bra. Her breasts, still full with milk, stood firm and hard. Her nipples saluted him. Stephen began to suck and hum as the sweet fluid ran into his mouth. Now he knew why his sons were always attached to her.

"Damn, this is so good." He gulped heartily and then moved to the other titty so it wouldn't feel neglected. Massaging her breasts, he didn't care that his hands were covered with milk. She was his wife and he loved it.

Doing something she used to do before having children, Dasia reached toward her own breasts and began sucking.

"Aw shit, that's what's up!" Stephen drawled and then shook his head, watching his wife. "Um . . . um . . . um . . ."

While they took turns with her titties, Dasia began to grind her crotch against his dick. Her pussy was wet and she needed it filled. Getting up off him with her skirt still around her waist, she noticed she had left a pussy stain on his lap, but she didn't care. She unzipped his BDUs, stuck her hand inside, and pulled out her husband's assault weapon. It was hard, hot, heavy, thumping, and waiting for her. She knelt down in front of him and, from his angle, all he could see were big-ass titties and a fat pussy he was dying to get in. As if she were starving, Dasia took Stephen's dick and made it disappear inside her hot, wet mouth. She knew how her husband liked to have his dick sucked and she liked to do it. Up and down, light, hard, rough, and commanding. She was ravaging his dick. The juices in her mouth began to run down his thick dick and she slurped them up. She liked sloppy oral sex and he loved it. Stephen continued to watch as she sucked, jacked, licked, hummed, and deep-throated him. Feeling his back arch, she realized that she was doing her job. Sucking harder, stronger, and pumping him, her mouth became even wetter and so did his dick. Stephen began to fuck her face and she gagged. Each time she gagged, she took his dick out of her mouth, spat on it, and put it back in to take more.

"Give it to me real nasty, baby," Stephen demanded, and that she did.

He reached down and grabbed one of her titties, pulling it hard and pinching her nipples the way she liked. Despite the wetness, she didn't stop him.

"Do that again. That feels so good," she urged with a mouth full of dick.

Just when he was about to, Stephen became rigid. "Babe, I'm about to—"

Dasia knew what she was doing but didn't move. Her wet mouth went farther down on his dick and Stephen felt something he hadn't felt in a long time—the back of her throat.

"Oh, shit!" he grunted. "Oh . . . god . . . damn . . . shit . . . girl!" Stephen's body began to jerk. Between Dasia's mouth and hand action, she worked to help bring up the milky white nut that he wanted to give her so badly. Always loving how he tasted in her mouth, Dasia gulped the backed-up love he'd had inside him. Even though some ran from her mouth, she used her fingers to ease it back in.

After his orgasm, Stephen wasn't through. The thought of sex with his wife always brought up an instant erection. Even after cumming, he was ready to go again. He helped her up off her knees and placed her on her back on his desk. Expertly, he shoved her knees toward her shoulders and slid her bikinis to the side to get a look at her fat, hot, cream-centered pussy. It was

trimmed neatly with an X that marked the spot. Stephen became aggressive and bit on his wife's titty, hard, while he ran the
tip of his dick up and down her center. Pushing for a moment at
anything that would give way, he searched for an opening and finally found it. Dasia's pussy welcomed him into the warm, deep
wetness of her mocha tsunami.

"Baby, this shit is so tight. Goddamn, girl!" He stroked her
deeper, then long and steady. "You're so wet. I love this shit!"

Opening her legs, Dasia wanted more and commanded,
"Deeper."

Stephen grabbed her and pulled her toward the edge of the
desk, pushing her back on his files, her knees at her chin. He did
as his wife asked, and went deeper. Stephen's dick was lodged
in his wife's stomach and jackhammered her pussy, giving her
pleasured pain.

The two found a hard fuck rhythm and rode it like he was
headed off on a tour with the navy reserves. She needed his reserves in her pussy. Stephen dug into the deepest part of her
ocean and Dasia moaned loudly. The deeper he went, the louder
she became. He didn't care who heard them. This was a long
time coming. He was pounding so hard, knocking the bottom
out of her pussy, that he was surprised she was taking his dick as
hard as he gave it. He knew she could do it, but there was just
something different about it this time. Her pussy craved his dick
and she told him with each stroke. He hit it faster and harder,
then removed it from its home and rammed it back into her repeatedly. The sound of their fuck juices was in the air. Stephen
continued to fuck his wife for the next fifteen minutes, and nearing the sixteenth minute, her eyes rolled into the back of her
head and her body shook. She grabbed his shoulders and held on

to his muscular body as she came all over his dick. Stephen felt a warm gush of sticky wetness cover his dick, and her hard pussy contractions forced him to erupt.

"Damn, baby," Stephen called out, thrusting into her deeper, squeezing out another round of reserves deep inside of her to the point of no return.

Afterward, he lay atop her on his desk. She kept her legs wrapped around his waist, not wanting to break their connection. Their breathing was still accelerated. They heard a commotion in the main area of the precinct and Stephen moved his head.

"Damnit!" he exclaimed, and reluctantly took himself out of his wife.

She got up off the desk and readjusted her clothing. With a smile on each of their faces, they kissed good-bye and Stephen promised that he'd be home soon.

Two months later, Dasia sat behind the microphone at WSB-TV and smiled into the camera, delivering Atlanta's local news. On the set, Stephen watched her and smiled. After she was done, they would leave to pick up the kids from daycare and drop them off at her mother's for the weekend. He'd made reservations for a weekend getaway at Chateau Elan and they were both looking forward to it. Unfortunately, it took another woman's misfortune for Dasia to appreciate what she had, but Stephen finally understood how Dasia felt and realized how important communication was. He promised that she'd always know he wanted her, despite what unexpected turns life may throw at them.

Intimate Strangers

Michelle Janine Robinson

It was hard to believe that either of them had any fluids left. After meeting at a bar the night before, they had talked, flirted, and drank martinis until they decided that the finger fuck he was pleasuring her with behind the bar might actually get them thrown out; especially when she realized her cum juice had found its way to the barstool on which she sat. Not only could she feel it, but she could smell it . . . and so could he.

They checked into a nearby hotel and fucked feverishly until dawn. Two hours later he was back for more. Even though he was half asleep, his hard cock was insistently poking at her thigh and once again she was lubricated by his fiery intentions. She moaned at the prospect of his cock once again being buried deep inside her and reached down and grabbed a handful, insistent that he fuck her immediately.

"Hmmm baby, I love a woman that takes control," he murmured with the thickness of sleep still in his voice.

Without a moment of even the slightest foreplay, he rolled over and entered her pussy. There was no positioning of bodies, no search for just the right position, nor the building of momentum. His cock was like a motorized drill, spreading her open and making her wet beyond belief.

He was fucking her so hard, she was sure her head would

have a knot on it the size of an orange if it kept striking the headboard the way that it was.

Her pussy expanded and contracted, gripping tightly to his cock, reluctant to let it go, even though she was sure to be late for work.

"Oh, baby. This is too fucking good. You know I have to go to work. Stop, baby, please. It's just *too* good."

"I know, baby. I know. It's good to me, too. And, after all these years, your pussy is still as wet and tight as when we first met. This is my pussy!"

"Yes, baby," she said breathlessly. "Your pussy . . . this is your pu . . . pu . . . pussy. Oh, baby. I'm gonna . . . I'm gonna . . . I'm gonna cum!"

She convulsed beneath him as her orgasm rocked her deep.

"Here it comes, baby. Take it! Take it!"

And, with that, his detonation was immediate.

"Ahhhhh . . ." he sighed. "God, that was good."

She jumped up from the bed, took a quick shower, and made every effort to get to work on time.

" 'Bye, baby," she whispered, as she left him lying prone in bed. "You and that nasty cock of yours have now made me late for work. Maybe I'll get fired, come back here, and we'll lie in bed and fuck all night and all day. Would you like that?"

She had worn him out. He had barely enough strength to raise his head from the pillow and say good-bye.

"Flight 318 to London, now boarding at Gate 14."

He sat in the airport, wound tighter than a drum and anxious to get away from it all. He was determined to enjoy this trip and leave his cares behind. Lately he had gotten into an awful rut.

Hers was the first face he saw upon boarding the craft. After seeing her, everything else around him paled in comparison.

Her smile would have welcomed him into her arms even if she were the ugliest woman on the face of the planet. Fortunately, she was not. She was unbelievably beautiful. But her smile . . . her smile was more than merely beautiful. Her smile was legendary. He was a man who seldom daydreamed but, at that moment, he was hard-pressed to relinquish the thought of what the combination of her silk sepia tones and his bold complexion might produce.

"Good afternoon," she said.

"Good afternoon," he responded, with a little *too* much bravado.

He couldn't help himself. In her presence, he felt like a lovesick teenager.

He found his seat, placed his carry-on in the overhead compartment, and waited for the inevitable moment when he would be close to her once again; maybe even close enough to touch her.

"Uhm, did you see that hottie in row twelve? Suddenly I'm craving a tall, wet, steaming cup of hot chocolate," Karen's colleague Wendy said.

"Hands off, you she-devil. I saw him first."

"Don't worry about me. Georgie is sticking it to me on the regular; and girl, that shit is *good*!"

"Yuck. You're sleeping with Captain Saneval. He's gross. You know he's married with children, right?"

"Shit yeah. I know, but we have an understanding."

"Oh" was her only response.

Finally, she made her way over to row twelve.

"What would you like to drink this afternoon, sir?"

His eyes lingered longingly over her moist, freshly glossed lips. "A Coke, please."

She left and returned a moment later with his drink. "Here you go, sir."

"Thank you."

Whether it was by accident or accidentally on purpose he wasn't sure, but the tips of their fingers touched and he was immediately aroused. She might as well have touched his cock directly; he would have been no less hard if she had. His erection poked insistently at his gabardine slacks, eager to find itself safely ensconced between her lips. Either set of them would have sufficed.

In an attempt to distract himself during the lengthy eight-hour flight to the UK, he decided he would catch up on some reading. Even under her severely buttoned flight attendant's uniform, he couldn't help but be aware of her breasts straining against the fabric, her nipples erect—maybe from the air conditioning on the craft, or just maybe she wanted him, too, just maybe? There was such grace in her walk, yet that same grace was edged with the faintest hint of raw sexuality. He wanted her more than he wanted to breathe.

"Would you like a blanket?" she asked.

"Yes, thank you."

The polite banter of it all, remarkably, fueled his rising libido. He wanted to take her right there, in the middle of the aisle. He wanted to bend her over the edge of the armrest, hike her skirt above her waist, rip her pantyhose from her succulent thighs, discard her hopefully saturated panties, unzip his pants, and slide his blood-engorged cock deep inside her. He wanted to fuck her until neither of them had anything left. So, as he visualized her hips grinding deeper and deeper into his manhood, he realized that instead of the two of them giving the flight crew and passengers a hot and steamy show, they were talking about whether or not he required one of the airline-issued blankets to keep him warm. It made him hotter than he could have ever imagined. The duality of it all was somehow intoxicating.

Finally, in the midst of going over some financial reports for work, he drifted off to sleep. Even his dreams were of her.

The wind was blowing and her hair cascaded over her shoulders. She was clothed in a white, sheer, organza-like garment, her nipples playing peek-a-boo beneath the covering. She giggled, then appeared to run in slow motion toward him. As she ran, her breasts bounced in time to her movements. Her arms were outstretched and it felt as though she was coming toward him, but it seemed to be taking longer than it ought to. Why hadn't she reached him yet? The anticipation of her presence was unbearable. He had never wanted anything or anyone as much as he wanted her at that exact moment. He busied himself with stroking his cock, waiting for her. He could feel the soft, gentle folds of her tight pussy walls drawing him in—and he stroked—and he stroked—and he stroked, as she closed the distance between them.

"Sir, sir. Can I get you anything?"

"No, I'm fine," he said with a twinge of embarrassment.

He hoped that none of what he had seen under the cover of sleep would be revealed.

She reached over past the sleeping passenger sitting in the aisle seat next to him, and she gently stroked his cock through his pants, pleased with the result. As he sprang to life beneath her fingers, she left him a note and walked away.

He opened the note and read it, more excited than he had ever been.

"Meet me in the restroom; the one right behind you."

His heart pounding, his skin warm to the touch, he did as she had instructed and, after waiting a few seconds, joined her in the cramped airplane restroom.

"So, Row Twelve. You've been staring at me the entire flight. Why is that? Do you wanna fuck me?" she asked.

He was speechless.

"Oh, I guess you don't," she said.

As she pretended to exit the bathroom, he grabbed her around the waist, gripping her tightly, unwilling and unable to let her go. He opened the buttons to her uniform and turned her toward him. Her breasts were beautiful. They were so full and her nipples seemed to ache for him to suck them, and so he did. Licking and biting at her tasty globes, he spit on one of her nipples, eager to see her response. He lapped at her wet nipples, fascinated with the slow descent of his own saliva on her beautiful breasts. It was truly a work of art. His juices were the paint and her body the canvas. He desired to paint her from head to toe.

"Oh, baby," she moaned. "I need you to fuck me now. I want your cock inside of me. Fuck me please!"

"Where do you want it?" he asked.

The cramped quarters of the restroom mattered not to either of them. Neither wanted anything more than to be engulfed. While one hand was on her mouth to prevent her cries from being heard by the passengers and the crew, his other hand played with her juicy, hard clit. As she ground her pussy roughly against his hand, urging him to plunge his fingers deep inside her, he entered her ass, feeling her tight hole slowly welcome him. With her body pressed against the bathroom door, several of the passengers had to be well aware of what was going on as he drove his cock harder and deeper into her ass, feeling her welcome him in more and more.

"Fuck my ass, baby. Oh, your cock is so fuckin' hard. Fuck me, baby, fuck me," she murmured against his hand.

"Take it, baby, take it. Open up, I want to go deeper, deeper inside of you. You are so fucking tight. It feels soooooo good, baby; so fucking good!"

He yearned to feel the inside of her pussy next and before he could spray the inside of her ass with his juices, he lifted her in the air and sat her pussy directly on his cock, gripping her body in his hands as if she were a rag doll.

He bounced her up and down his cock with great ease; gripping her waist and watching the various contortions of her face, twisted in ecstasy as he reached even farther back inside her quivering pussy. And, just when he thought this state of nirvana would go on without ending, he exploded inside her. She bucked and jerked, her eyes rolling up in her head. She breathed in the scent of his sex, wanting to suck him, but realizing that outside the doors of the bathroom, duty called. As they came together, he held fast to her, biting at her neck, aroused by the reddish love bites he left.

The two of them, left heaving and gulping for air, were satisfied, but still very much in need. There was so much he wished he had done; and he hoped for an opportunity (soon) to give her all that she deserved.

"To be continued," she uttered, reading his thoughts as she reluctantly peeled her body away from his.

She adjusted her clothing and exited the bathroom, returning to her duties on the aircraft.

"Where is he?" her colleague asked.

"He?" she questioned, just as he subtly returned from the bathroom.

"Don't act coy with me, missy."

"Coy? I'm quite sure I don't know *what* you are talking about."

"Uh-huh. Yeah. I believe you. That banging and knocking I heard on the bathroom door was just turbulence, huh?"

"Yeah, that's it. It was turbulence, plain and simple."

As he returned to his seat, her colleague followed him.

"Hello, Owen. Your heifer of a wife here didn't tell me you'd be flying with us today. I had to find out from another member of the flight crew."

"I'm sure it was nothing personal. I think maybe Karen wanted to ensure that I got enough rest before we start our holiday; three fabulous weeks in Europe and no work to speak of. I think she has plans for me."

"Sounds to me like those plans already got well under way."

"I'm sure I don't know *what* you are talking about."

"Why, of course, you don't," Wendy responded sarcastically. "That banging against the bathroom door was just a figment of my imagination."

"Yeah, that's it," he chimed in. "It was a figment of your imagination or maybe it was just good, old-fashioned—"

"Turbulence!" both he and Wendy chimed in unison.

"Yeah, I know, that's what your wife tried to sell me on. I'll tell you the same thing I told her, I'm not buying it."

Owen couldn't help but laugh out loud. Karen's partner in travel was everything she'd said she was. And he was convinced the two would have *lots* to talk about once Karen returned to work, after their vacation. In the meantime, Owen shut his eyes for a moment, anxious to replay the events of the day. He suddenly felt so lucky. No matter how many role-plays he and his wife engaged in—how many stolen moments in bars, pretending they were convenient strangers—when all was said and done, they each returned home to the same bed and the same home they had built . . . together.

Collecting trash from the passengers, Karen stole a quick glance at her husband, Owen, and winked.

He grinned back at her, replaying in his mind yet another stolen moment the two of them had created for themselves. It was what kept their love alive and their desire for each other ever strong. He still wanted her (and she him) just as much as when they had met more than ten years earlier. From headboard-battering sex within the confines of their one-bedroom apartment to stolen moments as members of the Mile High Club, they had no desire to be the perfect couple, but they were perfect . . . for each other. So, whenever work got to be too much and either of them forgot what *it* was all about, they brought the spice that they hoped would allow them to sizzle for years to come.

"I love you," she mouthed silently as she extracted a small piece of garbage from his hand.

"I love you, too," he mouthed back.

Twins

"I think you've lost your mind! I'm not wearing that—that damn nun's uniform!"

"It's called a suit, and if you're going to bible study, you have to at least look like a respectable woman."

"Uh, respectable woman? What are you saying? That my fine ass ain't respectable? Hell, I demand respect every time I step out! But just because I don't dress like a pastor's wife—"

"Hold up, Iesha. I'm no nun either. I just know how to dress to get a man worth having. I'm not one of those women who needs her breasts hanging halfway out of her blouse or her pants so tight she can't breathe—unlike some of us."

Close couldn't even describe the relationship between Iesha and me. Even though we were twins, we were complete opposites. I was the slightly taller, awkward one while she was so beautiful and confident. Her smooth, caramel complexion always brought her the male attention she desired, but somehow it didn't work for me. Sometimes, I found myself a little jealous of my sister because of her appeal to men.

We stood in my bedroom and I watched as she put on the black suit that I'd picked out for her, almost feeling guilty that I was covering up her perfect body. Iesha completed her ensemble by brushing her shoulder-length hair into a bun and downplaying her makeup, smoothing on clear lip gloss and ditching the spicy red, her usual color.

"But, sis," she pleaded, "don't you want a man to at least think about what it would be like to spread you open and—"

"Stop! Don't say it." I shuddered in disgust. "I can't believe I'm having this conversation with you. I can't believe I even agreed to this silly bet!"

"As I was saying," Iesha continued, practically ignoring me, "a man wants to at least imagine what it would be like to get the punany. He wants to smell its sweetness, love it . . ." She inhaled sharply and smiled. "Taste it."

"I'll pass," I said, folding my arms. "Better yet, I'll wait."

"Look, I'm not saying that being all sanctified is bad, but damn, sis—you gotta eat."

"What on earth does sex have to do with eating?"

"Picture this, Yana. You come home from a long, stressful day at work and yo' man had the same kind of tiring day. He sees you and he fucks your brains out!" She sighed. "Steak and potatoes all night!"

"Whatever!" I chuckled at her ridiculous analogy.

"Okay, Miss High and Mighty. How long has it been since you've gotten laid? Better yet, when was the last time you let a man just touch the kitty?"

"Well . . ." I thought back. "That was Solomon."

"So that was like what? Five, six years ago?"

"Seven," I blurted out. *Damn, seven years already?* "But I have a man. Someone who will never forsake me, cheat on me, or make me feel unworthy."

"Oh, hell naw, you've been holding out on me? You've been fucking somebody and you haven't told me?"

"Honey, I'm talking 'bout God. He will never cheat on me and it's all good!"

Iesha was sarcastic with her loud sigh. "I can't believe I fell for that lame shit. After that outburst, I'm even happier we made this bet because if we didn't, I'd have you committed. You're thirty-nine, not seventy-nine."

"I'm not crazy, Iesha. The only reason I considered this bet is because I think once you discover who God is, you'll be able to find some purpose. Maybe even close your legs and wait for a husband."

"Okay, Mother Teresa, don't push it." She puckered her lips. "That reminds me, the location changed for your date with James. He's cooking you dinner at his house on General Drive. Remember, you agreed to one night with him in exchange for my month in sex rehab—I mean, the church house—so no funny business. God help yo' ass if you don't show up."

"I don't know about all that, now. We didn't agree to something that personal."

"You're right, we didn't, but he's working on a special project at home and figured that it would be easier. Just try not to be you for one night, please!" She eyeballed my boot-cut blue jeans and red sweater. "Uh, you might want to get dressed because you need to be there in an hour. Your outfit is on the bed."

"Uh, no, those aren't clothes. That's hooker attire."

"Look, if I'm dressing like a damn missionary, you're dressing in what I would wear on a date. So the red bustier, black skirt, and three-inch platforms are it for you, tonight."

I stared at the bed in disgust. "I don't know. This is too much."

"Look, Iyana, I love you. You're my sister, best friend, and confidante, but you need to know that all of your little friends at church ain't who they pretend to be. Hell, half of those little choir members and ushers are in the club on Saturday night grinding to Jamie Foxx's '15 Minutes,' and deciding whose ass they gone ride home with."

She picked up my bible off the table and did a quick look through in the mirror. "Look at me," she stated. "I'm off to bible study, at a church, and I'm doing this all for you, Yana. So enjoy yourself and relax. I promise it won't be near as bad as you make it out to be. Take my car. There's a small duffel bag in the passenger seat for tonight. Take it to James, but don't open it. Text me and let me know when you get there."

I swallowed hard, unprepared for what my sister had planned for me. "Okay, I will."

"Oh, one final thing. I met James once about a month ago, but we've chatted a few times on the phone. He's really a great guy, so have fun!" With that, she headed out the door.

"Hey, wait a minute!" She was gone.

It took me twenty minutes to get dressed in the outfit she'd set out. The skirt was too short and I almost fainted fastening the bustier. I looked at myself in the mirror one last time, pulling my shoulder-length hair back into a banana clip.

I cannot let my neighbors see me like this. I grabbed the long faux fur coat that Iesha let me borrow last month.

I walked slowly toward the car, tripping twice in such ridiculous shoes, hoping that no one was outside that I knew. Still, I couldn't believe I was doing this—and to think, she's only met this guy once. I thought she'd hooked me up with a prospect, not a stranger.

Dear God, I just hope he's cute . . . and not expecting to get any.

• • •

The GPS directions were perfect and as I neared the exit, my stomach started doing somersaults. Exiting, I decided to pull over and collect myself before turning onto his street. I parked the car in an empty lot.

Where are her tissues, towels—something. I scoured quickly underneath the passenger-side seat and pulled out a silver flask.

"Please, God, forgive me." I took a swig of the vile-tasting substance, but it didn't help.

"Vodka!" I chuckled. I pulled down the driver's-side mirror and patted away beads of sweat from my forehead.

I pulled back onto the road when my purse started buzzing. "What the hell?"

Turning onto General Drive, I stopped at the entrance of the gated community and checked my phone. Iesha had sent a text message.

"Hey, sis. Hope you're close. I txt James and said you were running late. Remember to have fun!"

"Okay," I responded.

The gate code was already programmed into the GPS and his home was barely two minutes away. I pulled into his circular driveway, admiring the white stucco, two-story home. James's lawn was well manicured with gorgeous oak trees scattered throughout.

"I can do this . . . I need to pray."

My silent two-minute prayer turned into a long, ten-minute one. I swallowed hard, taking one last gulp from the flask, and carefully placed it back underneath the seat. I grabbed the duffel bag and opened the car door.

"Amen."

I approached the front door and tried not to wince as my stomach started turning again. My nerves were getting the best of me.

I'm stronger than this. Just eat and go home, Yana. And no more sisterly bets. Ever. I rang the doorbell and waited. After getting no response, I went to knock and mistakenly pushed the door open.

"Hello, is anyone home?"

I looked past the entryway and noticed that there was a portrait of a couple hung on the wall over the fireplace to my right. She was scantily clad in white lingerie and they were both holding glasses of wine—ready to kiss. Candle sconces framed the portrait. I looked down to see a small round table covered in a red cloth. In the center of the table were a long-stemmed red rose, a glass of white wine, and a note:

Good evening, my love. Please leave your indiscretions at the door. This glass of wine will assist you. Your instructions are down the hall.

My Love? Instructions? Indiscretions? I was flabbergasted—and confused.

I picked up the glass of wine and started down the hall, taking small sips, remembering I'd just had a little vodka. I entered the next room—a small sitting room. James was obviously a lover of art because the walls had more artwork of men and women in different sexual situations. Candlelight danced everywhere and I was starting to wonder if I would be eating dinner at all. I spotted another table, this time with a purple tablecloth, another glass of wine, and a second note:

Indulge me with another glass of wine. I promise this will be the best night of your life. Prepare to have fun and we will do everything we talked about.

What does he mean, "Everything we talked about"? Oh, my God! Does he think I'm—No, she wouldn't do that to me. I'd never spoken to him and Esha said that they've talked and texted and that she told him about me.

My heart was beating hard in my chest, and I thought about leaving before I got in too deep.

No, I'll simply greet him, thank him for the wine, and leave.

I sat on a white plush sofa and continued to sip. After I'd finished half the glass, I wasn't as nervous but still slightly apprehensive.

Where is he?

The candlelight had me in a trance as I ran my fingers across the sofa with my eyes closed, feeling the softness of the fabric . . .

One more minute and I'm gone . . .

"Welcome to my lair, my queen. Don't speak, just relax." I could hear his deep sexy voice, but I didn't see him enter as he stood behind me. Was I asleep?

"Baby, I want you to know that last text you sent made my dick hard as a rock. I've been waiting to see you and watch you run your tongue all around the shaft of my cock."

It was a setup! My sister sent me there, knowing that she wanted me to be her for the night. I shot up. "James . . . look . . ." But the alcohol had taken effect and I was a little light-headed. "Shhh, baby, I want to do all of the talking tonight, just like we planned." He unzipped my black duffel bag. "I see you brought the goody bag." He opened the bag, pulled out a blindfold, and quickly tied it on me. The wine was in full effect and though I was mortified by the thought of seven years without sex, this man wanted to make me feel good.

I sat there in a daze, terrified on the inside and completely clueless on the outside.

What in the world am I supposed to do? What would Iesha do?

"Okay, baby, take my hand, and let me lead you to our secret place tonight."

It took everything I had to smile. I took his hand and he helped me up. "Baby, don't be shy now; look at me." He raised my blindfold and just stared at me. "You are so beautiful, more beautiful than the first time I laid eyes on you." He cupped my face with both hands, and I looked up at his face. He is handsome. Caramel skin, salt-and-pepper goatee, gray eyes, and bald. His hands were so soft, so sensual, and when he touched my face and swept his fingers across my lips, he almost took my breath away. He was dressed in black slacks and an open white shirt, revealing his well-manicured chest. I closed my eyes and inhaled the scented candles for the first time. I tried to hide my excitement at being in the presence of a man so fine.

He replaced the blindfold over my eyes and kissed me.

Immediately, I kissed him back, feeling my sweet spot betray me as it began to quiver. He picked me up and I wrapped my hands around his neck as he began to walk. I rested my head on his shoulder.

My final destination had the smell of fresh vanilla as he lowered me onto the bed. He knelt before me and proceeded to take my shoes off, massaging my feet.

"I can't wait to taste you, feel you, to be inside you." He took each toe into his mouth and sucked on it. "Mmmmm . . ." It felt so good and I knew it wasn't supposed to. "Oh yeah, Iesha, baby, you taste so good."

I shuddered at hearing her name, but came to the realization that I didn't care anymore. I heard him fumbling with something. "Let's see what else you have in this bag."

I didn't know what was in that bag, but I did know that James was amazing at sucking my toes and kissing my ankles. He rose up and pulled me to my feet, holding my waist. It dawned on me that he was unzipping my skirt. I grabbed his hand.

"It's okay, baby, I'll take really good care of you. I promise."

Whether it was the wine or simply the yearning of my body, I released his hand, letting him continue. That voice was getting to me. It was so relaxing, mesmerizing. My skirt and thong fell to the floor.

Next he unbuttoned my blouse, and my nipples responded immediately as he unfastened my bra. I could feel his eyes on me.

"Damn, baby, your titties are huge." He cupped one and I gasped. "You are absolutely beautiful naked."

He placed each breast in his mouth and sucked, running his tongue around my nipples. *Oh, my God, he makes me feel so good . . .*

"C'mon, Iesha, I want to take you to the brink, baby. I want you to call me Daddy tonight."

We kissed again, the warmth between my legs growing, my body betraying me. That voice—sweet, sensual, deep voice from this man was making my center ache with anticipation, a throbbing that I hadn't felt in a long time. I threw away the blindfold and watched as he fumbled around the bag. After a few seconds, he pulled out something and showed it to me.

"You have a lot of nice toys in this bag. I would love to see what this rocket does to you." He pulled me close and kissed my cheek, putting his tongue in my ear. "Shit, girl, you smell so good." He ran his tongue along my shoulder up my neck to my ear, kissing my earlobe.

He pushed me back onto the bed and placed his hand in between my legs. He gently pushed my thighs open and I let him, realizing that it might be my one opportunity to let go.

"Yeah, let Daddy in, let me feel that pussy. I want you to cum for me, baby. I wanna feel you cum for me." His fingers slid in and out of me and I was sure I had wet his bed with my love. "Yeah, mama, there you go."

Jesus, he was pressing my button and . . . *Oh my, what is that— that is not his finger. Not vibrating like that.*

"Yeah, baby, you like that, don't you? Doesn't that feel good?" He set the vibrator on top of my clit and I jerked forward.

"Oooooohhhhh . . . mmmmm . . . that feels so good."

He continued to finger me, the sensation incredible as the vibrator continued its buzzing. "Oh, my Jesus! Oh, shit!" *Forgive me, Lord!*

"Yeah, mama, c'mon and cum for Daddy. I knew you had it in you."

"Please don't stop, please . . ." *How could I have forsaken my body for this long?* "Oh, yeah, baby, that's it."

I needed to touch him—to bring him closer to me. I began to rub his head, my feet perched on his shoulders. He kissed my belly and I felt warm all over. I was so wet and it felt so good. He proceeded to taste me, his tongue tossing my love button around in his mouth. "Oh, shit, James! I can't—I can't . . ." and I felt something I hadn't in years.

He took my hand in his and placed it on his stick. "Touch me," he said. "Touch my cock and squeeze it, baby."

He placed my hand on his dick and I squeezed the tip, in awe. It was thick and so hard. My pussy throbbed from the thought of being taken by James. My body was ready.

Without a second thought, I took him into my mouth. I was overwhelmed as I began to go up and down the shaft of his stick. I moved to the head of his stick and began sucking harder, letting him grind himself into my mouth.

I needed more. I started to touch myself and grew more aroused as he continued fucking my face.

"I see you need me, baby. You ready?"

"Uh-huh."

He laid me down and put my legs on his shoulders and entered my center.

"Oooooh . . . James . . ."

"Yeah, Iesha . . . you like that, huh? Damn, you're tight. You've been saving this pussy for me, haven't you? Damn this virgin pussy, girl . . . so good."

I winced as he pushed deeper, but as soon as he slid in, every nerve in my body exploded.

"Oh, my God, I'm . . ."

"Yeah, baby, that's what I'm talking about. Let Daddy have it . . ."

My climax was strong and long. "Ahhhhhh shit! James!!!"

"Oh baby, you know just what to do. Damn, this pussy feels so good." He pulled himself out of me and knelt in front of me. "Sit up, baby."

I sat up and instinctively sat Indian-style. I watched in awe as he brought his dick to my face and perched it on the tip of my nose. I smiled at him before opening my mouth as wide as I could so he could push his stick into my mouth.

"Yeah, baby, suck this dick. Go up and down the shaft. Yeah, just like that."

I glanced up at the first man I'd had in many years. His face was serious, his hips gyrating as I tasted myself on him.

"Oh yeah . . . Oh yeah . . . oh shit . . . ooooohhhhh yeah . . . fuck!"

He pulled his stick out and commanded me. "Get on all fours, baby. I wanna really fuck you; I need to see your ass, boo."

I turned over onto all fours and before I was ready, he slapped it and immediately pushed his dick inside of me.

"C'mon—raise yo' ass in the air!" I cried out while raising my ass in the air. "That's that shit, ma. Yeah!"

He rammed me, harder and deeper with each stroke. I loved the pain of his dick pounding against me, all while he mercilessly slapped my ass.

"Yeah, baby, you're mine now! Damn, this pussy is good, oh, shit!"

My body started to speak for me, my vagina got wetter and then I realized that I was moving in rhythm with him.

"Oh yeah, baby, that's what I'm talking about. Make Daddy work for that pussy. I don't mind a little fight. Work that shit, girl. Show Daddy how that pussy talks."

Oh, my God—I'm getting that feeling again. He sensed my release and slammed into me harder and deeper.

"I'm ready to explode, baby. Where do you want it?" I turned around, opened my mouth, and let him fill it, his seed squirting into my throat and down the sides of my face. Smiling, I licked my lips and tasted the man who'd verified what my sister had always said: "No matter who you are and what you do, there's a little bit of a freak in all of us. You just have to let it out!"

Sleigh Ride

Amazonia

If I had a quarter for every time I was late, I'd be filthy rich by now, Faith said silently to herself as she searched for her keys and her purse. Her son's Christmas play was supposed to start promptly at seven p.m., according to the invitations that were sent home with the students two weeks in advance. Faith would be attending the function alone. Faith and Jabari's dad were still together, but they weren't married. They weren't perfect but they worked well together.

When Faith finally made it to the elementary school, she wondered how many students were participating in the program, seeing as how it took her ten minutes to find a place to park. By the time she got to the auditorium, it was half past seven and the auditorium held no empty seats. She found a spot at the back of the audience, falling in line with the rest of the late arrivals. Lucky for her Jabari's class had not yet performed. The first-graders were doing their own rendition of "Santa Claus Is Coming to Town."

Faith scanned the crowd of children seated in front of the stage and found her fourth-grader tucked between two girls that captivated his attention instead of the chorus of six-year-olds, who had composed the song well but completely destroyed the performance. By the end of the song, the stage had lost two little boys who had to potty, a couple of shoes from various little girls that had been tossed away by overly dramatic kicks during the dance routine, and a couple of Christmas ornaments that hung from the tree onstage had been knocked off their branches and stampeded by almost everyone as they exited the stage.

Faith was laughing so hard after this that she could barely breathe. That's when she noticed that she had left her bottle of water in the car. As the third-graders gathered themselves to perform, Faith snuck out of the auditorium to find the water fountains. When she found one she realized how low and undersized they were. But she didn't care. She kneeled down into a squatting position, pursed her lips, leaned against the plastic "push" bar for extra support, and allowed the icy cold water to flow over her tongue and splash the back of her throat until she was satisfied.

"Ahhhhh," she said aloud.

"Well, that seemed refreshing," a deep voice said from behind her.

"Yes, it was," she said as she spun around and laid her eyes on what had to be the most gorgeous man she had ever seen in her life. He was taller than her, which meant that he had to be at least six feet. She was five foot seven without her heels, so right now they stood eye-to-eye. His head was bald and his eyes were green. He was the sweetest piece of extra-dark chocolate that she ever did see. He smelled of cologne, but right now she couldn't figure out which one. He was dressed in a pair of black slacks, a green shirt, and dark green tie. Faith hadn't realized that she'd been staring at the man until she noticed a confused look on his face.

"What?" she asked him when he just stared back.

"I said, I have some soft drinks in my office if you wanna come and get one. The kids won't be finished for another hour and it's too cold out here for you to be running back and forth to this water fountain. Want one?" he asked for the second time, although this was Faith's first time hearing it.

"Oh, sure," she replied, and followed his lead down the hall. "So, what grade do you teach?" Faith decided to start a conversation so that the journey wouldn't be too awkward.

"All of them. I'm the music teacher, Mr. Hall. Nice to meet you." He looked at her and smiled.

Faith wanted to melt right there in the middle of the hallway. Who was this man? And why on earth was she just coming in contact with him now? *Damn, I should attend more parent-teacher meetings*, she thought to herself.

When they reached the music room, he held the door open and waited for her to catch up. Once inside, they made their way to his office. He opened a mini fridge and told her to take her pick. Faith did so. Once she had opened the container of grape soda and took a quick gulp, she turned around to find that Mr. Hall had disappeared. She scanned his office and noticed that there were no pictures of him or his wife, just a photo of a little league team. She assumed he had a son who was a member.

Faith didn't even know if the man was married and here she was fantasizing about him. As she sipped the carbonated syrup, she daydreamed that he would come back into his office, wipe everything off the desk, and put her on top of it. Faith dreamed that he would trace images with his tongue on her neck and between her breasts. She imagined that he would trace her silhouette with his fingertips, from her scalp to her ankles. She rubbed the cool aluminum against her ear and down to her breasts. She had gotten hot; she was blushing from a little fantasy.

Damn, I want him! Faith thought. She hopped off the music teacher's desk, where she had placed herself there in all her imagination. There was a throbbing between her legs now. If he didn't touch Faith now she would have to touch herself. But she would much prefer that the cause of this problem be the solution.

She walked to the door of the office to see where Mr. Hall had wandered off to. Assuming that he had started back toward the auditorium, she turned out the light and closed the door. She found him at the front of the classroom, sitting in a sleigh that had been decorated by his students.

"I still haven't decided what else I could do with this thing. It cost too much for me to just throw it in storage until next Christmas," he said to Faith, who only stared back.

"I know what you could do with it, Mr. Hall." Faith had a smirk on her face because of the thought in her head and the wetness in her panties.

"Really?" Mr. Hall asked, anticipating her answer.

"Uh-huh." She placed her soda on the piano and glided the rest of the way to Santa's sleigh.

Mr. Hall sat and waited for her response, but the look of curiosity that he had on his face turned to pure astonishment as she straddled his lap and leaned in for a kiss. She would know whether she was disrespecting him if he pulled back or pushed her off, but to her surprise, he grabbed her ass and initiated the kiss. He sucked her bottom lip, which tasted of sweet grape soda, and she decided to get the ball rolling. If it didn't happen tonight, she had a feeling she wouldn't sleep until it did.

Mr. Hall grabbed a handful of Faith's hair and ran his fingers through it. That drove her crazy, to feel those big fingers run across her scalp. She undid his tie and unbuttoned his shirt. Her skirt had been pulled up when she climbed into the sleigh. Mr. Hall's pants were undone and halfway down. She didn't know when he had done this and she didn't bother to ask. He pulled her thong off and dropped it at his feet before he gripped her ass again and entered her slowly.

"Mmmmmm . . ." she moaned as she tilted her head back and held on to the back of his head. She had a feeling this was going to be the ride of her life. To her surprise, he kept a steady motion of slow, long strokes. Instead of speeding up and making him catch her pace, she decided to go with his once she thought about the point of climax.

He grabbed her legs and placed them on his shoulders, allowing himself deeper access and more control. Faith did not oblige. In fact, she leaned in closer and let the pain become her pleasure as she kissed him again to intensify the feeling. Faith opened her eyes, not remembering when she had even closed them, to notice that she still had on her shoes. *Oh, well,* she thought. She closed her eyes and concentrated on the feeling. Mr. Hall stood up with Faith sitting in the palms of his hands and decided to speed up his pace.

This was new to Faith. She had done a lot of things but never had she met a man that could do this. She was in love with the moment. Once her moans got louder, Mr. Hall decided to withdraw and switch positions again. Faith knelt on her knees on the sleigh bench, facing the rear end of the carriage. He entered her wetness again, slow and hard, amusing himself with the moans and the head tilt that he had assumed was to come. Faith bent a slight arch in her back and Mr. Hall found her G-spot, which not many men had accomplished in her twelve years of love-making.

Faith, who was thirty now, felt all her fantasies come to life as he gripped the back of her neck and guided her into the doggy-style position. *This is it,* she thought. What would make this particular climax so special was that neither of them had uttered a single word since they had begun, and neither of them would know when the other would break.

While Mr. Hall was still behind Faith, he reached in front of her, unbuttoned her shirt, and unhooked her bra. While he pulled the shirt off, Faith allowed the bra to fall onto the sleigh bench. Mr. Hall bent forward and kissed the back of Faith's neck as he rubbed and tweaked her nipples, hoping to make her climax before he did.

Faith could not utter a single word, even if she tried. Her leg began to shake and, as it did, Mr. Hall flipped her over and sat her on the bench facing him. He bent down to his knees and spread her legs as wide as they would go. He buried his face in her soft place and entered two fingers inside Faith so that she could still get the full experience. Faith continued to rub her own breasts and tweak her own nipples while Mr. Hall drank her juices and came to his own climax using his other hand. He felt her vaginal walls contract before she exploded. Faith's legs were still shaking when Mr. Hall stood up in front of her. She could barely move, until she heard the applause.

"Oh, shit! Jabari!" she said, and jumped up to get her clothes on. Before Mr. Hall could get his pants on straight, Faith had her bra and shirt back on and was bending down to pick up her thong, which had been abandoned at the beginning of this little escapade. She tucked it into her purse, straightened her hair to the best of her ability, kissed Mr. Hall one more time, and exited the music room.

She ran into one of the bathroom stalls on her way down the hall and cleaned herself up with the wipes that she never traveled without. She reapplied her lip gloss as she approached the auditorium. Jabari's class was assembling on the stage once she got inside. There were a couple of empty seats now, so Faith found one at the back of the crowd.

The fourth-graders began to sing "Silent Night" and Faith smiled and waved to her baby. He waved his hand quickly, embarrassed that some of the girls in his class would think that he was a momma's boy. She giggled on the inside because she knew.

Faith's legs finally stopped shaking. She had no idea how she had managed to wobble all the way back from the music room, and she was just glad that there was a chair available. Faith could hear the kids singing but all she saw were the images in her head of that damned Mr. Hall. That dark chocolate skin, that shiny bald head, and that huge—

"Is this seat taken?" she heard his voice behind her again. He didn't wait for her to respond. Instead, he moved around the row of chairs and claimed the seat as his own.

Faith looked straight ahead. For some reason, she was nervous. She was still in a relationship with the father of her child and she had no idea of Mr. Hall's background. She had never done this before. It was wrong for him to allow her to do it. But it felt so right. Mr. Hall said nothing as he stood up and walked behind the row of chairs. He dropped a piece of paper into Faith's lap and continued to walk. Faith attempted to open the piece of paper before she noticed it was a letter. She folded it back into the small square it was when it had been given to her and tucked it into her purse.

Once the fourth-graders had finished all of their performance Jabari ran toward his mother and occupied the seat that Mr. Hall had first claimed.

"Baby, you were great!" she said to Jabari. He smiled and looked toward the stage where the final act was about to begin.

"Ma, I don't wanna watch them. I'm hungry. Can we leave now?" Jabari asked, waiting for a response.

"Sure, baby. Let's go." Faith and Jabari exited the auditorium and headed to their car.

"Oh, I gotta use the bathroom." He ran into one of the restrooms next to the water fountains.

Faith couldn't wait to read the letter that Mr. Hall had given her so she pulled it out of her purse while Jabari was in the restroom. It read:

Dear Miss,

You never gave me your name. I would enjoy seeing you again, since I see that you enjoyed me. I wanted you when I first laid eyes on you. Jabari was in the second grade, and the first day you came to pick him up, I wanted to say something to you, but I didn't want you to feel disrespected. I'm glad that you made the first move. You ran out in such a hurry tonight. If you ever think about me again contact me.

Alexander

Mr. Hall's phone number and e-mail address were written at the bottom of the page. God, if he only knew she probably would never stop thinking about him. She tucked the paper back in her purse and Jabari walked out of the restroom.

"Where's Daddy?" He looked at his mother.

She didn't know how to answer that. Hell, she couldn't answer that.

"He had to stay late for work tonight," she lied.

"Oh, I hate his job. He's never home," Jabari said with a frown.

Faith thought about the music teacher again. "Well, did you have fun tonight?" she asked her son.

"Yeah," he replied.

"Then that's all that matters," she said, and kissed him on his forehead.

"Oh, yeah. I forgot to tell you my teacher wanted to know if I could join his baseball team this year."

"Sure. I don't see why not. That should be fun!" she told him.

"Yes! I'll tell Mr. Hall in the morning!" he exclaimed.

"Who?" Faith asked to make sure she wasn't hearing things.

"Mr. Hall, my music teacher. He has a little league baseball team. He's my favorite teacher! Now you finally get to meet him!" Jabari said with lots of excitement.

Faith smirked and opened the car door for her son to climb inside. She had a feeling that she would be experiencing many more sleigh rides.

Coosawhatchie

Zane

If you've ever driven down Interstate 95, to or from Florida, then you've passed Coosawhatchie, South Carolina. In fact, you've even driven over the Coosawhatchie River. Probably never noticed it, though. When I was a little girl, I used to sit by the banks of the river, watching the cars and trucks speed across the overpass, wishing that I could hitch a ride in just one of them. I never even gave a damn where they were headed. I yearned to escape the small town of 11,407 people residing in 4,164 households, according to the latest United States census.

By now, you must realize that everyone in town has to know each other, definitely by face if not by name. Saying that nothing exciting ever happens in Coosawhatchie is an understatement. In fact, the last "newsworthy" event dates back to the Civil War when General Robert E. Lee utilized our little slice of heaven as his headquarters as he sought to fortify the coastal defenses of South Carolina and Georgia. Yep, since 1862, life has been pretty dismal here. Unless you count the occasional bar fight in the one bar in town, or someone reporting a freshly baked apple pie being stolen off their screened-in porch.

My name is Betsy Smith. Exotic and original name, don't you think? I'm twenty-eight years old but I feel like I am living the life of an eighty-two-year-old woman. My mother is the town seamstress so I am her junior seamstress by default. There aren't many jobs here and my old, rusty '72 Ford pickup can't make it far; especially not in the dead heat of summer.

Summer. August to be exact. What I like to call "the long-suffering winds of August." Nothing but dry heat, a ton of mosquitoes, and the scent from Robert Carlock's moonshine still lingering in the air. No breeze, no rain, no mercy. Just heat.

Last summer, around this time, things were a tad different for me. I had the most exciting experience of my entire life; at least to date. You see, up until then, my experience with humans of the male persuasion was rather limited. In Coosawhatchie, there are my cousins, cousins of my cousins on the other side, and cousins of their cousins of their cousins on yet another side. Outside of Perry Brown, the town stud because he is the only truly attractive man in town, pickings are slim.

I won't even form my mouth to tell a fib. I fucked Perry . . . once. He was my first. In fact, he was also a lot of my friends' first. The older men around town call him Cherry Bomb because he has popped so many cherries that the number is rising on a daily basis. I was never sure whether Perry's dick was good dick since I didn't have anything to compare it to . . . until last summer.

Even though I was scared to death, I ventured out with my best friend, Colby. She wanted to go apply for a job at a bar in Savannah, Georgia. She figured that waiting tables couldn't be so hard and she does have a high school diploma. So we borrowed her dad's 1993 Cutlass and made our way there.

Compared to Coosawhatchie, Savannah seemed like Paris, France. At least how I had imagined Paris to be. People were walking around, laughing, shopping, hugging and kissing all over each other like it was Christmas in the summer. A cloud of sadness instantly fell over me. I realized that my life was at a standstill and millions and trillions of other people were making the most of theirs.

We arrived at Bottlenecks, a small roadhouse on the outskirts of Savannah, about nine that night. Colby was dressed to
impress, and to tantalize, in a pencil-cut black dress and four-
inch heels. I didn't even know where she had acquired the getup
but she was looking hot. Me, not so hot. I had on some jeans and
a faded T-shirt from the previous year's Jasper County Fair.

When we walked in, all eyes were on us; presumably because
we were what city slickers call "fresh meat." Colby sashayed over
to the bar to ask for the owner, some dude named Melvin, while
I surveyed the patrons. My heart started beating faster in my
chest and I struggled to keep from hyperventilating. I had never
seen so many fine men in one place in my life. Well, hell, I had
never seen so many fine men even spread out in various places.

I decided to go stand by a wall. I felt uncomfortable posing
in the middle of the floor. No sooner had I picked a good, empty
spot when a man in a navy blue suit approached me.

"Hi, I'm Dean."

I was speechless. He was about six inches taller than me, a
dark chocolate, with smooth skin and a low-top fade. But what
drew me to him the most were his eyes. They were mesmerizing, like two black diamonds.

"So, do you have a name?" he asked, losing his patience.

"I'm Betsy."

I reached my hand out to shake his. I did have at least that
much common sense. Even though I rarely got to greet someone
whom I had never met in Coosawhatchie, I did have manners.

Instead of shaking my hand, he brought it up to his soft lips
and kissed it. My uterus damn near dropped clean out of me. I
jerked away and he seemed offended.

"I'm sorry. I'm just not used to . . ." I paused, realized that I
sounded plum foolish.

"You're not used to what? Men kissing your hand?" I dropped my eyes to the floor. "Or men period?"

I didn't respond and Dean chuckled.

"It's all good, Betsy. Can I buy you a drink?"

"No, no thank you. I never drink."

"Maybe you need to live life on the edge a little, at least for tonight."

Live life on the edge! I had to admit to myself that I had thought about that a time or two in my life. After that night, whether Colby got hired or not, my tired, eighty-two-year-old–acting ass was headed back to sitting on the side of the riverbank watching people speed by on the highway.

I glanced over toward the bar and Colby was talking to an older man who was presumably Melvin. Dean was staring at me with those diamonds and something awakened in me that I never realized was even there.

"Dean, would you mind taking me someplace local and fucking me until I black out?" I slapped my hand over my mouth, wondering who the hell had just said that! "I mean . . . I didn't mean . . ."

Dean placed the tip of his index finger over my lips. "Your pleasure is my pleasure, Betsy."

Before I could respond, he was leading me out of the club and getting me situated in the passenger seat of a luxury automobile that I could not even recognize.

You're really tripping, I thought, as he walked around to the other side to get in. *Get out! Get out now!*

Needless to say, I didn't get out but you knew that already. There would be no story to tell if I had gotten out. I just had to "live life on the edge."

We ended up at his place, a very nice cottage-style house on the water. His place was decorated like a model home. He was way out of my league, that was for sure. I live over the local feed store in a one-room flat.

As soon as we were in the door good, Dean was all over me. When he gently slid his tongue in my mouth, I felt my pussy thumping. The difference between him and Perry a.k.a. Cherry Bomb was obvious from the very first second. He leaned into me and I felt his dick growing hard in his pants.

Dean pulled my T-shirt up while we continued kissing and pulled my tits out of my bra so he could caress them. I started calling on Jesus that he would swallow them whole. I'm not sure if it is just me—my friends and I never discuss sex since most of us lost our virginity to the same man—but my breasts are my weakness. Whenever I masturbate, all I need to do is concentrate on them and I have orgasms that make my eyes roll back up into my head.

Yep, he broke the kiss and started devouring my breasts. He sucked them so good and so hard that all I could do was hang on for the ride. I had never imagined a man so hungry, not even in my fantasies. We stood there in the doorway as I rubbed his head while he moved back and forth from tit to tit. It was amazing!

I have no clue how much time elapsed but he must have sucked on me for at least fifteen minutes before he finally picked me up and carried me upstairs. I locked my legs around his back and started kissing him again. He moaned. I moaned. We moaned in unison and then I almost freaked when he lowered me down on the steps halfway up and started going at my breasts again.

That did it. I exploded, right there in my jeans. He must have realized that I was experiencing aftershocks because he chuckled as he clamped down on my left nipple.

"You like that, huh?" he asked.

"Yes . . . I like that a lot," I struggled to say with bated breath.

Dean grabbed me by the back of my head and licked my chin in one long, slow stroke. "Then you're really going to love what I do next."

"Oh, God!" I started shaking like a leaf. "You're going to fuck me now, aren't you?"

Dean shook his head and grinned. "No, not yet. I skipped dinner. You're not going to deny a hungry man, are you?"

"Oh, shit!" I exclaimed. "You're going to eat me!"

Dean didn't respond and I was too shocked to say anything else. Now Perry was known for a lot of things around Coosawhatchie but performing oral sex wasn't one of them. In fact, most of the women in town wouldn't perform oral sex on him, either. Unlike most situations where women have to wonder where else a man's dick has been, we all saw each other on a damn near daily basis so there was no speculation there. Everyone made Perry use a condom and no one was trying to suck his dick . . . that I knew of. We did not discuss sex openly but that was common knowledge among the masses. Even the menfolk talked about that.

Dean unzipped my jeans and pulled them down halfway over my hips. He stuck his face down there, moved my panties to the side and, before I could blink twice, he was licking and slurping down there to the point where I had to clamp my hand over my mouth again to keep myself from screaming.

His tongue was warm, soft, and incredibly moving. He ate me like that for a few minutes and then pulled my right sandal off so that he could take my right leg out of my jeans and panties. Then he spread my legs open right there on the steps and really went to town on my pussy. I decided to let go, removed my hand, and screamed like there was no tomorrow.

I watched his head bob and weave up, down, and all around between my legs. I decided to try to do more than just lie there—I've heard how men despise that—so I started moving my hips to his rhythm and even put my foot up on the stair railing to get more leverage.

"Oh, yeah, you love this shit!" Dean said, obviously proud that he was turning my ass out. "You taste so damn good!"

Dean removed my other sandal and got my bottom half completely naked, then shocked me again by telling me to turn over.

"Right here on the steps?" I asked. "You're not about to fuck me in the ass!"

Dean laughed. "I have the feeling that might be a little bit too much for you. At least for tonight."

I sighed in relief and turned over, with pussy juices dripping all over him, me, and the steps.

I assumed he was going to fuck me from behind but, instead, he lifted up my ass and started eating my pussy from behind. His nose was buried in between my ass cheeks while for the next ten minutes he ate me like I was his last meal. By the time he was done, I couldn't even move. My legs were weak so he finished carrying me to his bed.

His room was dark—only the moon shone slightly through the sheer curtains—but I still freaked when he started taking his dick out in the near blackness.

"Hold up," I said. "Can you make it darker in here?"

He laughed. "Darker, why? I was actually planning to turn on the lights. I want to see every inch of you."

"Oh, heavens no." I sat up on my elbows. "I felt the size of your dick through your pants. If I actually see it coming toward me, I might faint."

He fell out laughing and I couldn't help but do the same.

"I'm not that experienced," I admitted. "I'm not a baby or anything but it's just that—"

Once again, he shut me up but this time with a kiss. I tasted myself on his tongue and realized that I was turning into a true freak.

When he broke the kiss, he said, "I like the fact that you're 'inexperienced,' Betsy. I could tell that from the moment I laid eyes on you."

Damn, it was that obvious?

Dean walked over and turned on the overhead light. When he turned back around his dick was out, and he was coming out of the rest of his clothes. I decided not to protest. I was too hypnotized by his huge, beautiful-ass dick.

"Lie down," Dean instructed me, and I did as I was told, but he laid me sideways on the bed, with my head near the edge. "It'll be fine. Just take your time."

Dean's dick hit me in the forehead and then slid down my face, over the ridge of my nose and into my open mouth. I wanted to suck it, I yearned to suck it.

I tried to relax my throat so that he could get as much of it inside as possible. Before I realized it, I was moaning and licking and sucking and gulping everything I could down into my throat. I had never imagined that sucking dick could be so fantastic.

Once Dean realized that I had his dick on lockdown, he bent over and started sucking my tits again, and then my pussy. He put his left knee on the bed so his dick could get deeper in my mouth and so he could gain easier access to my pussy. He ate, I sucked. He ate some more, I sucked some more. Then Dean came in my mouth and I know that I came all up in his.

Dean stood up straight and gazed down into my eyes, watching his glimmering dick extract itself from my cum-filled mouth.

"You ready for this dick, baby?" he asked.

I couldn't even manage to respond. My mind was suspended somewhere between reality and illusion.

"Turn around." Dean reached for my ankle and pulled me around on the bed. Then he climbed on top of me and rammed his dick inside me in one swift motion. I stifled a scream but somehow managed to clamp my legs behind his back as he started moving in and out of me like a jackhammer. He really intended to make my ass black out!

He lasted for what seemed like forever and I enjoyed every second of it. I reached down between us and rubbed my pussy while he worked it over, hoping that it wouldn't freeze up and go out on me. Colby told me that once, she got fucked so hard that her pussy collapsed. I didn't want that shit happening to me.

Dean fucked me without mercy and I have no idea how many times I came but I actually started squirting all over the sheets and the walls. It was insane! Suddenly, I had a migraine from so many orgasms but I still kept going.

After about two hours, Dean was spent and collapsed on top of me. We both fell asleep like two newborn babies.

The next morning, at dawn, I asked Dean to take me back to Bottlenecks to look for Colby. I was sure she was pissed and was hoping she hadn't called my parents back in Coosawhatchie, claiming that I was missing. I had left my cell phone charging in her car and when I had tried hers, the network was busy.

When we pulled up in the parking lot, Colby was sitting on top of her daddy's car practically in tears. Melvin was standing there trying to console her. I could tell that she wanted to strangle me but once I emerged from Dean's car, looking like I had been in rehab for a month, she grinned and then giggled.

"You fucking slut!" she exclaimed.

I couldn't help but smile as Dean wrapped his arm around my shoulders and walked me to her car.

Dean and Melvin, who knew each other, exchanged pleasantries and then Colby and I said our good-byes. Dean gave me his number and I gave him mine, but guess what? To this day, he has yet to call me. I guess that it was all a dream, the magic between us. He probably does that kind of freaky shit with a different woman every weekend.

Colby ended up getting the job at Bottlenecks and always asks me to come to Savannah and live with her. I'm kind of leery because I don't want to run into Dean. She said he still comes into the club and she has never seen him leave with another woman, but she's probably saying that to prevent my feelings from being hurt.

Either way, I enjoyed the intense dick down that Dean gave me that night. It was enough to last me for a few years, until I can get out of Coosawhatchie. I plan to "live life on the edge" again someday soon. The world is a big place and if I can get fucked like that in one night of venturing out, the sky is the limit.

I am about to go back to my place on top of the feed store and call it a night. There are too many mosquitoes out here by the river. Wait, my phone is ringing.

Oh, shit! It's Dean! He must be hungry!

"Hello . . ."

About the Contributors

Michelle Allen is a native of Baltimore, Maryland. She resides there with her young daughter, and is pursuing a degree in nursing at Coppin State University. She is currently attempting to turn her short story into a full-length novel.

Amazonia is a single mother in her early to mid-twenties. She lives in Savannah, Georgia. Her greatest strengths and weaknesses are her three children.

T. Ariez is a Texas native currently working and living in Austin. She enjoys spending time with her family and laughing with her kids. She loves to write and is currently working on her trilogy, *Toxic*. Recently she has shown an interest in screenwriting and hopes to one day have her films seen in mainstream theaters. Please visit T. Ariez on Facebook at www.facebook.com/t.ariez3 or she can be followed on Twitter @tariez12.

Mr. Harold Dean Armstrong was born in Kansas City, Missouri. He was voted Most Likely to Succeed by his high school classmates, and in his senior year, he won first place in the 1983 Black Heritage Essay Contest, sponsored citywide by the 4-H Club. He is a graduate of Robert Morris University. Mr. Armstrong has published four manuscripts, two fiction and two nonfiction. All are currently available at www.lulu.com/hdarmstrong.

Asali is a native of New Orleans and newcomer to the literary world. She is an avid reader and versatile writer who has made a declaration to pursue doing things she is passionate about, such as photography and writing. "Tres Leches" was featured in the erotic anthology *Between the Sheets* from Delphine Press. Check out her work or comment on her website at www.asaliwrites .com.

Gemini Blaque is currently residing in Chicago, Illinois. When Ms. Blaque isn't creating titillating works of fiction, she balances her time between working in social services; volunteering with her organization, Kappa Alpha Lambda Sorority Inc.; and spending time with family and friends. She plans to become more involved in uplifting, projecting positive well-rounded images of, and addressing issues concerning the LGBTQ community through her professional career and personal life in whatever way that manifests itself in true Gemini style, with passion and creativity.

Camille Blue is an information professional living in southeastern Wisconsin. Her first short story, "Anais," was published in the anthology *Succulent: Chocolate Flava II*. Camille Blue may be reached at Camilleblue2007@yahoo.com.

SA Brown began her literary career as a contributing author for *Sugar and Spice: Anthology for the Grown and Sexy*. SA hopes to inspire, encourage, and entertain readers with compelling characters and thought-provoking story lines. Her first solo effort, *Still Not Satisfied*, chronicles the journey of a young man who might have to lose everything to gain anything. Stop by www .sabentertainment.com to learn more about SA Brown.

Landon Dixon's writing credits include *Forum, Naughty Neighbors, Score, Voluptuous, 18eighteen, 40 Something, Leg Sex, Buttman, Clean Sheets,* and stories in the anthologies *Sex & Seduction, Sex & Submission, Sex & Satisfaction, Five-Minute Fantasies, Spank Me, Satisfy Me, Ultimate Submission, Ultimate Sex, Ultimate Sins, Seriously Sexy, Naughty Spanking 2, The Mammoth Book of Best New Erotica 8,* and *The Mammoth Book of Erotic Confessions.*

Jeremy Edwards is the author of the erotocomedic novels *Rock My Socks Off* and *The Pleasure Dial,* and the erotic story collection *Spark My Moment.* His quirky, libidinous tales have appeared in more than fifty anthologies, including four volumes in the *Mammoth Book of Best New Erotica* series. Jeremy's greatest goal in life is to be sexy and witty at the same moment—ideally in lighting that flatters his profile. Readers can drop in on him unannounced (and thereby catch him in his underwear) at www .jeremyedwardserotica.com.

The sky is the limit for this sassy, sundry, and prolific author. **Elissa Gabrielle** has broken the ceiling of literary excellence with her gift in the skill of multigenre writing. The author of two poetry books and four novels and contributor to multiple anthologies, Elissa has proven herself to be well versed in artistic creativity. Her colloquial and imaginative creations have led to sensual and seductive inclusions in Zane's *Purple Panties, Erogenous Zone: A Sexual Voyage, Mocha Chocolate: A Taste of Ecstasy,* and more. As a literary entrepreneur, Elissa is the founder of the greeting card line Greetings from the Soul: The Elissa Gabrielle Collection, collaborator and creator of *The Triumph of My Soul,* and publisher of Peace in the Storm Publishing (www .peaceinthestormpublishing.com). Elissa has managed to turn relatively unknown authors into household names and has molded and shaped the careers of some of today's brightest literary stars. In addition to these innovative achievements, Elissa has graced the covers of *Conversations* magazine, *Big Time Publishing* magazine, and *Disilgold Soul* magazine and has been featured in *Urbania* magazine and *Black Literature* magazine. Peace in the Storm Publishing has been nominated in several categories in the African American Literary Awards Show, and has won Independent Publisher of the Year in 2009, 2010, and 2011. In addition, Elissa Gabrielle was named Self-Published Author of the Year in 2010 for her explosive novel *A Whisper to a Scream.* Her writing and publishing passion is rooted in her desire to give a reader's soul a rise, one page at a time, and grounded in her quest to bring forth the Triumph Anthology series, an ongoing testament of faith. The first anthology in the series was the highly acclaimed *The Triumph of My Soul,* which will be followed by *The Soul of a Man* and *The Breakthrough* respectively. "I started the Triumph series because in life, we all fall down, but by the grace of God, we get back up. There is always victory in tomorrow," Elissa says about the Triumph series. From the novelty of her writing to her highly regarded greeting card line and the successful culmination of her publishing company, Elissa Gabrielle remains an ingenious and creative force to be reckoned with in terms of delivering distinct, fulfilling, and entertaining literature. By pushing herself to stay a cut above the rest, Elissa Gabrielle brilliantly and consistently delivers literary best.

Shaniqua Holt's true love is writing, as it has been since the third grade. She sometimes thinks her love for writing has turned into an obsession. Besides writing she is also an avid reader with an unhealthy passion for reading from all genres and subgenres. She lives in the South with her family and pets.

Eva Hore's work is seen in magazines such as *Hustler, Forum, Desire,* Australian *Penthouse, Leg Sex, XL* magazine, *Naughty Neighbors, For Women, Playgirl, Erotic T, Three Pillows*, and *Swank* magazine. Anthologies with Accent Press in the UK, *Delicate Friction, Best Lesbian Fiction 2005, Skin Deep 2, Mammoth Book of Erotic Fantasies UK, The Collective, Best Women's Erotica 2006, The Perfect Valentine, After Midnight Anthology, JustWatch Me* with Cleis Press, *The Sexiest Soles, Misbehavior, Gay Quickies, Mammoth Book of Erotic Confessions UK, Reality or Fantasy* with Dark Roast Press, *The Long Weekend and Other Stories* with No Boundaries Press, *The Best of Eva Hore* with JMS Books, and *The Big Book of Bizarro*.

Author **Jusme** is a writer in her early forties who is employed in social services. Presently residing in San Antonio in the great state of Texas, Jusme began writing at the young age of eleven by journaling. "I've found that journaling is therapeutic, you can be whoever you want to be." Jusme was first published in 2010 in Delphine Publication's *Between the Sheets,* in 2011 with Surviving Lives through Literature's *Voices Behind the Tears,* and most recently Naughty Ink Press's *Untapped Collection of Erotic Firsts.* She began writing erotica by accident, just to have fun, and found her niche. Jusme grew up in a very strict, Christian household and was raised to believe that a woman's enjoyment of sex was a no-no, and that she definitely must *always* make sure that her partner is satisfied and *never* worry about herself because she isn't important. Yeah, well, the reality is that should never be the case, and women should always make sure that they are taken care of because it is guaranteed that their partner will get theirs.

Sex is a part of everyday life and what's normal is different for everyone. Hell, who's normal? Remember this: When it's all said and done . . . no one is more important than Jusme . . . Please visit Jusme's fan page @Author Jusme on Facebook.

Lynn Lake's writing credits include *Leg Sex, 18eighteen, Desire, On Our Backs, Feminine Zone,* and stories in the anthologies *Truckers, After Midnight, Sex & Seduction, Ultimate Sins, Ultimate Uniforms, Seriously Sexy, Girl Fun, Purple Panties 2, Z-Rated: Chocolate Flava 3, The Mammoth Book of Lesbian Erotica,* and *The Mammoth Book of Erotic Confessions.*

Damian Lott is a native of Rochester, New York. A competent, versatile writer of fiction and nonfiction. Currently working on a debut novel. The son of Brenda Lott. The husband of Vonjula Thompson-Lott, and father of Domanique, Kamille, Damisa, Korrine, and Celeste Lott. A lover of nature, humanity, and philosophy. An avid reader of diverse literature who draws inspiration from all aspects of life. Motivated to reach all cultures through writing. In hopes of gaining knowledge, bringing ideas into circulation, and causing the minds of people to grow. I wholeheartedly thank Zane and her staff. This opportunity is a blessing, and I look forward to giving readers more. Sincerely, Damian Lott.

Cynthia Marie currently resides in St. Louis, Missouri. She has edited and written street and urban lit for the past seven years and has been credited as the editor of many *Essence* best-selling titles. She is the editor behind the 2010 African American Literary Award nominee *Romance for the Streets* and a contributing author to Destiny Carter's erotic anthology *Freak Files Reloaded* with two stories of her own, "Who's the Boss" and "A Hard Ride Up." Cynthia Marie will tantalize you with hot, erotic, and sexy urban tales as well as thought-provoking, relatable, and sexy urban stories.

Niyah Moore was born in Sacramento, California. Her latest novel, *Guilty Pleasures* (Nayberry Publications), is now available. She is one of the contributing authors of the 2008 African American Literary Award–winning erotic anthology *Mocha Chocolate: Taste a Piece of Ecstasy* (Nayberry Publications), the anthology *Chocolat Historie D'Amour* (LadyElle Publishing), the anthology *Souls of My Young Sisters* (Kensington Publishing), the anthology *Mocha Chocolate Remix: Escapades of Passion* (Nayberry Publications), and the anthology *The Heat of the Night* (Peace in the Storm Publishing). She currently resides in San Francisco, California, as a divorced mother of two.

Nadia is a New Orleans native who is new to published writing but very ambitious. She is an accounting assistant, licensed massage therapist, and a part-time accounting student, but is passionate about engaging others through her inspired writing. Nadia is a wife and mother who loves spending time with her family more than anything else, and she hopes to continue sharing her inner thoughts with her readers. Feel free to contact her or leave comments at nadianeworleans@yahoo.com.

After graduating at the top of her class from an all-black high school in Prichard, Alabama, where she currently resides, **Carla S. Pennington** went on to further her education at Spring Hill College in Mobile, Alabama, where she received her Bachelor of Arts degree with a concentration in journalism in 2002. Upon receiving her degree, it didn't take her long to realize that her heart was set on writing fiction. Therefore, she quickly began pursuing that dream.

In 1996, Carla was diagnosed with multiple sclerosis, a neurological disease that has no known cure but for which there are many treatments that can slow down the progression. She refuses to let the disease interfere with her life and continues to pursue her dream of becoming a bestselling author while also an active mom.

In 2005, Carla published her first novel, *Fling,* and in March 2008 one of her short stories, "Crusin," was featured in an anthology of erotica called *Mocha Chocolate: Taste a Piece of Ecstasy.* In February 2010, her short story "Deceitful Love" was featured in another erotic anthology, *Chocolat Historie D'Amour.* In July 2010, her short story "Point and Click Lover" was featured in the follow-up to the 2008 erotic anthology called *Mocha Chocolate: Escapades of Passion.* In 2011, her second novel, *The Available Wife,* was published through Life Changing Books, and the sequel, *The Available Wife 2,* was published with LCB in November 2011. Carla is currently working on a few other projects that will be released in the future.

Michelle Janine Robinson is the author of the Zane Presents novel *More than Meets the Eye,* published in 2011. Michelle is also the author of *Color Me Grey,* published in 2010. Both books were published by Simon & Schuster/Strebor and are available wherever books are sold. Recently published is Michelle's thriller *Serial Typical,* and coming in 2013, *Strange Fruit* and *On the Other Side.* Michelle's short-story contribution "The Quiet Room" was a featured story in the *New York Times* bestseller *Succulent: Chocolate Flava II.* She has contributed to several other anthologies, including *Caramel Flava, Honey Flava, Purple Panties,* and *Tasting Him*. In 2009, *Tasting Him* won the IPPY (Independent Publisher) Award for Erotica. Urban Reviews listed Michelle's first book, *Color Me Grey,* as one of the best reviewed books on UrbanReviewsOnline.com for 2010. In February 2011, Michelle was voted *Writers POV* magazine's Annual Winter Writing Contest Winner of the year and in March 2011, Michelle was voted a National Black Book Festival finalist for best new author of the year. Michelle is a native New Yorker and the mother of identical twins.

R.W. Shannon is a native of the east coast. She is an avid Ravens fan but will tolerate watching the Redskins. When not writing, the single vamp can be found at a yoga studio, taking a walk on the Appalachian Trail by her house, or shopping at the nearest outlet mall. Her work can be found at Cobblestone Press, Beautiful Trouble Publishing, Phaze books, and other fine e-publishers.

W. Biddle Street is a Baltimore expat living in Tennessee. Born and raised in East Baltimore, he spent twenty years traveling the world at the expense of the U.S. Army before retiring and settling in Tennessee. He says Tennessee is his home, but Baltimore is never far from his heart.

Ran Walker is the author of the novels *30 Love* and *B-Sides and Remixes,* as well as the novellas *16 Bars: A Short Story Mixtape* and *The Last Bluesman*. He has participated in the Callaloo and Hurston-Wright writers workshops and is the recipient of a Mississippi Arts Commission/NEA fellowship for creative nonfiction. A former practicing attorney, Walker lives with his wife,

Lauren, in the Hampton Roads area of Virginia. He can be found online at www.ranwalker.com and on Twitter @ranwalker.

Cee Wonder is a pseudonym for a longtime educator and coach who holds a master's degree in professional development. He tapped into erotic literature when he first read *The Sex Chronicles: Shattering the Myth* by Zane. It was a welcome discovery and inspiration. Now, he aspires to write his own book of erotic sexcapades. He can be contacted at fw3026@yahoo.com.